THE
LAST TALK WITH
LOLA FAYE

THOMAS H. COOK

ISIS
LARGE PRINT
Oxford

Copyright © Thomas H. Cook 2010

First published in Great Britain 2010
by
Quercus
by arrangement with Harcourt, Inc.

Published in Large Print 2011 by ISIS Publishing Ltd.,
7 Centremead, Osney Mead, Oxford OX2 0ES
by arrangement with
Quercus

British Library Cataloguing in Publication Data
Cook, Thomas H.
 The last talk with Lola Faye.
 1. Murder victims' families - - Fiction.
 2. Adultery - - Fiction.
 3. Fathers and sons - - Fiction.
 4. Alabama - - Fiction.
 5. Psychological fiction.
 6. Large type books.
 I. Title
 813.6–dc22

ISBN 978–0–7531–8882–8 (hb)
ISBN 978–0–7531–8883–5 (pb)

Printed and bound in Great Britain by
T. J. International Ltd., Padstow, Cornwall

For my mother,
Mickie Cook,
with love and devotion

When what we hoped for came to nothing, we revived.
— MARIANNE MOORE

Three Months Earlier

So, Luke, what's the last best hope of life?

The memory surfaced as it often did, out of the blue, for no apparent reason: Julia, my lost wife, glances up from something she's been reading, takes off her glasses, and, knowing that nothing will ever open inside me until I answer it, she bluntly poses her question.

I was standing before a glass display case filled with old frontier blankets when this memory last came to me. The blankets were thick and rough, and I imagined those first westward settlers curled up beneath them, whole families pressed together as they waited out the night. How fiercely the prairie winds must have lashed their little wagons, shaking the spindly frames and billowing out the canvas. Later they'd no doubt used these same blankets to ward off the frigid cold that had so ruthlessly whipped the plains, spreading them over the dirt floors of their dugouts, or layering them over their own shivering bodies, where they'd huddled with their dogs as the wind howled outside. How much warmth these blankets must have provided, I thought. How often they must have seemed the only warmth.

It was this sense of physical suffering in the service of some great hope that had once formed the basis for all my human sympathy, the one deep feeling that was truly mine, and that had once fired my dream — boyishly, perhaps, but yet more powerfully for that — of writing my own great books.

In those books, I'd hoped to portray the physical feel of American history, its tactile core: the searing bite of a minié ball, the sting of a lash, the muscular ache of hard labor and the squint of small chores — what it had actually felt like to pick cotton, hew a tree, fire a locomotive, thread a needle made of whalebone, shape a candle by another candle's light. Mine would be histories with a heartbeat — palpable, alive, histories that pulsed with true feeling.

I'd done none of that, I knew, as I turned from that glass case, those neatly stacked frontier blankets. I'd written a few books, the most recent to be published just three months from now, but I'd never created anything that approached the works it had been my youthful ambition to write.

It's one thing to bury an old dead dream, however, and quite another to attempt, again and again, to resurrect a dream you can't let die, which is what I'd done, always beginning with a passionate concept, then watching as it shrank to a bloodless monograph. I'd repeated this process many times, and later that same afternoon, only a few minutes after I'd stood before those frontier blankets, I prepared my desk for yet another run at my old best hope, but stopped and found myself thinking about where it had all begun.

Then, rather suddenly, it came to me, a memory of my mother's wedding ring. Just before leaving

4

Glenville, I'd picked it up and looked at it closely, like a jeweler, recalling all the times I'd seen her delicately remove it before washing dishes because she feared it might slip off and disappear down the drain. At the heart of those memories, I should have felt some gritty aspect of her life: the weight of an iron as she pushed it across a shirt, the oily touch of dishwater, the gooey damp of batter, and if not these, then at least I should have been able to infuse the ring she'd cherished with that power of time and remembrance we trivialize with the phrase *sentimental value*.

Surely, I should have felt *something* at such a moment, but tellingly, I hadn't. Unless one could call numbness a feeling, for that was the only sensation I'd actually had, a numbness at the core, everything dry, brittle, dead, all of which should have told me that no matter how many times I tried, I would never write the deeply sentient books it had been my dream to write, that I was, and always would be, as Julia had once said, a strangely shriveled thing.

Standing at my desk, recalling the unfeeling way with which I'd stared at my mother's ring, I heard again her earlier question: *So, Luke, what's the last best hope of life?*

I glanced out the window, into the chill September rain, and thought again of how life's darkest acts pool and swirl, but never go under the bridge.

So, Luke, what's the last best hope of life?

I'd had no answer then.

Now I do.

PART I

CHAPTER
ONE

She had one of those hayseed names, Lola Faye Gilroy, and that night I would more easily have expected an apparition of my father sitting down to his last meal of corn bread and buttermilk or my mother reading *Anna Karenina* in her bed than Lola Faye herself, particularly given the darkly inquisitive look in her eyes, the same look she'd had at my father's funeral, as if she were still trying to sort it out, determine if she alone had caused so much blood to be spilled.

Even on that day, eyeing her from across the black hole of his still-open grave, I'd thought her the last person in the world to be the "other woman" in my father's life, though by the time he sat down for that final, profoundly unromantic meal, I'd known about their relationship for several months, a terrible truth I'd kept from my innocent and unsuspecting mother.

I'd not seen her again until some months later, when my bus had pulled out of town. On that occasion, I'd noticed her sitting alone on the same concrete step my mother and I had often shared. She'd looked up as my bus went by, and there it was, that same vague look of quizzical dissatisfaction I'd first noticed at my father's funeral, as if she'd been going over it all yet again, the stark facts of his murder, gnawing at them in that little rodent way of hers, which had made me only more anxious to rid myself of Lola Faye Gilroy, my father, my mother, Glenville, and anything else that might stop my heart and chill my soul, make me ask the dreadful question Lola Faye would later pose near the end of our talk: *Oh, Luke, can life really be like that?*

I'd flown to Saint Louis at my own expense, the purpose being to hawk my new book, *Fatal Choices*. I'd done a yeoman's job of discussing certain disastrous tactical decisions — the failure of the Confederate high command to storm Washington after First Manassas; the shooting-gallery layout of our fleet at Pearl Harbor — and in that way had illustrated the larger but hardly unfamiliar point that otherwise intelligent men can go monstrously wrong.

The Museum of the West had provided a room for my talk, and the museum gift shop had agreed to order a few copies of my book and set up a table where I could sign them at the end of it. The museum's events planner had balked, however, at supplying wine and cheese.

I arrived at the museum early that evening, checked to make sure my books were actually in the gift shop, then, with time on my hands, toured the modest Charles Lindbergh exhibit. The great aviator's empty flight suit hung in a glass display case, oddly deflated, like his reputation. For years he'd lived in the ill favor his prewar flirtation with Hitler had created, less a maker of history, in the end, than the diminished

10

product of its unforgiving judgment. Staring at that suit, its ghostly folds, I had an idea for another book: *History's Outcasts*.

I snatched the little notebook I carried with me for such purposes, scribbled a reminder, then walked to the lecture room where I was to give my talk. Inside the room, I found a young man putting out folding chairs. A museum identification badge hung from a black cord in a pouch of rectangular clear plastic. The front of the badge bore the likenesses of the great explorers Meriwether Lewis and William Clark, both looking eager to map the far reaches of the West, to penetrate its unknown vastness, their courage so indomitable, their adventure so thrilling, their achievement so stupendous that beside such towering figures the rest of us seem but sidelined players in a small-town game.

"Proceeded on," I said softly.

"Excuse me?"

"Oh," I said, faintly embarrassed by the abrupt wandering of my own mind. "It's a phrase Meriwether Lewis often wrote in his journal. 'Proceeded on.' It means, I suppose, not giving up, proceeding on . . . toward something great."

The young man peered at me like one in the presence of a space creature. "I have to finish up," he said.

I realized that I blocked the row of chairs the young man was attempting to complete.

"Oh, sorry," I said, and immediately stepped out of his path. "I'm Dr. Paige, the speaker here this evening."

For a moment we stared at each other, the young man working to decide what he should do next, I awaiting his decision.

Finally he said, "We have a little garden."

By this he meant that I should go there to cool my heels until it was time for me to speak.

"Yes, of course," I said. "I'll wait there."

In the garden I found a few aluminum tables with round white tops and matching chairs. A little fountain spurted arcs of water from the mouths of four leaping fish, and over them a loosely draped girl with flowing hair poured another, larger stream of water from a wide-mouthed pitcher. The sculpted fish seemed happy enough to receive this offering, but the girl's face remained oddly grim, as if she were aware, as the fish were not, that the water she offered them was poisoned.

The tables were all empty save for one at which a young man kept glancing about expectantly. It struck me that I'd once had that inner tapping of the foot as well, especially at those moments when escape had seemed impossible and I was forced to consider that I might live my whole life in Glenville, the moribund little Alabama town in which I'd been born and had grown up, and which my vast ambition had demanded that I leave. In quick succession these thoughts of Glenville brought back my mother and father, brought back Miss McDowell's jangling need and Debbie's dread; brought back Sheriff Tomlinson in his thoroughness, Mr. Ward with his disturbing news, Mr. Klein's grim revelation; brought back that whole departed world, and yet, for all this parade of figures from my distant past, no thought came to me of Lola Faye.

She was very near, however.

In fact, she had to have been cruising down Lindell Avenue at that very moment. But had I thought of her as I sat in the chill shade of the garden, watching that vaguely malicious girl pour vaguely sinister water into a pool of happily oblivious fish, I doubtless would have recalled her not as she was now, bent upon her mission, but as she'd been during the relatively brief time I'd known her: twenty-seven years old, dressed in solid-color skirts, usually pastels; her blouses often adorned with small designs, mostly flowers, though sometimes snowflakes or little furry animals, like the wallpaper one sees in the rooms of young children. There'd been a sunny quality in her style of dress that seemed forced, and even a little silly, like believing a fairy tale one should have outgrown. "She dresses against the facts," my father explained when I mentioned it once, and by which I assumed him to mean that Lola Faye dressed against the brutal facts of Woody Wayne Gilroy, the distraught husband whose sobbing phone messages she never answered; the rented wood-frame house, with its water-stained ceiling and creaking floor; and perhaps even against the dead-end job she'd taken at Variety Store, the eternally struggling little five-and-dime my father owned and in whose back storeroom he had enjoyed the fruits of their tawdry love affair.

13

Or had it been lust alone that had driven him to betray my mother?

I had never been able to say, since desire and love are often so impossibly mingled that to ascertain where the one begins and the other ends is simply more than we can do.

This much was obvious, however: Lola Faye Gilroy, at the time she met my father, was nearly twenty years younger than my mother and had what any Victorian would have called a comely shape. That said, she was by no means beautiful, and certainly not dazzling. Among ladies of the court, she would not have caught the king's eye, nor even that of a lowly minister.

In terms of personal habits, she smoked like a young woman who had no expectation of ever impressing anyone with either her style or her grace, and her desk, as I noticed many times, was covered with coffee-cup rings, the ashtray boiling over with butts and charred matches.

As to education, Lola Faye had graduated from high school but had gone no further, and I never saw her with a book. She spoke in the accent of our region, and in every way appeared to be exactly what a life lived in Glenville had made her. Nothing about her suggested worldliness or sophistication. Her smile was warm and open, but any attempt at a sultry pout would have made her look clownish. She would not have known how to turn away, then look back fetchingly; how to flip her hair seductively or languidly close her eyes. The art of coquetry would have been as beyond her comprehension as anything in French.

14

Was she sensitive? Was she knowing?

I never thought so, but in some people, these qualities emerge only at intimate moments when, in the soft quiet of a darkened room, one suddenly betrays a depth of understanding wholly unseen before, some piercing bit of painful wisdom that peeps out like a scar from beneath a cuff, and often with an implied sense of secret sharing that is powerful in itself: *This is for only you to see.*

I could never imagine such a moment passing between Lola Faye and my father when I thought of them together, but perhaps this was because it was at this moment in any recollection of that sour time that my mind inevitably, and as if in flight from far darker thoughts, returned me to my fondest memory of my mother.

She'd been working in her garden long into that afternoon, a woman in her late thirties. I was a boy of ten, with nothing to do but watch her. After a while, she straightened herself, then unpinned her hair so that it fell in a thick dark wave down her back and over her nearly bare shoulders. Caught in the sun, she had suddenly looked beautiful to me.

I think Mr. Klein must have seen this same beauty at that moment too, because when I noticed him standing on the other side of the fence, his face conveyed a look almost of awe.

"Good afternoon, Miss Ellie," he said.

My mother turned toward the voice and saw Mr. Klein, the man in whose jewelry store she had worked before I was born, a tall, dark, and thoroughly foreign man, our town's only Jew.

"Good afternoon, Mr. Klein," my mother said.

Mr. Klein handed my mother a book. "I thought you might enjoy this."

My mother took the book. "*Middlemarch*. Thank you, Mr. Klein. I'll be sure to return it."

"There's no hurry at all, of course," Mr. Klein told her.

He was a man in his mid-fifties, and he spoke with a slight accent. Everything about him struck me as graceful and refined, so that he seemed perpetually to stroll some beautiful Old World square. He had lost everything in the war, according to my mother, his parents and his two brothers. It was the kind of loss, she said, that could "increase" a person, because "some people get larger, Luke, as things are taken away."

"I read *Silas Marner* again only last week," my mother told Mr. Klein. She smiled. "Allow me to give you something in return." She drew her basket from the ground. It was filled with lush red tomatoes. She took the largest and most fully ripened one from the basket and offered it to him. "Please."

Mr. Klein reached out and took the tomato, but from the bottom, so that for just the slightest moment, the back of his hand rested against my mother's palm, an instant during which their eyes locked, and in that locking, sent and returned a tiny but palpable charge.

"Ellie!"

It was my father's voice, but when I turned, I didn't see him. This was not unusual, since it had long been his habit to announce himself from a distance, as if he felt his wife and son should be alerted to his approach.

He came steaming around the corner of the house only seconds later, dressed, as he always was, in baggy trousers and a flannel shirt with a perpetually frayed collar. He was carrying a large brown bag and for a moment seemed to use it almost as a shield as he approached where my mother, Mr. Klein, and I stood at the old wooden fence.

"Good evening," Mr. Klein said to my father.

My father nodded, then glanced about. "Pretty evening," he said.

Mr. Klein's eyes returned to my mother. "Yes, quite lovely," he said.

"Mr. Klein brought me a book, Doug," my mother said. She lifted it into the air with a flourish. *"Middlemarch."*

My father stared at the book as if it were a serpent, something that twined and hissed.

"That's nice," he said. He looked at Mr. Klein. "So, you getting much trade these days?" he asked.

Mr. Klein shrugged. "About the same as always."

My father appeared at a loss to continue this conversation, and in lieu of talk, roughly shook the brown bag. "Ham," he said. He looked at my mother. "I thought you might bake it with apples." He turned to Mr. Klein. "You like ham?"

Mr. Klein shook his head softly.

"People of the Jewish faith don't eat ham, Doug," my mother informed him gently.

It was the first I'd heard of this, but it served only to elevate Mr. Klein in my esteem; all things remote were beginning to draw me, images of castles and rivers and ancient battlefields now playing continually in my child's mind.

"Is that right?" my father said. He looked genuinely amazed. "You don't know what you're missing, Abe."

"I suppose not," Mr. Klein said. He looked at my mother again, now with a slight smile playing on his lips, one she returned as if in soft conspiracy.

"Well, I should be going," he said to her.

"Thank you so much for the book," my mother said. "I'll return it to you when I'm through."

Mr. Klein touched the brim of his hat. "Good evening, then."

"Good evening," my mother replied.

Mr. Klein turned and headed back toward his car, a figure moving smoothly through the twilight.

"Nice fellow," my father said. "Smart too. Good head for business."

My mother took the bag from my father and tucked her one free hand beneath his arm. "Come, Doug," she said as one might gently coax a child to follow.

I turned away from them and watched Mr. Klein go, something lonely and isolated about him, like a deer cut from the herd, so that as he drifted across the green lawn, I felt the nature of his foreignness, how he would always be the "other" in other people's eyes.

Within seconds he'd disappeared around the corner of our house. I turned toward the back door that led into our kitchen. A light went on inside, and from my place on the lawn, I watched as my mother busily removed the ham from the brown bag, placed it in a metal pan, then began peeling apples, all of this done with what struck me as unearthly grace while my father sat at the kitchen table, oblivious to her service, his body kicked back in his chair, his boots pressed against the side of the table, his dusty old . . .

Your life is oedipal as hell.

Julia's voice sounded so vividly in my mind at that moment that I had to keep myself from turning around in my chair to look for her. Then, just as suddenly, the world returned to me in its actual detail: the chairs, the fountain, the stone maiden whose expression now seemed quite cleverly malicious as she fed the unsuspecting fish their final draft.

I looked at my watch and realized that the young man must have long ago placed the last chair in a neat row and that no doubt a few people had already taken their seats and were awaiting my arrival.

What I didn't know as I rose and made my way toward the room that had been prepared for my talk was that Lola Faye Gilroy, for very different reasons than the rest of the audience, was waiting for me too.

CHAPTER
TWO

A few people turned as I came into the lecture room, but others continued to read whatever books they'd brought with them or to chat with those nearby. With one exception, all of them were women, most seated alone, their damp raincoats neatly folded and placed in the empty chairs next to them. The single man in the audience looked to be in his mid-sixties. He wore a Vietnam veteran's cap, the name of his unit emblazoned on the bill, the sure sign of a military history buff.

They were all museum regulars, or so it seemed to me, and I had no doubt that they would gather in this same room on the following night and from these same metal chairs respectfully listen to a talk about the development of the Winchester rifle or the ritual importance of Native American chants.

I offered a warm smile as I stepped behind the lectern. "I should say right at the beginning that my book will be available in the museum shop after my talk." The smile became self-deprecating. "I always forget to mention that, which my publisher doesn't appreciate."

There was a twitter of laugher at this, though it was the sort that is sympathetically offered for a joke gone flat.

From this already tenuous opening position, I began my talk. I had chosen to speak about certain military decisions, I told my listeners, because their consequences were particularly dramatic. Following the formula of such talks, I gave the usual examples from American history: General Santa Anna's catastrophic timidity at the Alamo; Grant's sanguinary charge at Cold Harbor, the only decision that famously passionless commander regretted.

Here a hand lifted. It was the veteran, of course.

"Why did Grant regret that charge?"

"Because so many Union soldiers died," I answered. "And the charge proved to be futile."

"Lots of bloodbaths turn out to be futile," the veteran said. "You can't know that when you give the order."

"No," I agreed. "You can't. But looking back on it, you —"

"What about Iraq?" the veteran interrupted. "Do you think we'll come to regret all that?"

"I don't know," I said. "Because the war in Iraq has not become history yet. At least not in the way the charge at Cold Harbor is now history."

The final results of the Iraq War could not yet be determined, I went on to tell my listeners, because the issues in play had not yet been resolved.

"As forces, they are still alive, and they may still be alive when all of us are dead," I concluded. "Whereas the futility of that charge at Cold Harbor was so quickly established that Grant himself thought it almost murder."

Murder.

Strange, it would occur to me later, that it was on so dark a word that she had appeared.

Even if I'd gotten a much closer look at Lola Faye Gilroy, I wouldn't have recognized her. Twenty years had passed, after all, so that what I saw skirt by the open doorway of the lecture room was not the relatively youthful figure that had drifted down the wide center aisle of Variety Store, blond and well-proportioned, with slender white arms emerging from the short sleeves of a baby blue blouse but a woman whose body was considerably fuller, though by no means heavyset, and whose clothes were darker than before, covered more of her than before, and whose somber hues and extended coverage seemed no longer in contradiction to the facts.

She hadn't paused at the door as she passed, however, and if I had by chance glanced down at my notes at that moment, I wouldn't have seen her at all. Even as it was, she made only an impression of movement in the corridor, so I immediately returned my attention to the audience.

By then I was several minutes into my talk and able to judge how it was going, which wasn't very well; the attention of my audience was clearly flagging. As that was so often the case, I'd found a way to make light of it, a device I now routinely employed.

22

"You know," I said with a laugh, "when I start to talk, I always want it to sound sweeping, like the talks I imagine my graduate-school idols would have made: historians like Gibbon, Macaulay, and Carlyle." I laughed again, this time in an even more self-deprecating spirit. "I think if I'd set out to carve Mount Rushmore it would have ended up a cameo."

My listeners offered a hint of amusement in response to this, but only a hint.

From that point, I had no choice but to plunge ahead, and so, with a show of retaking some oddly lost ground, I proceeded on through various other military debacles until I reached the end of my talk.

"Any questions?" I asked.

There weren't any.

"All right, thank you for coming."

My listeners began to struggle up from their chairs and gather their belongings.

"Again, my book is available in the museum gift shop," I reminded them. "I'll be there if any of you would like a signed copy."

I added nothing to this, but simply drew my few notes from the lectern and stepped away, politely trailing the last of my listeners into the corridor, moving slowly so as not to pass them, before heading to the museum shop.

My books rested on the little card table the museum had provided, their arrangement exactly as I'd seen them earlier, so it was clear that they'd not attracted the notice of even that cursory browser who idly picks up a book only to set it immediately down, though always a tad askew, as if in haste to rid himself of it.

Still, I'd been assured that I could at least attempt to sell my book, and on the wings of that faint hope, I took my seat at the little table and waited, my hands cupped together so as not to seem threatening, a friendly smile pasted on my face.

Time passed.

No one came.

And so, to pass what remained of this time upon the cross, I retrieved a book from my briefcase, the latest biography of George Washington, and began reading. I was tramping through the snows of Valley Forge with him when a voice drew me back to the present.

"Fatal Choices."

I looked up to see a woman clutching my book with an odd severity, as if it were an unruly baby. She wore a black overcoat, and her head was covered with a tight wool cap exposing only a few strands of lusterless blond hair. A pair of thick-framed glasses rested not quite halfway down her nose, as if they'd slipped from their place. She'd wound a dark green scarf around her neck, the loose end flung over her shoulder in the way of a boa. Something about her seemed ragged and out of whack, so that I wondered if she was one of those mad or homeless people who sometimes find themselves in libraries and museums because, quite literally, no other doors are open to them.

"Hello," I said politely.

She didn't respond at once, but only looked at me silently, one hand rising to push back her glasses,

24

though even then they remained slightly askew. Then she said, "You don't recognize me, Luke?"

The features of her face shifted, reformed, achieved focus, then burst forth in a flash of chilling recognition.

"Lola Faye?" I asked unbelievingly.

And suddenly, it was as if all those many years simply fell away, and she sat once again on the steps of the Confederate monument, sunlight glinting in the bus window as her gaze lifted toward me, a dark inquisitiveness in her eyes.

"Lola Faye," I repeated starkly. "Gilroy."

She made no threatening move, and yet I felt as if I'd just been handed an adder in a basket. I could almost hear it crawling about, probing for some break in the weave.

"I guess you're surprised to see me," she said.

Astonished, I thought, *stupefied*.

And yet, here she was, standing before me now, the woman, then a very young woman, with whom my father had fallen in love or lust so many years before, Lola Faye Gilroy in a frayed cloth coat, her hair covered with a woolen cap, a dark green scarf coiled around her neck, her once slender arms grown thick, her skin now dry, her eyes magnified by the thick lenses of her glasses, not yet an old woman, though surely getting there.

"Lola Faye Gilroy," I repeated again. "Yes . . . surprised."

I looked at her more closely, and nothing that met my eyes suggested anything but that Lola Faye had matured into a drab middle-aged woman, clearly one of quite limited means. Her clothes, for example, were anything but luxurious, so there was little doubt that money remained as elusive for her in later life as it had in her youth. Her face seemed more pale than before, and the rings beneath her eyes appeared a little darker because of that. There were wrinkles at the corners of her lips, and the usual middle-aged webs at her eyes. The slight scar on her chin, and another on her forehead, gave her the battered look of inmates in public institutions, the habitués of prison cells and asylum wards. Or maybe it was more the look of an old suitcase, something that had been tossed about and kicked around, that bore the dents and bruises of misuse. Her eyes, once rather sparklingly blue, had dimmed considerably and now appeared vaguely sunken, so that she seemed to be looking out from the mouths of two small caverns.

"Can I call you Luke?" she asked in a voice that was decidedly tense. She pressed the book toward me, the name of the author flowing beneath the title: *Martin Lucas Paige*. "Because I thought you might go by Lucas now."

Was there a hint of mockery in that, I wondered, a sly insinuation that I was self-inflating, self-important? I didn't know, but even so, it heightened the physical uneasiness I felt in her presence, the sense of something tightly wound.

"I just use Lucas for my books," I told her.

She looked as if she had no notion of what to say next, but her gaze remained steady and unflinching, as if she were peering at a man in a line-up. Then, in a movement so quick it startled me, she dug into the depths of a black canvas bag, yanked out two crumpled twenty-dollar bills, and thrust them toward me.

I didn't reach for them.

"You pay at the cash register," I informed her.

She squinted, as if suspicious that I was giving her wrong directions. "The cash register?"

"Over there," I said.

She looked to where I'd indicated, then turned back to me. "Okay," she said, and headed down the aisle. She'd gone only a few feet before she stopped, as if in response to a sudden command, and whirled around to face me. "I'll be right back," she said.

Be right back, I thought. *Why?*

As she continued down the aisle, I tried to imagine what had compelled Lola Faye Gilroy, of all people, to come here, to this little museum, and buy a book she would likely never read, the book of a man she had never known save as a boy, and that boy very angry at her, as she could imagine, and the man probably still angry, perhaps murderously so.

By then Lola Faye had reached the cashier, paid for my book, and placed it in her bag. After that, she nodded, mouthed *Thank you* to the clerk, then came back down the aisle to where I remained, as if fixed in a strange suspension, behind the little table.

"Okay, it's mine now," Lola Faye said with what seemed an edgy smile. She removed my book from the bag, placed it on the table in front of me, and opened it to the title page. "Would you mind?"

Would I mind?

A moment of unreality seized me, disbelief that this woman, my father's lover, had actually made such a request. I knew that it was a lowly thing, an autograph, and that mine was more lowly than most. But how could she ask me to inscribe a book for her knowing the dreadful part she'd played in the lurid scandal that had destroyed so many lives? What could she expect my inscription to say? Did she think I would ignore the past and write *Best wishes* or *Nice seeing you in Saint Louis* or *Thank you for your support?* And if I wrote something of that sort, what would she gather from my willingness to do so?

In answer to those questions, I decided that only one course of action was open to me, and so I quickly took the book, wrote *To Lola Faye Gilroy* on the title page, signed my name, and slid it back across the table toward her.

"Thank you," Lola Faye said. She picked up the book and now seemed to nestle it in her arms. "Are you proud of what you did?" she asked.

A quiver of anxiety coursed though me, as if I'd been summoned unexpectedly to the witness stand. "Proud of . . . what I did?" I asked tentatively.

"Getting a great education," Lola Faye said. "Writing books." Her tone was matter-of-fact, but something in it seemed rehearsed, as if she'd stood before a mirror, a different book in her arms, practicing her lines like some B-movie actress. "Making your dream come true."

Her nearness, so profoundly physical after she'd had no more substance to me than a fleeting thought for all

28

these many years, struck me as powerfully invasive, like a stranger lurching into your yard, big and dark and ominous, and at the sight of whom you close the door, snap the dead bolt into place.

"I mean, you must be proud of doing all that, right, Luke?" Lola Faye asked. Now her tone seemed gently probing, though in a way I couldn't quite nail down, part affirmation of a prior conclusion, part uncertainty with it.

I offered only a soft shrug as my answer, a response with which I hoped to end my talk with Lola Faye but which had the opposite effect, so that she suddenly seemed intent on lingering a moment longer.

"So, do you ever think about Glenville?" she asked.

A murky pool of memories boiled up from the chamber in which I'd kept them sealed since leaving that very town.

"Old times, I mean?" she added.

I could hardly believe my ears. Old times? Could it be that Lola Faye Gilroy actually saw the dreadful events that had benighted my last days in Glenville in sepia tones, little faintly golden photographs of times past?

"Well, those old times were rather painful, as I'm sure you remember," I answered bluntly.

"Yes, they were," Lola Faye agreed, though something crazily nostalgic still clung to her voice. Or was it simply a tone of regretful inquiry I'd heard, a dry digging through the ashes?

"I think about them a lot," Lola Faye told me. Her gaze abruptly intensified, as if some unexpected

29

thought had fired in her mind. "We'd have a lot to talk about, wouldn't we?" She shrugged. "I mean, who else is left?"

This was at least factually accurate, I thought, in that they were all dead, the others: my father in one pool of blood; Lola Faye's husband, Woody, in another; my mother lifeless in her bed; poor inconsequential Glenville for a moment transfigured by all this into a redneck Shakespearean stage.

Lola Faye offered a smile that seemed little more than a small ray in a stormy sky. "I'm forty-seven years old, Luke. I've seen a lot of water go under the bridge."

"Forty-seven," I repeated without emphasis. "Really?"

She didn't answer immediately, and during that interval of silence I saw a strange urgency build within her, tense and growing more tense, like the trigger finger of an assassin as the target nears.

"Luke, there's one thing I always wanted to tell you," she blurted finally. "What Woody wrote in that note he left . . . that I made him do it? He didn't mean it that way. He didn't mean that I put him up to it."

A wave of relief passed over me. So *this* was why Lola Faye Gilroy had dragged herself from God knows where over to the Museum of the West on a wet December night. She'd come to make her case before me, clarify the issue Woody Gilroy had raised in his suicide note, rid herself of the guilt he'd laid at her feet, revisit all that in a talk with me, then enter her plea at the end of it: *not guilty*.

"Woody never mentioned your daddy and me one time," Lola Faye declared in the firm way of a witness under oath. "Never once mentioned he thought we were doing something."

Doing something? Lola Faye's euphemism for the back-street affair that had ended in so much death sent a streak of pain through me.

"Well, things happen," I said quickly, like one turning away from some blood-soaked crime scene. I nodded toward the book she held in her arms. "Fatal choices," I added. "We all have to make them."

Lola Faye drew in what appeared to be a relieved breath and looked at me as if she'd completed the task she'd set herself, told me what she'd come to tell me, and in return had received a small measure of understanding.

And yet, she didn't leave.

"Are you staying in town for the night?" she asked in a voice that was now quite casual, as if we'd passed a hostile border check and were now on our way to a safer place.

I nodded. "At the Shady Creek."

"It's nice there, I bet," Lola Faye said. "I passed it on the bus. It looked very expensive."

I shrugged. "Well, I don't get pampered very often."

"Not since your mom, I guess."

I found it curious that Lola Faye had brought up my mother, though by then I'd noticed the distinctly zigzagging nature of her mind, the way her thoughts rushed around like rabbits in a field, as did her tone of voice and physical demeanor, tense at first, now almost chatty, as if her mood rose and fell, shot this way or that, like a balloon carried by strong but unpredictable currents.

"Actually, it's since my wife and I got divorced," I said with a quick smile. "Although I can't say she pampered me very much." I let the smile grow a bit in length, though not in warmth. "She was a modern woman, if you know what I mean. She wasn't much for babying a man."

"That's what Ollie said about me," Lola Faye said in a voice that was now plainly conversational. "That I wasn't soft and cuddly."

"And Ollie is . . . ?"

"My husband," Lola Faye said. "I married late, you see. Because I guess I was a little put off, you know, by men."

There was a pause, and during it something changed in Lola Faye's eyes so that for the first time she resembled the Lola Faye of old, a simple country girl without ambition, undesigning, as artless as a wooden slat, perfect for my father.

"Maybe we could find a place to talk," she said. "You must be tired, giving a big lecture, all those people out there listening."

"Actually, it energizes you," I said. "Being the center of attention."

The way her face softened slightly went perfectly with the way she briefly lowered her eyes. "I wouldn't know," she said quietly.

Was that the moment she hooked me into agreeing to have a talk, the moment I began to feel somewhat less guarded in her presence for the simple reason that she'd allowed me to feel bigger than I was, more important, the great man I'd once hoped to be, the jewel in my mother's crown? I wondered if that same humbleness had attracted my father to her. Had that been her secret charm? Had she made poor, ordinary Vernon Douglas Paige feel big and strong and important? Perhaps if we had a little talk, I might unearth at least that part of the mystery, find the tiny, innocuous seed from which the poisonous plant had sprouted.

"My hotel has a lounge," I said. "It looked pretty quiet. We could go there." I glanced about the shop. The cashier was counting the receipts, and the store had emptied. "We can go now, if you want."

Lola Faye started to turn, then stopped. "I wouldn't want to force you, though," she said. "Maybe you have friends in town, people you need to see."

"Not at all," I told her.

"You're not meeting anyone while you're here?" Lola Faye asked.

"No one," I said.

"Really? No one?"

"Not a soul," I assured her. Something caught in me, a little hook in my heart. "I'm entirely alone."

Lola Faye's eyes gained a hint of brightness, like those of a runner who'd leaped over an obstacle and so could continue toward the finish line. "Good," she said with the tiniest of smiles.

CHAPTER
THREE

Tiny, and yet something in that smile gnawed at me, as if behind her thin, cracked lips were small white fangs.

And so as Lola Faye and I made our way toward my hotel, I wondered if I hadn't possibly been tricked into this talk, Lola Faye's soft "I wouldn't know," the way she'd lowered her eyes rather sadly as she'd said it, all of that simply a well-laid trap into which I'd foolishly fallen.

But if that was the case, it was too late to reverse course, particularly given that Lola Faye's mood had brightened considerably during our walk. She'd even delightedly pointed out various Christmas decorations: snowmen and reindeer, Santa Claus and "baby Jesus." Saint Louis seemed a wonder to her, magical as Paris, dreamy as Venice.

Through all of this, I simply walked on beside her, listening absently, resigned to the fact that I could find no way to escape at least a few more minutes of conversation but determined to get away as soon as I could, not only because I fully expected to find our talk boring but because something remained troubling about her sudden appearance, a sense that it was anything but casual, so that her reversion to this new version of herself, happily delighting in the splendors of Saint Louis, struck me as less than genuine.

Once in the lounge, Lola Faye took a moment to appreciate a décor that seemed to strike her as indescribably opulent. "You've come a long way from Glenville, Luke," she said as we took our seats at one of the lounge's small tables. She took off her coat but left on her dark green scarf. She peered about, noting the flowers, the grandfather clock, the elegant curtains and carpet. "A real long way."

It was a perfectly ordinary beginning to a conversation, but I found it peculiar that in returning me to the past, Lola Faye hadn't mentioned some innocuous person we'd both known in Glenville or a particular event that had occurred during the time we'd both lived there: the Flower Festival no one attended, or the Grand Tour of Homes that had been equally a bust. No, it had been Glenville as a whole, you might say, that she'd first referenced, Glenville as a world we'd shared, and which for some reason she'd brought up in the way of one beginning a story whose ending one knew but would not reveal.

"A long way, yes," I said, trying to sound relaxed, casual, intent on concealing the fact that even after so many years, any talk of Glenville still sent little ripples of disturbance through me. "A long way from the blinding country of youth."

Lola's Faye's eyes snapped over to me. "The blinding country of youth," she repeated, sounding appreciative, though I wondered if there might not be something else lurking within, like a figure behind a curtain. "You were always so smart, Luke."

"Thank you," I said lightly, "but I have to confess, it's not my line. 'The blinding country of youth,' I mean. Dylan Thomas said that."

Lola Faye stared at me quizzically.

"He was an English poet," I explained. "Or I should say, Welsh."

"A poet," Lola Faye said. "So you read poetry? When you're not writing books, I mean. It must take years to write a book."

"It takes a little while, yes," I said.

Lola Faye's laugh was a tad too broad, better suited to the stage than this quiet lounge.

"A little while?" she asked. "Like it's nothing! Like anyone could do it. If they had . . . 'a little while.' Like I could do it if I'd ever had the time or the chance, or like just anybody could. Like it's not the most important thing in the world, writing a book."

I waved my hand, dismissing the lavish appreciation of authorship Lola Faye had offered. "It's hardly the most important thing in the world," I said. "Writing a book, I mean."

The blue of Lola Faye's eyes darkened by an infinitesimally small increment. "But to you it was, wasn't it, Luke?"

There was something in those eyes that discomfited me, and so rather than answer, I quickly glanced away from her and toward the bar, where a waitress in black pants, white blouse, and burgundy vest leaned against a short column.

36

"Miss?" I called to her.

The waitress heard me and quickly stepped over to our table.

"Hi," she said.

"Hi," I said. "Could we order drinks?"

"Sure." She looked at Lola Faye. "What would you like?"

"Do you have red wine?" Lola Faye asked.

"Merlot, cabernet sauvignon, and pinot noir," the waitress answered.

Lola Faye looked taken aback, as if she'd suddenly realized that lounges such as this, in upscale hotels, expected patrons to possess an esoteric knowledge that she didn't have.

"I think you'd like pinot noir," I said to her.

Lola Faye nodded softly. "Okay."

"Pinot noir for both of us," I told the waitress.

"Coming right up," the waitress said as she stepped away.

"I'm over my head," Lola Faye admitted with a faint and very uncharacteristic giggle, as if shifting from a woman to a little girl. "You saved me, Luke." She lifted her hand to her mouth. "I was embarrassed. Did I look embarrassed?"

"You looked fine," I assured her.

She drew her hand from her mouth. "So, you know all about wines?"

"I just know that pinot noir's a nice wine," I said.

"In Glenville it was just iced tea, remember?" Lola Faye asked in a way that struck me as pointed, as if she were determined to hold to the script she'd written in her head. "Sugar or no sugar. With or without lemon. That was it, the only choices we had."

"The only choices, yes," I said.

"Glenville," Lola Faye said, and with that word seemed miraculously to return me there. "Glenville, Alabama."

Imagine an idyllic Southern town, utterly Faulknerian in its entrenched Southernness. Imagine a grand courthouse, blindingly white, with high columns and crowned with a graceful dome. All the charming buildings that surround this courthouse are two stories high. They are all built of wood, and the wood is painted various colors but always pastels. They are each adorned by a gallery, these buildings, and in the shank of the evening, the town's merchants and professionals lounge upon these second-floor porches, easing back in white rocking chairs, sipping bourbon and smoking cigars. The shops below the galleries sell diaphanous dresses and broad-brimmed hats, and from some of the windows a glittering array of jewelry, wedding bands, and snow-white pearls winks at the townspeople who at their leisure stroll by them. The streets themselves, even the ones off the square, are immaculately clean and sunlit. An unhurried traffic of people and cars moves along these streets, languidly and gracefully, with much nodding by the citizens and stopping to greet, as if the population of this dreamy village lived in a perpetual spring of azalea-dappled perfection. It is a beauty that grows only more bountiful in the residential quarter, where large houses rise in roomy expanse over

38

spacious, perfectly tended lawns, and where, on a stroll in the evening, one might hear a favored daughter practicing her Chopin.

Now, take that domed courthouse and replace it with a gray-concrete monstrosity that sits on a parched brown slope overlooking a single narrow street of squat buildings artlessly festooned with crude hand-lettered signs. Take away the comfortably shaded wooden galleries and replace them with flat brick façades baking in a hellish heat. Take away the dress shops with their gossamer gowns and the twinkling windows of gold and pearls and replace them with Jesus-jumping storefront churches, wholesale outlets for car parts, and consignment stores cluttered with chunky costume jewelry, crumbling paperback books, and odd-lot glassware. Take away the twining lanes, the great houses with their ample porches, and replace them with a scorching grid of one-story single-family homes, a patchwork of brick, wood, concrete, and whatever can be covered with machine-cut plates of aluminum siding.

Replace your Faulknerian idyll with all that, and you still wouldn't have Glenville.

For Glenville, you'd have to add several abandoned storefronts, their empty windows staring like blinded eyes onto deserted sidewalks; twanging country music blaring from car-lot speakers; a park strewn with crabgrass in summer and mud puddles in the fall; and a windowless library housed in the basement of the police department. Rust and seepage would have their measure too, along with chiggers and kudzu and a thick jungle growth of pokeweed, outstretched limbs bending beneath the weight of bloated purple berries and oversize leaves.

And even after adding all that, yet more is required.

You'd need a trailer park perpetually pulsing in the light of a police cruiser, diesel trucks sitting like exhausted mastodons in red-dirt driveways, a makeshift Catholic church for the seasonal pickers of green beans and watermelon, and long lines of rusty cars and old pickup trucks streaming toward the dog-food factory as the third shift winds its way through the breaking of yet another dreary dawn.

You'd need all that, plus this: everywhere, everywhere, a sense of dazed and charmless struggle.

Or so, surely, Glenville had seemed to me.

"You never liked it, did you, Luke?" Lola Faye asked. "You never liked Glenville."

It occurred to me that all I'd just thought of Glenville, my low, cruel estimation of the place, must in some way have been written on my face.

"No, I didn't like it," I admitted.

"Because you never felt like you belonged there?" Lola Faye asked. "I bet that's the reason."

"Maybe," I answered, then quickly turned what seemed the knifepoint of our talk in her direction. "Did you like it?"

"Yeah, I liked it," Lola Faye said. "Your daddy did too."

As if summoned by Lola Faye, my father's image suddenly materialized before me, in that instant as real as Hamlet's paternal ghost, though my father had hardly been a king, much less a noble one. In fact, even at the moment when I'd realized what he'd done, the incontrovertible evidence clearly arrayed in front of me, my father's infidelity had struck me as impossible, given his staggering lack of any characteristic a young woman, even one as low-born and commonplace as Lola Faye, might find attractive. I knew that had he been a powerful man, a man of great achievement or learning or fame or even simply wealth, his affair with Lola Faye would not have left me stunned and incredulous, which was the effect it had had upon me at the moment I'd discovered it. For when it came to adultery, I'd read enough to know that great men dallied with shepherd girls and the daughters of farm hands and falconers, along with all the twittering ladies of the court. These men might be fat and boorish, of course, but they carried themselves with a separate weightiness as well, the gravity of the great matters with which they daily dealt. They were men of affairs, men of the world, men who traveled, drank claret, ate oysters.

Beside such men, my father possessed all the breadth and stature of a cottonseed. He had read nothing, gone nowhere, and never had the slightest desire to do either. The pork chop he ate at dinner had only days before been the slopped pig of some local farmer. He didn't know anything of history and didn't want to; didn't know anything of science and didn't care to. His religion, as far as I could tell, had been served to him like infant formula and had gone down smooth and silky without the resistance of a single fleeting doubt.

And so for me, the shock had been not that my father had betrayed my mother but that he'd actually had the opportunity to do so, that in tiny, hidebound Glenville, some creature of the opposite sex had returned what must have been his very awkward advances.

"Glenville was the perfect place for your daddy," Lola Faye said. "I'm sure he wouldn't have been happy anywhere else."

"Definitely not," I agreed.

"But it sure wasn't the right place for you," Lola Faye added in a voice that conveyed sympathy and understanding, a small-town girl's full recognition of big-city dreams . . . or did it? "You were always meant for something better, Luke."

Something better?

Was there an edge of mockery in her response, something unsaid but subtly biting? The problem was that I honestly couldn't tell. Lola Faye continually dodged any effort to pin down her mood, so I found it difficult to ascertain the exact meaning of anything she said. Iago's shadow seemed to hang all around her, her every remark a double-edged rapier whose blade flashed, then disappeared, then flashed again, always so quickly I couldn't determine its actual motion.

What I knew for certain about her last remark, however, was that its content carried a familiar ring, a not altogether complimentary estimation of myself that I'd heard before and against which I'd always bridled.

42

"Is that what my father told you?" I asked. "Because it sounds like something he'd have said about me. That I was too good for Glenville."

Lola Faye's tone of voice now turned unexpectedly breezy. "But you *were* too good for Glenville, Luke," she said. "You've proven that." She laughed with that same breeziness, a laugh that appeared to refresh her. "Goodness, Luke, you couldn't have done all you've done if you'd stayed in Glenville. Written books and all that. Who would blame you for wanting to leave Glenville? Not me. That's for sure."

"It's just that I always knew what my father thought of me," I said.

"Well, he had country ways, your daddy," Lola Faye said. She seemed to stare at me as if through the slit of an open door. "You wouldn't have liked that about him, his country ways."

Country ways indeed.

No, I admitted to myself, I hadn't liked them at all.

I remembered his sitting across the kitchen table from me, eating in that animal way of his, pouring so much salt on a sliced tomato that the salt lay unabsorbed in a dull gray coating, glistening and wet. He'd mashed jelly together with margarine and eaten it, as he ate everything else, with a spoon. He'd crumbled corn bread in buttermilk and drunk it in loud gulps. In fact, this had been his last meal, the remains of that dinner still sitting on the table above his sprawled, blood-soaked body.

"Yes, we were very different, my father and I," I said.

I recalled how he'd often deposited his dusty old work shoes on the kitchen table, as if they were a place setting, how he did everything with the same carelessness: mowed the yard in ragged strips, surrendered whole parts of the garden to the tyranny of weeds, allowed wasps to nest and bees to burrow anywhere they chose.

"The worst thing was that he was just so scattered in the way he did things." I shook my head at his many lapses. "He'd start something, then stop right in the middle of it and go on to something else. He couldn't concentrate on a single job for five minutes."

Lola Faye unaccountably drew the cloth napkin from the table and gave it a loud flap. "Things came at him," she said matter-of-factly.

"What?"

"Things came at him," Lola Faye repeated. "Like bats."

With the same unaccountable intent, she refolded the napkin and returned it to its exact position.

"That's the way he described it," she added. "Like he was in a room and things were just always coming at him."

That my father had even been aware of the disorderly nature of his own mind, his utter incapacity to focus on a task, was news to me.

"He told you that?" I asked. "Really?"

Lola Faye's attention fell to the place setting. She adjusted the fork, the spoon, the knife. "It bothered him, the way he was," she said. Her hand stilled and her eyes lifted toward me. "You must have known that."

"No," I answered softly. "I didn't."

Lola Faye nodded without saying a word, something disquieting in her gaze, so that I glanced away from her and over to the bar, hoping to see the waitress making her way toward us. But she was nowhere in sight.

"They don't have such great service here," I said when I faced Lola Faye once again. "They need to train the staff."

Lola Faye scratched her neck unselfconsciously. "Are you a big tipper, Luke?"

It was an odd question, but I answered it anyway. "Just average, I guess."

"Your father was a big tipper."

I found it surprising that my father had ever gone to a place where tipping was expected. "Where did you notice that?" I asked.

"Chattanooga," Lola Faye said. "He went there to buy sardines at the wholesaler's. He'd heard the price was good because some government shipment got sent by mistake. It was meant for the army or something, those sardines, but they got dropped off in Chattanooga. He bought fifty cases, and we loaded them into that old brown delivery truck he had. Then we went to get a bite to eat before we drove back to Glenville. It was a steak house. Nice."

"And he left a tip?" I asked.

"The waitress spilled," Lola Faye said. "It was her first day, she told him. He felt sorry for her."

"I see."

"He left ten dollars," Lola Faye added. "A ten-dollar bill. That was a lot of money in those days." She thought through the proportions. "I think the check was maybe thirty dollars for the both of us because we didn't drink. Wine, I mean. Just iced tea." She rolled her eyes up slightly in a way that suggested she was running the numbers again. "Yeah, it must have been around thirty dollars, the bill, so it was a nice tip your father left." Her gaze settled on me. "He shook hands with her when we left. I always remembered that. He shook hands with her and wished her good luck with her new job."

A memory flashed, this one of my father taking my hand as we crossed the main street of Glenville, looking both ways, reminding me to do the same: *You have to be careful, Luke. Things come at you fast.* With that memory, the rough look of his hands returned to me quite vividly, the many ways he'd scraped his fingers and bruised his palms, the gouges of metal staples, the tiny cuts of paper, all the many hapless wounds his hands had borne.

I don't know how long this recollection lasted, only that when it ended I found Lola Faye staring at me silently, almost pensively, like one studying some artifact long lost in time.

"Did you just have one of your great thoughts?" she asked in a tone whose exact position between admiration and something inexpressibly other than that I simply could not locate.

"No," I answered cautiously. "Just something that came back to me. A memory."

Lola Faye offered no response to this but instead turned her attention to the small laminated paper that had been inserted into a chrome display. "What's this?" she asked. "'Appletini,'" she read. "'Vodka and green-apple Pucker.'" She looked at me. "Green-apple Pucker? What on earth is that, Luke?"

"It's a liqueur," I answered. "It's very tart."

"Is it really green?"

"Yes."

She screwed up her face. "A green drink? That sounds sort of yucky. I bet you've had one, though. I bet you try things."

"No, I've never had one," I said.

Lola Faye's gaze was once again fixed on the card. "A green drink," she mused. "Green-apple Pucker."

"Most people wouldn't drink it straight," I told her.

Lola Faye nodded. "Yeah, it says you mix it with vodka. A green martini. Huh." She released a short, appreciative laugh. "The things people come up with." Her eyes found me again. "Actually, it sounds sorta good."

"Then have one," I said.

She shook her head. "No, we already got that wine coming."

"After the wine, then."

"Two drinks, Luke?" Her eyes actually twinkled, and her right hand slipped under the cloth napkin like a cardsharp reaching for an ace in the hole. "You think we'll talk that long?"

Oddly, truthfully, I said, "I do."

CHAPTER
FOUR

But *why* did I say that, I wondered at that instant, given the fact that I continued to feel uncomfortable in the presence of Lola Faye, continued to hear that little adder poking at the basket wall. Was I only being polite in suggesting to Lola Faye that our talk might go on a little longer than I'd anticipated, that there was no need to rush, plenty of time, that is, for her to try an appletini?

No, I decided. I'd offered more time because despite its initially jarring effect, Lola Faye's talk of Glenville, of the early life I'd lived there, those boyhood years, had returned me to a youth that had once been full of hope, to that boy who'd once striven for something good, even great. There had been a time when the world was tactile and aromatic, and when all my senses had been open to it. Lola Faye had hardly known me then, and so it struck me that I could possibly put aside all my uneasiness in her presence — those eyes behind a beaded curtain, that little snake poking at the straw — and for once look back with something other than anger and regret. And so I allowed myself to feel a certain pleasantness in being with someone who'd known me in my youth but only distantly, so that I

48

might briefly and safely return to those otherwise unpleasant waters, a return I hoped to achieve easily and without consequences, a river of time with no rapids ahead, no precipitous falls.

On that thought, and quite to my surprise, I found myself once again in a summer garden, Mr. Klein drifting away with a backward glance, my mother's hand reaching down to grasp my shoulder. *Let's take a walk, Luke.*

We'd taken that walk many times, always to the town park, which meant that we strolled down Glenville's one main street. We'd usually pass Variety Store on our way to the park, but on this particular day my mother took us by a different route so that we ended up at the far end of the park, where the Confederate monument stood in proud isolation within a grove of trees.

We sat down on the steps of the monument, and I expected my mother to draw a book from her bag and either read to me or have me read to her, as was our custom on these occasions. But this time she merely sat and peered out into the park. I was just a boy, but I could sense some kind of tumult in her mind, something unsettled, restive, pent up. It built in her steadily until she finally blurted, "Don't settle for Glenville, Luke." She took my face in her hands and stared at me fiercely. "Don't ever let yourself settle for Glenvi —"

"Pinot noir for the lady," the waitress said.

Now I was once again in the lounge of the Shady Creek Hotel, watching as the waitress placed a dark red paper coaster on the table in front of Lola Faye, then set the glass of wine on it.

"And for the gentleman," she added as she did the same for me. Her smile was toothpaste-ad white. "I'll check back in a few minutes."

I felt an odd comfort in having revisited and then returned from the past so pleasantly. "The lady might have an appletini at that point," I said cheerily.

Lola Faye girlishly waved her hand. "I don't know about that, Luke," she said.

"Whatever she wants, that's what she'll get," the waitress said brightly.

And I thought, *At last, perhaps, on this one night, in this small way, Lola may actually get what Lola wants.*

"That's so nice, Luke," Lola Faye said. "You know, what the waitress just told me, that whatever I want, I can have. It makes you feel special, being treated nice like that."

I looked at the scar on her forehead, the dent in her chin, and wondered in what less nice ways she'd been treated since my father's death, whether Ollie was kind or abusive, gentle or violent. My father had never lifted his hand against my mother, but there'd been a kind of violence in the way he'd distanced himself from her, going to Variety Store early and coming home late, never taking her out or buying her a present. In all the years of their marriage, I'd never once seen him embrace her, or heard him say a tender thing.

"Would you mind answering a question?" I asked.

"Sure," Lola Fay answered.

I leaned forward slightly. "Was my father nice to you?"

Lola Faye's eyes softened. "Your daddy was very nice to me, Luke."

"Always?"

"Always," Lola Faye answered, but now a little tense, clearly wary of the subject. She reached for her glass, then stopped, paused, drew back her hand. "It seems strange, Luke, us talking about me and your daddy."

When I gave no response to this, she eased her hand back to the glass, lifted it, took a quick sip, then returned it to the table. "Do you ever see him? Your daddy, I mean? Like the way I see Woody sometimes? I'll be at the Walmart or the grocery store, something like that, and I'll look up from the grapes or the lettuce, whatever, and I'll glance over, and there he'll be. Just standing there in those old blue overalls he used to wear. Woody, just like he was back then."

"I see my mother that way sometimes," I admitted. "But always as she was when I was around ten. Still a beautiful woman."

"When do you see her, Luke?" Lola Faye asked in a tone that was entirely conversational, as if we were chatting at a laundromat or over breakfast at the IHOP. "On her birthday, something like that? An occasion?"

"No particular occasion," I answered, and immediately recalled her dark eyes, how very expressive they'd been, with something I hadn't understood always playing in them, an emotion I couldn't comprehend at that age with so little of life behind me but that was starkly clear to me now: lost hope.

"And do you see your daddy too?" Lola Faye asked.

This time her tone seemed subtly interrogative, and it struck me that she had begun this line of conversation with my father, asking if I ever "saw" him, and that she had now returned me to him.

"On rainy days," I answered warily. "I don't know why."

Lola Faye considered this for a moment, then said, "Well, it was raining at his funeral." She glanced toward the window, the little rivulets of water streaking down the glass. "Drizzling, like now."

I took a quick sip from my glass. "It's supposed to change to snow, by the way. Snow by midnight, according to the local forecast."

Lola Faye appeared indifferent to any change of weather. "There was a rose on his coffin," she said, like one pointing out a disturbance in the brush. "Your mother put it there. So I guess she must have loved him, to do that."

My mother's love for my father, either its depth or its source, was not a subject I wanted to discuss, and so I shot back, "What made you think of the rose?"

Lola Faye shrugged. "Probably those red flowers over there," she said.

I glanced over to a holiday display of poinsettia. "Pretty," I said coolly.

"Or maybe it was just me putting a couple of things together," Lola Faye added with an innocence that seemed strained, so that once again I felt like I'd been returned to a planned route. "Those red flowers and that rose I saw on your daddy's coffin. They teach you to do that in therapy. It's called association."

"You've been in therapy?"

"No, but I read a book about it once," Lola Faye said. "I like to read."

She smiled quite brightly, then reached for the bag she'd tucked my book into after she'd bought it. The bag was turned at a different angle now, and I saw the words *Los Angeles County Coroner* written on the side, along with a comic chalk outline of a crime-scene murder victim.

"Interesting bag," I said.

"They have a gift shop at the coroner's office," Lola Faye informed me. "You can buy cups and T-shirts. It's a tourist stop because of all the bodies that have been there. Celebrity bodies. Murdered people. Like Robert Kennedy and Marilyn Monroe."

"Marilyn Monroe wasn't murdered," I reminded her.

"You don't think so, Luke?" Lola Faye asked. "I read a book that said she was."

"So, you're a bit of a conspiracy buff?" I asked.

Lola Faye looked at me quizzically.

"People who believe that Marilyn Monroe was murdered, for example, or that Oswald wasn't a lone assassin."

She shrugged. "Well, things aren't always how they seem," she said. A pause, then, "Are they, Luke?"

"I guess not, but —"

"Oh, and you can order stuff from them online too," Lola Faye interrupted. "From the LA coroner's." She dug into the bag. "Speaking of reading and things not being what they seem." She drew out a book and handed it to me. "I'm reading this now."

I took the book from her and read the title: *The Sheppard Murder Case.*

"The book's pretty interesting," Lola Faye said. "I think maybe he was framed. Dr. Sheppard, I mean. I think maybe the police just needed to pin his wife's murder on someone, and so they pinned it on Dr. Sheppard."

I handed the book back to Lola Faye. "Could be," I said crisply. "It happens, I guess. A person wrongfully accused."

"Yeah, it happens," Lola Faye said. She returned the book to the bag, then placed the bag over the arm of her chair. "Wrongfully accused, like you say. So the real killer got away. Anything can happen."

"Anything," I agreed, trying to trace back to how we'd gotten on the subject of unsolved murders, people wrongfully accused, killers still free, and wondering whether Lola Faye had intended our talk to go to such a place all along. I decided to change the subject.

"We forgot to make a toast," I said. "It's customary to make a toast before we drink."

"But I've already sipped," Lola Faye said. "Was that bad manners when I did that?"

I waved my hand. "I sipped too. Don't worry about it." I lifted my glass. "Here's to . . ." I stopped because I couldn't think of an appropriate toast. Here she was, Lola Faye Gilroy, sitting across from me in a shadowy lounge, the same Lola Faye for whom my father had evidently been willing to cast everything aside, my mother, me, even the little store he'd mismanaged for twenty years.

But this was a bitter recollection, and to avoid any further consideration of it, I simply smiled and said, "So, what shall we drink to, Lola Faye?"

"I hate that name," Lola Faye said with a sudden starkness, as if it were a long-suppressed resentment. "It's a redneck name, don't you think, Luke?"

I shrugged. "I've never thought of it one way or the other."

"Like Wanda Jean or Betty Sue. Hillbilly girls in those stupid dresses with big prints on them, cut down to . . ." She indicated her bosom. "People make fun of girls like that. Girls like I was." She appeared momentarily returned to that place and time. Then, with a quick laugh and a lightning twist of mood, she was back in Saint Louis and smiling brightly. "I've been thinking of changing it."

"Changing your name?"

"Yep."

"To what?"

She shrugged. "Maybe just plain Lola or maybe just plain Faye." She thought this possibility over briefly, then shook her head. "But I probably won't change it at all."

"All right," I said. "So, what shall we drink to, then?"

My father's one true love grabbed her glass and clinked it against mine in a motion that was a little too fast and hard, the sound of our glasses a little too loud. "To us," she said. "To the survivors."

CHAPTER
FIVE

To the Survivors?

This was certainly not the toast I'd expected Lola Faye to make, but I offered no objection to it. For in a way, I had to admit, we *were* survivors, the only two people in the dreadful saga of my father's infidelity who had lived to talk about it.

On the wings of this thought, my father insistently stepped back into my mind. As a boy, I'd tried to imagine him as the strong, silent type, had bestowed noble characteristics upon him that my very growing older and smarter had later stripped him of. I wondered if in Lola Faye's estimation he'd actually had those characteristics, and with that thought I recalled a time I'd overheard a conversation of theirs, recalled it vividly, which surprised me, and almost word for word:

How much do you think I oughtta ask for these Christmas dolls, Lola Faye?

My father's voice had come from behind the barely open door of Variety Store's backroom.

I don't know. They're pretty nice. Maybe ten dollars?

Her reply had been hesitant and unsure, no doubt because she had no retail experience, and yet here was my father asking advice of Lola Faye Gilroy.

Ten dollars? You think many folks could afford that?

Asking advice as to his wares and prices, as to what might or might not be profitable, advice he'd never asked of me, nor would he have taken it had I offered.

I'd shaken my head at the sheer ludicrousness of this exchange, my father with no head for business, Lola Faye with no experience in business, the blind leading the blind, and yet their talk had carried within it an element that had never existed in any conversation between my father and me, an intimacy and trust, a sense of shared endeavor.

Now I wondered if Lola Faye had come to me in search of that kind of talk, hoping to have that kind of conversation out of some bizarre and inexplicable need to rekindle her feelings for my father, touch him again through me.

"Okay, to the survivors," I said, and clinked my glass against hers, knowing full well at that moment in our talk that I would never be a party to any such plan, never allow myself to serve as medium between her and my dead father.

Still, I could see how seriously she considered this last talk to be from the way she put down her glass very slowly once the toast was made, all her earlier breeziness now muted, her gaze, by the time the glass returned to the dark red coaster, quite noticeably subdued.

Then, as if suddenly determined to resist her own descending mood, she yanked the dark green scarf from around her neck in a peculiarly festive manner, like a girl arriving at a party.

"I liked what you said about your mother, the way you see her, I mean," she said. "All young and beautiful." She took a sip from her glass. "She was really nice, your mother."

It wasn't my mother's niceness that struck me then, however, but her sacrifice, how from the moment she'd urged me to get out of Glenville, she'd done everything she could to make sure I'd be able to do just that. I thought of the little metal box she'd secreted in the back of her closet, how tenderly she'd opened it with her long pale fingers, saying, *This is for you, Luke. This is for your journey.*

"A nice woman," Lola Faye added. "Always nice to everyone."

I started to offer some expression of polite agreement, but she abruptly changed the subject.

"Do you remember your speech, Luke?" she asked brightly. "That great speech you made at Glenville High?"

She couldn't possibly have heard it, and it surprised me that she'd even known about it. I'd only been in the ninth grade at the time, a full two years before she'd been hired to work at Variety Store and thus long before she'd ever heard of me. The speech had been a rousingly patriotic affair that I'd given as the ninth-grade representative in a school debate tournament. I'd won the contest and in winning it had gotten noticed and written about by the town newspaper, an article above the fold, complete with a photograph, entitled "Glenville's Smartest." The fact that each week produced another champion of one sort or another had done nothing to dampen my own enthusiasm for myself, and I'd basked in the attention for a month.

"I remember the first line of it," I admitted, and that, truthfully, was all I remembered.

"Oh, then say it to me," Lola Faye said happily.

"I couldn't," I said with fake modesty. "It's embarrassing."

"Oh, come on, Luke," Lola Faye pleaded in a voice that shifted to a nearly childlike playfulness. "Come on, say it to me. It's just the two of us. Come on, Luke, I dare you."

I leaned back in my chair, lifted my head as if to address an eagerly awaiting throng, and delivered the line. "An American, I believe, is one who at a bullfight roots for the bull."

Lola Faye clapped her hands enthusiastically. "Oh, that's great, Luke."

"Well, it put the crowd at ease, at least," I said casually.

"And you've probably done that every time since then," Lola Faye said with the same enthusiasm, though I wondered if this enthusiasm was simply a form of flattery she was using to relax me as I had relaxed the crowd, and after which, I'd lowered the boom.

"You must have made so many speeches by now, Luke," Lola Faye continued with what appeared to be unabashed admiration. "In big rooms, I mean. Big halls."

Big halls? I all but cringed. For I'd never spoken in any big halls. Only classrooms with twenty students at the most, or sometimes a packed house of listless freshmen, and that room packed only because History 101, the staple of my academic year, was a required course.

"Anyway," I said. "It was a successful speech, I guess."

"'Roots for the bull,'" Lola Faye repeated in a mock oratorical tone, as if the line might reverberate within her forever, be an eternal source of amusement. "'Roots for the bull,'" she said again. "That's so great, Luke. How did you ever think of that?"

"Actually," I confessed, "it's not my line."

Lola Faye's expression was pure puzzlement.

"I mean, it wasn't a line I wrote myself," I explained. "I read it somewhere. Probably *Bartlett's*."

"*Bartlett's*," Lola Faye said. She seemed to think it might be a department store, so I explained a bit further.

"It was the first book I ever owned," I told her. "My mother bought it for me."

It had been my tenth birthday, and the book had been wrapped quite beautifully in gold paper and a silver bow. "All the wisdom of the world is in here," she'd said as she gave it to me.

"I bet it was a history book," Lola Faye said.

"No, it was a book of quotations," I told her. "Famous things that famous people said. You know, like from Lincoln: 'With malice toward none, with charity for all,' that kind of thing." When Lola Faye said nothing, I added, "*Bartlett's* was a book of quotations like that."

"What other people said." Lola Faye nodded softly. "Like that line about Americans at a bullfight rooting for the bull."

"That's right."

"Like 'the blinding country of youth,'" Lola Faye said. "Not your own words."

"Not my own words, no," I said.

She thought about this for a moment in a way I found impossible to decipher, though her expression appeared somber and uncertain, as if she were weighing some great matter in her mind. Then, in a complete turn, her face brightened.

"Well, you picked a perfect line to start that speech with, Luke," she said, like one who'd decided to forgive some small sin. "Even if it wasn't yours."

There was no hint of accusation in Lola Faye's remark. Or was there? I couldn't be sure, and yet it reminded me rather piercingly that I hadn't credited anyone for the line that opened my little talk, not then nor ever after, when students or teachers at the high school mentioned what a terrifically apt and funny line it was. I'd wanted to say, *Well, actually, it wasn't my line*, but I never had, and now it seemed to me that my lips had been sealed by some sadly needful part of me that had craved attention at all costs and so had been willing to sacrifice some ineffable but real element of moral character. At that thought, I felt an odd emptying of myself, as if Lola Faye had inserted an ice pick and left a puncture from which I would leak forever.

"Even if it wasn't mine, yes," I whispered almost to myself, thinking: *Is that where it began?* Fitzgerald said that you lose yourself in pieces. Was that little corruption, that small deceit, where the first piece of me had fallen away and away, like Satan over the rim of Heaven?

Lola Faye shook her head. "Boy, that was a long time ago, Luke, when you gave that speech."

As if transported back by her words, I found myself once again behind the podium peering out at the crowded assembly hall as the students and teachers of Glenville High exploded in applause, basking in an admiration that, as it turned out, I would never know again.

"A long time ago," I repeated when I returned to the present.

My momentary lapse into remembrance appeared to make no impression on Lola Faye.

"Doug was really sorry he missed that speech," she said.

It struck me that I'd never heard Lola Faye use my father's first name before. In the store she'd always called him Mr. Paige, and so far during our talk, she'd called him "your father" or "your daddy." Now, quite suddenly, she'd called him Doug, familiarity that came upon me stealthily, like a night crawler into my bed.

"Doug told me he'd planned to go hear your speech, but this shipment came in from the wholesaler, and he had to unload the truck," Lola Faye sped on. "But you won, and Miss McDowell gave you that certificate, and then you were invited to speak at the Rotary Club and the Lions Club."

The added details Lola Faye had garnered surprised me, and I felt vaguely like the subject of some official inquiry, the way you might feel, for example, if you learned that FBI agents had been talking to your neighbors about you.

"How do you know all that?" I asked. "Where I gave that speech, the Rotary Club and the Lions Club."

"I saw it in the scrapbook," Lola Faye answered. "The one your daddy had."

"That scrapbook was my mother's," I corrected. "She's the one who cut all those articles out of the paper and made a scrapbook."

She'd done it with meticulous care, sitting at the kitchen table, the scissors held delicately in her hand, *snip, snip, snip,* accomplishing it all with great attention, keeping straight edges and pointed corners, and she'd finally achieved a kind of small perfection, pasting the article with equal care in the scrapbook she rather poetically called *Luke's Journey.*

"She made that scrapbook like an artist would have done it," I added. "Like a painter or a sculptor would have made it. My father didn't have anything to do with it."

"He liked it though, your daddy," Lola Faye chirped. "He brought it to Variety Store. He showed it to people."

One of whom, quite obviously, had been Lola Faye Gilroy, the young woman with whom he'd fallen in love and had an affair and in that way had thrown my life into turmoil.

"Not enough," I said sharply. "He didn't care enough about anything. Not about my mother and certainly not enough about me."

This remark erupted from me before I could stop it and with a bitter loss of control I'd not intended, and I strove immediately to take back.

"But he was like that," I added with a clear effort to show my indifference to my father's indifference. "He came first. That's just the way he was."

I was quite certain that Lola Faye had had a very different impression of my father, of course, given what had happened between them. Even so, and as I also expected, she didn't offer a contradictory opinion of the man who had seduced her when she could not have been more needy and abject, an unskilled, penniless shop girl with an estranged husband crazed by the loss of her, a man who, rather surprisingly, she mentioned at just that moment.

"Woody was like that too. Most men are." She smiled as if she thought I must be an exception. She let this settle in, then added, "Woody didn't understand the situation."

I thought of the pleading messages Woody had left in Lola Faye's dented tin mailbox after she'd stopped taking his calls, changed her number, irrevocably turned away from him.

"Clearly," I said.

"That we were through, Woody and me," Lola Faye said. "He didn't understand that."

"Well, some men are a little dense," I allowed, trying to drop the subject, though not before an awful image

64

came into my mind: poor, baffled, overweight Woody Wayne Gilroy, kicked out of Lola Faye's bed and sprawled on his cousin's sofa a mile from the little house they'd shared, nearly headless, according to the *Glenville Free Press*, the shotgun barrel lying on his chest, all above it a gooey mass of exploded bone and flesh, bits of brain hanging like wads of gum from the wall behind him. The generally reticent *Glenville Free Press* had spared our town's eager readers no detail.

"Yes, but what happened to him, Luke," Lola Faye said softly, "that was really terrible." She released a small sigh. "Of course, what he did was terrible too." She added nothing to this, so I couldn't be sure to which of her husband's ghastly acts she was referring.

"So fast," she added, lowering her gaze again, like a penitent before her confessor. "It all happened so fast."

We were both briefly silent, then Lola Faye raised her head abruptly, as if that earlier penitent had just been given full absolution, the girlish sparkle in her eyes now fully regained. "So, there." She smiled softly, then took a quick sip of wine, after which she fanned herself as if overcome by heat. "You don't want to get me drunk, Luke," she said with a comic grin.

"Why's that?" I asked casually.

"Because I'm a mean drunk."

A mean drunk, I thought, *like Woody was rumored to be*, though the police investigation had revealed that he'd only started drinking big time after Lola Faye left him.

Lola Faye took another sip. "Just kidding," she said perkily. "I'm an easy drunk, is all. I get drunk easy, I mean. It never took much. So I have to watch myself when it comes to drinking wine."

"But you don't drink wine much, do you?" I asked, leaving out that her less than rudimentary acquaintance with even quite common varietals had given me this impression.

"No, I don't, Luke," Lola Faye answered. "It's expensive, to begin with. Even big bottles. I mostly drink Co'-Cola. Pepsi, I mean. I can tell the difference. People say you can't, you know, with your eyes covered. But I can tell the difference between Diet Coke and Diet Pepsi." Her hand shot up and she gave a violent snap of her fingers. "Like that!" she said.

This power of subtle differentiation between diet sodas was a skill in which Lola Faye took quite obvious pride, so I went along with it in the indulgent way I went along with golf-course stories in the faculty lounge and English-teacher tales of meeting the Great Writer who turned out, of course, to be a lush or a skirt-chaser or, in any case, a searing disappointment.

"Really?" I said admiringly. "I hear it's not good for you, diet soda. Not good for your stomach."

"Maybe not, but that's in the long run," Lola Faye said. "Years down the road, right?" She shrugged. "And who has years?" She took another sip of wine. "But wine is supposed to be very good for you, isn't it, Luke?"

"So they say," I answered, and took a sip myself. "'For thy stomach's sake,'" I added when I set the glass down. "'Take a little wine for thy stomach's sake,' the Bible says."

66

"The Bible, right." She took another quick sip from her glass. "Did you ever join the church, Luke?"

Oh, please, no, I thought. Please don't tell me that Lola Faye Gilroy is now a born-again proselytizer of some backwoods fundamentalist faith come all this way into the heathen North to save the soul of Glenville's only published writer.

"No, I didn't," I said flatly. "Because I never believed a word of it. Not a whit. Not a smidgen." I made a pointed pause in order to emphasize what I said next. "And never will."

There, I thought, *done with it*. Now perhaps Lola Faye Gilroy can gather her things and leave the rest of the devil's brew in the glass, and we can both get back to our lives.

But instead she said, "Me neither. Which makes it hard sometimes. I mean, to think that there's nothing, that it will all be over, and that when it is, you'll be nothing. Your daddy didn't believe in anything either."

"Yes, he did," I protested. "He went to church every Sunday. Tithed that damn ten percent when we barely had food on the table."

"Yeah, but it was all fake," Lola Faye said matter-of-factly. A humorous recollection appeared to grip her. "One time, he said, 'You know, Lola Faye, when you've been dead a million years, you've just started being dead.'"

"My father told you that?" I asked.

"Yep," Lola Faye said. "And that's not all. One time, he said, 'You know, Lola Faye, religion is just Santa Claus for grown-ups.'"

I wasn't convinced of one word of this. "Why did he do all that church stuff then?" I asked.

She shrugged. "I guess he thought it might be good for business."

I laughed. "So that was his business plan?" I looked out into the night. "Going to church?"

When I looked back at Lola Faye, there was a troubled expression on her face.

"You okay?" I asked.

"I'm fine." Her eyes fell to her glass. "I just went back for a second." She chuckled and took up the wine. "It can be depressing, but really, a person should go back. Otherwise, it goes missing. Your whole life."

I offered no argument to this, but Lola Faye seemed to find an argument in my silence.

"So why don't people do it more often?" she asked. "Think back over the past."

"Because there's no point," I answered brittlely. "You can't change anything."

"Is that why you never came back to Glenville once you left it?" Lola Faye asked.

I nodded, though I knew that the real reason was my sense that some places, like unstanched wounds, never stop bleeding.

"Me, I go back to old memories a lot," Lola Faye said. "I think it helps us go on from where we are. Which we can't do unless we go back over things, find out what really happened."

What really happened?

For some reason I wondered if she could possibly be referring to that night, the desperate anger, the annihilating blast, all that blood and shattered glass, my father sprawled across the cheap linoleum that covered our kitchen floor.

"What really happened?" I asked hesitantly. "To whom?"

"To us," Lola Faye answered in a tone that was quite leisurely, even relaxed, as if she'd just come to a place in a book where she could pause, briefly think over what she'd read. "To all of us."

"I don't quite know what you're talking about," I said cautiously.

"Life," Lola Faye explained. "I'm talking about life."

"Your life?"

"Mine," Lola Faye answered. "Yours." Her eyes took on an aspect that seemed different from any of the ones I'd seen before, hard and in some way throwing off sparks, like an instrument being sharpened. Then that thin smile again as she lifted her glass in a second toast. "To continuing our talk."

PART II

CHAPTER
SIX

But we didn't continue our talk.

At least, not in terms of anything further about Lola Faye's life, or mine, or even life in general.

Instead, Lola Faye launched into a discussion of the park across the street, how she'd had some time to "scope it out" earlier in the day. While she droned on about what she'd seen along this pathway or beside that pond and how nice the people she'd met there were, I went back again, back to Glenville, Variety Store, the affair that was being carried on in its back storeroom and that, as it continued, became a gathering storm within my family.

I'd never held Lola Faye entirely responsible for any of it, for compared to my father, she'd seemed little more than an innocent bystander: a young woman separated from her husband, in financial straits, no doubt in need of comfort. But at the same time, I'd never completely excused her. It was just that my father had seemed to me the truly guilty party, mainly because he'd accepted my mother's deep devotion then repaid her with betrayal. I had resented Lola Faye, certainly, but it was only my father I'd actually despised.

Lola Faye's taste in men was another question, however, and as the current, middle-aged version of that once vulnerable young woman now went on to discuss how nice people were in Saint Louis, I tried to imagine how ham-handed my father's initial advance must have been, as well as how desperate or bereft Lola Faye must have been to entertain it.

I'd always imagined my father acting quickly, impulsively, since he'd never been capable of formulating what could remotely be called a plan for anything. This utter lack of calculation had been the bane of Variety Store, the small profit it made immediately used up by something my father had neglected, usually taxes, which he never filed on time and so interest and penalties continually accrued. He would neglect a leak in the toilet until the floor gave way beneath it; allow carpenter ants to have their way until whole sections of woodwork had been reduced to sawdust. For all that could be determined from his actions, he didn't believe wind and rain actually weathered anything. His tools rusted in dank pools; bolts of fabric turned to rot in the moldy dampness of the store's more or less unlighted cellar.

So it must have come without forethought, my father's first adulterous approach, a moment when the urge swept over him like a hot wind, and before he could stop himself, and quite without calculation of either his actions or their consequences, he'd reached out and touched Lola Faye Gilroy, or perhaps simply said . . . what?

Had it been *I love you?*

74

If so, they were words I'd never once heard him say to my mother. A certain distance had seemed to define them, one that a particular memory always brought back.

It was the Christmas following my discovery of my father's affair, all of Glenville adorned with lighted trees and decorations. My mother had been somewhat unsteady on her feet for the last few days and for that reason she hadn't left the house. But she had always loved the season, delighting in the Nativity scenes and displays of Santa and his reindeer that people placed in their front yards. And so on that particular evening she'd emerged from her bedroom with her hair brushed and wearing a little make-up, her mood uncharacteristically light, almost girlish.

"Your father and I are going to drive around town a little to see the decorations."

I had zero interest in such things, of course, and the knowledge of what my father was doing in the backroom of Variety Store soured the notion of my mother's dressing up for this pathetic tour even more. But for all that, it was clear that my mother was looking forward to getting out, even if it was only for a brief cruise around Glenville, and so I said, "That's nice, Mom."

And it would have been, at least for her.

But it never happened.

A few minutes later, my father came rattling home in that old delivery van of his, strode into the house, yanked off his shoes, and plopped down into his recliner with a great show of exhaustion.

During all of that he hardly seemed to notice my mother, and certainly he saw not a bit of the effort she'd put in to make herself attractive.

"Doug?" she said, standing before him then, lipstick applied, earrings dangling, as if she were going to a fancy restaurant.

"Hey, Ellie," my father said as he released another weary breath.

"Are you ready to go?" my mother asked brightly.

My father had closed his eyes, but they fluttered open. "Go where?"

"For our drive," my mother said. "To see the Christmas decorations."

My father waved his hand. "Naw, they's no need for that," he said. "I been all over town already. They's nothing to 'em."

And with that, he closed his eyes once more and left her there, standing before him, mute, awkward, bereft of a love and devotion and certainly of a loyalty she fully deserved but would never have.

I had never seen her look more utterly alone than she did at that moment. Watching as she remained in place before my father's slumped figure, I felt the weight of her fruitless preparation, the pull of her earrings, the dry flecks of her make-up, all of it united in a single, tactile sensation of the arid, shaved-down life that had been imposed upon her.

It was a spur to action, and so I sprang to my feet.

"I'll take you around town," I said. "I'd like to see the decorations."

My mother melted at the offer, particularly because she knew I cared nothing for Glenville's holiday display. "Oh, Luke," she said. "You're so kind."

So kind, I thought now. Where had that boy gone?

On that brutal thought, I shook slightly, as if my spine had been raked by a cold finger, and in response to which discomfort I grabbed my glass and downed what remained of the pinot noir in a single gulp.

"Goodness, Luke," Lola Faye blurted.

I returned the glass to the table. "What?"

Then, as if in solidarity, Lola Faye grabbed her glass in exactly the same way I'd grabbed mine and drained it. "Wow." She looked at her glass and appeared genuinely surprised that there was nothing left in it. "I didn't think I could get it all down."

"Now we're both running on empty," I said a little starkly, the whole dreadful saga returning to me in a series of images: Woody's uneaten fries, the hole in my father's chest, my mother's hand gripping the banister, Lola Faye's eyes lifting toward me as my bus cruised by.

Lola Faye's hand fluttered to her mouth. "How weird," she said. "It was like I saw you do it and —"

"Saw me do it?" I interrupted with a sudden startle.

"Like I saw you gulp down your drink and just said to myself, *You can do that too, Lola Faye.*" She shook her head. "How weird, me slugging wine down like that." She shrugged. "I guess I'm sort of not myself tonight."

"Then maybe you should have that appletini," I said.

She looked hesitant. "Do you really think I should try one, Luke?"

"What's life without experiment?" I answered with a flourish.

Lola Faye laughed. "The things you say, Luke," She looked at me jokingly. "Or did someone else say that and you just stole it?"

"I guess a lot of people have said it," I answered, and nodded toward her empty glass. "So, another pinot noir, or do you throw caution to the wind?"

She thought a moment, then announced her choice. "I'll have an appletini," she said with a casual flip of her hand. "I'm going to live dangerously."

"Good for you," I said, and with a broad motion summoned the waitress.

"Another pinot for me," I told her. "And for the lady, an appletini."

The waitress smiled cheerfully. "Coming right up."

Once the waitress had departed, I expected Lola Faye to return to her description of the park or the amiability of the local population, since both topics had appeared to lift her mood, divert her from the dark elements of the past we shared. During the last few minutes, she'd laughed several times, shaken her head almost playfully, and seemed truly to become, in some sense, a quite different person. She'd made a little joke at my expense, ordered an appletini, and appeared more relaxed than before. All of which pointed to the possibility she'd say nothing more about "old times."

But instead of continuing down that lighter road of talk, she abruptly returned to the past.

"He would have been sixty next week. Woody."

"Would he?"

Lola Faye burst out laughing. "Would he? Woody? You are so hilarious, Luke."

I hadn't actually intended this peculiar homophone as a joke.

Lola Faye continued to laugh. "I bet you keep your students in stitches."

"Not at all," I told her. "As a matter of fact, my students say I'm pretty dull."

Lola Faye stopped laughing. "They say that to your face?"

"No, they do it on the Internet," I answered. "They have this site where they can say whatever they like about their teachers. Nothing really vulgar. They can't do that. But they can say you're dull, plodding, boring, whatever they want."

"Well, I think it's just rude," Lola Faye said. She appeared angry for me. "They should have more manners, kids that go to an expensive school like where you teach. A school that's hard to get into and all that. The cream of the crop."

"Maybe so," I said, not wanting any further discussion of either my decidedly dull students or the less than impressive academic status of Clarkston College. "We were talking about life. Looking back over it. You said you thought it was a good idea."

She looked at me as if she were now uncertain about the statement she'd previously made. "You probably think I'm all wrong," she said cautiously. "You probably think I'm stupid for thinking that."

"Not at all," I assured her. "I just think it's a complicated subject."

Lola Faye nodded in agreement. "One thing I know, it goes by in a hurry," she said. "Life goes by in a flash."

She continued on this topic for a time, using the usual phrases to describe the fleeting nature of human existence, one's days on earth gone "in a blink" or "before you know it." But she added nothing to what she'd said earlier, and even seemed a little hesitant to elaborate on it, so I finally decided to bring the whole subject to an end.

"Time flies, yes," I said flatly, like a closing bell.

That would do it, I thought, that would get us beyond any more futile *tempus fugit* talk. I glanced about the room, the few occupied tables, an older couple just leaving, a younger one preparing to leave.

"So, what now?" I asked when I returned my attention to Lola Faye.

Before she could answer, the waitress arrived with our drinks.

"An appletini for the lady," she said as she placed a new red coaster in front of Lola Faye and set her drink down on it.

"Thank you," Lola Faye said softly.

"And for the gentleman, pinot noir," the waitress said, then repeated the process. "Enjoy."

Lola Faye carefully picked up her drink and very slowly brought it toward mine in an exaggerated effort not to spill any of it.

"Martini glasses are tricky," I said.

Lola Faye nodded, but her eyes never left the drink.

"So, what do we toast to this time?" I asked.

"This time you choose."

"Okay," I said. "To you, Lola Faye Gilroy."

She raised her glass. "And to you . . . Martin Lucas Paige. To all the truly innocent," Lola Faye said with a loud laugh.

To all the truly innocent?

It seemed a bizarre toast, but we were on a roll and so I lifted my glass even higher than hers. "And the guilty too," I intoned.

"Yes, the guilty too," Lola Faye said softly, and with that toast, brought the glass slowly to her lips, her eyes visible just above the rim, and in those eyes, it seemed to me at that moment, the same question I'd first seen in Sheriff Tomlinson's gaze: *Luke, what did you do?*

CHAPTER
SEVEN

He'd come across me by accident, as far as I ever knew, though there seemed something calculated in the slow way he'd approached me that afternoon. I'd been sitting on the steps of the Confederate monument, not reading, but thinking. My father had been dead for only a few days at that time, but my mother, weakened by the blow as well as by the scandal, had already taken to her bed.

"Hello, Luke," he said. He glanced about the park. "Pretty much deserted this time of day."

"I like it that way," I said.

"Better for keeping your focus, I guess," Sheriff Tomlinson said. His eyes narrowed somewhat. "You're very focused, aren't you, Luke?"

"I guess so," I answered quietly.

"Very focused on your future," Sheriff Tomlinson added. "Everybody says that."

Everybody? I thought, trying to guess just who this *everybody* might be: Miss McDowell? Debbie?

"A boy with a plan," Sheriff Tomlinson said. He smiled his friendly, avuncular smile. "You sure didn't get that from your daddy."

"No, I didn't."

"Poor soul, Doug couldn't keep his mind on anything for long," Sheriff Tomlinson told me. The smile left, then returned, soft, unassuming. "Remember when he decided to paint the front of Variety Store?"

The idea had come to my father in the way all his ideas came to him, on the wings of chance. Suddenly, for no apparent reason, he'd decided that the front of the store needed to be "spruced up." Its current appearance wasn't eye-catching, he said. It needed to be brighter, shine out distinctively, like neon. That same day, he'd gone to the hardware store and bought fourteen gallons of orange paint.

"How much did he get done before he stopped painting that first time, Luke?" Sheriff Tomlinson asked good-humoredly, as if we were old friends recalling a rascally acquaintance.

"Half of one side," I answered. "About as far up as his head. Then he stopped. A few weeks later he took it up again and got about a third more done before he stopped. That's the way he did everything."

Sheriff Tomlinson shook his head and laughed. "I noticed just the other day that there was still a spot up on the left side that he never got to." The laughter hadn't entirely trailed off when he added, "That must have driven a boy like you nuts, Luke."

"Yes, it did," I admitted.

"A boy who's got plenty of focus would have trouble with a daddy like that."

I nodded.

Sheriff Tomlinson's eyes settled upon me. "Did you two have much trouble?" he asked. "You and your daddy?"

"No," I lied.

Sheriff Tomlinson remained silent for a moment, and during that time I wondered if this was some kind of interrogation technique, a way of letting me twist slowly, slowly, in the wind.

Finally he said, "You don't have any questions, do you, Luke?"

"Questions?"

"About what happened to your father that night?" Sheriff Tomlinson asked.

Why had he asked me that? I wondered. Was he seeking an odd reaction, a misspoken word, some sign that the truth had not been entirely revealed by the note Woody Gilroy had written before he'd put a shotgun to his head?

"No," I answered, and left it at that.

Sheriff Tomlinson glanced about the park again, then, to my surprise, he sat down next to me. "So, you going to miss this little town when you leave, Luke?"

It sounded like an innocent question, idly asked, but the scrutiny of Sheriff Tomlinson's gaze when he asked it made me feel like the desperately paranoid murderer in *The Tell-Tale Heart*.

"Yes," I lied. "There are things I'll miss."

"Like what?"

Now I could tell the truth. "My mother," I answered.

"How's she holding up?"

"Not particularly well," I said.

Sheriff Tomlinson peered out toward Main Street, the darkened windows of Variety Store only a few blocks away. "Sorry to hear it." He drew a cigar from his pocket and lit it. "Must've been hard on her, finding out about your daddy."

I recalled my father in all his staggering lack of business acumen, shoving receipts into whatever nook was nearest, granting credit to whoever requested it, forgetting to bill, so indifferent to inventory he couldn't tell what sold and what didn't so that the store was often flooded with items that could be as easily obtained at the town dump. But this had been nothing compared to his betrayal of my mother, the devastation it had caused.

Sheriff Tomlinson drew his gaze back to me. "Must've been a blow to you too."

"Yes," I said crisply, though I'd known about my father's affair with Lola Faye long before the sheriff had read Woody Gilroy's scrawled note.

The sheriff looked up toward the mountain. "So, when will you be leaving for Harvard, Luke?"

"I don't know for sure," I answered.

"You don't know for sure?" Sheriff Tomlinson asked.

He was clearly surprised by my answer, for how could a boy with a plan not know for sure what lay ahead of him?

"No," I said.

"Why not?"

"Arrangements still have to be made," I answered cryptically.

But even then, I'd expected to leave Glenville at the end of August, though under vastly different circumstances than the ones that later emerged.

Sheriff Tomlinson nodded heavily and got to his feet. "Well, I'm sure you're going to be very successful, Luke," he said. "It's good to have a dream."

"Luke?"

It was Lola Faye's voice, and it seemed to strike at me from the far reaches of space.

"Yes?" I said. I blinked rapidly, embarrassed, surprised, and even a little shaken by the depth of my latest backward journey. "I get lost sometimes," I sputtered. "In thought, I mean."

"That's what Debbie told me," Lola Faye said with a casualness that seemed not altogether genuine; I suddenly felt I'd once again been led back to a path that she had only briefly, with that talk of the park and Saint Louis's friendly citizens, allowed us to leave.

"I had a nice talk with her just a few weeks ago," Lola Faye added with the same casualness. "She remembered how funny you were."

Funny.

As if cued by the word, I made another return to Glenville. On this occasion, I went farther back in the timeline, to when I was sixteen, by then confident of my powers and that I would one day be a great writer of epic American histories.

She'd been a mountain girl, Debbie Todd, from one of the tiny towns that dotted the Appalachian foothills surrounding Glenville. The most popular girls at the school were the daughters of the local lawyers, doctors, bankers, and mill owners, and so Debbie must have been surprised when I approached her, since I'd already garnered the reputation of being the smartest kid at Glenville High, the one everyone felt certain was destined for great things. Certainly she'd appeared surprised the day I first approached her.

"Hi," I said.

We were standing in a crowded corridor, and I suppose, like any other boy of my age, I'd been attracted mostly by her face and figure, the luxuriant way her long blond hair fell down her back in gentle waves. She had piercingly green eyes, the sort poets call emerald, but seemed hardly to notice how pretty she was, though I'm sure she was aware of it. It was simply that she gave it only fleeting worth, a coin she had to spend, and quickly, and which she valued only because she knew others did.

"Hi," she said back; she started to say something else, then stopped dead, and waited.

"I'm Luke Paige."

"I know who you are." She drew her books more tightly to her chest. "I heard you were applying to some big-name college."

"Yeah, I am," I said.

"I'm applying to Mountain Community," Debbie said, a response I took to mean not only that she would not be applying to elite schools but also that she had no interest in pursuing anything but an ordinary life, one lived in Glenville or, if not in Glenville, some nearby town.

I'd known at that instant that Debbie would not be the girl I fell in love with, that she would never be my wife, the mother of my children. But I had rarely dated and didn't want to be thought of as shy or, worse, a queer, so the urge seized me, and I followed it.

"You know about the Sadie Hawkins Dance?" I asked.

Debbie shook her head.

"The Sadie Hawkins Dance is where the girl asks the boy," I told her.

Debbie waited.

"I thought you might want to ask me," I said with a big smile.

Debbie laughed. "That's a funny way to ask me out," she said. She thought this strange approach over for a moment, then shrugged. "Okay, I'll ask you."

Now it was my turn to wait.

"Will you go with me to the Sadie Hawkins Dance, Luke?" Debbie asked.

I thought it over, then shook my head. "Nah," I said.

A huge smile burst onto Debbie's face, and I knew in that instant that I'd won her.

"That you were smart and funny, that's what Debbie thought," Lola Faye said now. She took a quick sip of her appletini. "Debbie and I really weren't that far apart in age," she went on. "It seemed like it back then because ten years is a lot when it's between twenty-seven and seventeen. But when it's between forty-seven and thirty-seven, that's not a lot, really. You've both had the same experiences by then. Gotten married. Learned about things. People." Her maddeningly emaciated smile returned. "The way life can turn on you."

I leaned back smoothly, laboring to camouflage how odd and troubling I found the fact of Lola Faye just calling Debbie out of the blue, having a "nice" talk with her.

"Debbie said you were like a statue the last time she saw you," Lola Faye continued. "In the cemetery, I mean." She glanced toward the large grandfather clock that stood a few yards away, its great brass pendulum moving rhythmically back and forth. "I told her you'd been through a lot," she added. "That I got kind of cold and hard too after what happened back then." She drew her gaze to the right of the clock and stared out the distant window, the cold drizzle beyond, her attention fixed on a dark red car as it pulled up to the curb. "Cops can make you that way." Her eyes slid over to me. "Once they start looking into things, trying to connect things. They can turn you into stone." She paused a moment, thought something through, then went on. "Of course, Sheriff Tomlinson had a job to do. I mean, nothing like that had ever happened in Glenville."

It seemed strange that the conversation had moved to the police investigation that had followed my father's murder, and for a moment, and as I had so many times before, I wondered if I'd been rather slyly directed from one stream into another. I couldn't tell, but the thought now hit me in a way that was so unsettling I abruptly decided to bring my last talk with Lola Faye to an end.

"Well, it's getting late," I said. "And I have an early flight tomorrow morning. So I think maybe I should be —"

"I mean, you have to be careful what you say to the police," Lola Faye interrupted sharply, like a woman rushing to close the gate before the animal escaped. "Or even careful about what you do. Like even your father's funeral, whether to go to that or not. I had trouble deciding about that, Luke. Because I didn't know what your mother was thinking or had been told, you know? Or you either, Luke. I didn't know what you were thinking either."

"But in the end, you came to his funeral," I reminded her. "I remember seeing you there."

She nodded.

"Why did you come?" I asked, then realized that I'd been stopped cold in my effort to end this conversation, stopped cold and drawn back into it, that in some sense I had become a moth to her flame.

"I was sort of out of it, really," Lola Faye answered with a shrug. "I don't remember getting up and saying, 'I'm going to Doug's funeral.' Getting dressed and all that, getting in the car, going to the cemetery. Maybe it was the drugs, to tell you the truth. Those drugs they gave me to calm me down. You don't always think straight when you take those things. They can make you a little nuts. They affected me that way. They still do."

"Did you say 'still do'?"

"Yep," Lola Faye said without the slightest reluctance to reveal such a dependency.

"What drugs are you taking?"

"Whatever the doctor writes out," Lola Faye answered with a shockingly dismissive flick of her wrist. "They keep switching me around." She laughed. "Got to keep Lola Faye under control." She saw the strained look on my face. "But I'm under control," she explained hastily. "As long as I take my medications." She nodded toward the drink that stood before her. "I like this, Luke. Good suggestion. Appletini."

"I'm glad you like it," I said distantly. "Of course, with medications, maybe you shouldn't be drinking."

"So the doctors say," Lola Faye replied with a second dismissive wave of her hand. "But they don't know everything, do they, Luke? They may be smart, doctors, but they don't know everything." She laughed again, this time with an unsettling ferocity, almost a howl. "Besides, the way I look at it, a girl's gotta do what a girl's gotta do. That's been my motto ever since he died."

"Since he died?" I asked. "You mean my father?"

"No, I mean Danny," Lola Faye said. "My little boy."

Some measure of that which is most lost and irrecoverable within a single human life suddenly settled over Lola Faye.

"He was eight," she added softly. "Hit by a car. Hit and run. The guy got away with it."

"I'm sorry," I said. "I didn't know. You hadn't mentioned that."

"Got away with murder, that's what Ollie said."

I stared at her.

"But, hell, people don't like sob stories, do they, Luke?" Lola Faye asked. She took another sip from her drink, and with that sip, or so it appeared, her mood lifted like a circus tent, a hint of cotton candy in the air. "So, you thought I meant ever since your daddy was killed that I started living by that motto of mine?"

"Yes."

Now that same tent abruptly collapsed and a solemn sense of dark remembrance came into Lola Faye's voice. "Maybe it did start with all that," she said. She put down her glass softly. "You know, Luke, if it had just been Woody, it wouldn't have mattered as much. I know that's a terrible thing to say, but truth is truth, and I'd lost any feelings I ever had for Woody. If I'd ever had any in the first place, I mean." She shook her head. "He was sweet, Woody. But love, that's something else, don't you think? Like with you and Debbie."

"I never loved Debbie," I said.

"But she loved you, right? She looked like she did. She had that look in her eyes, like you were the one, and she knew it, the one you don't get over, no matter how much time passes. She had that look when she was with you, don't you think, Luke?"

I knew that Lola Faye couldn't have seen me with Debbie more than a few times, usually just quick drop-ins at Variety Store, so I wondered if she'd come to this knowledge of Debbie's love for me by observation or just from the talk she'd had with her.

92

"We romanticize first love," I said mordantly. "Make more of it than is really there."

Lola Faye shook her head. "Not when it's real, Luke." She lowered her eyes a bit, then lifted them and offered a bizarrely cheerful smile. "Your daddy liked Debbie," she said brightly. "He said she was down-to-earth." She smiled quite warmly, but it was a heat her eyes drained away. "Opposites attract, they say."

CHAPTER
EIGHT

Opposites attract?

Was that an accusatory remark?

And if so, what did Lola Faye mean by it and what was she getting at?

These were questions that for a moment took me out of the conversation, so I hardly paid attention as she diverted our talk to a staggeringly unlikely discussion of how ideals of attractiveness had changed, how there'd been a time, according to a program about art she'd seen on A&E, when chubby women had been the most desirable females, though now it was the skinny ones. There'd also been a time when girls with brains had had a certain appeal, she said, but now it was just the ones who were "made of plastic" who were considered attractive.

From there, she'd offered a brief survey of the magazines she read, mostly women's magazines that featured articles telling their readers "the fifteen ways to please a man or the twenty ways to please yourself." At that point, she'd giggled self-consciously and said, "You know what that means, right, Luke?" She read crime magazines too, she said, a type of reading she'd gotten into because of Ollie. "So I guess you could call me a crime buff."

Throughout this long monologue I could think only of that previous remark, how, according to Lola Faye, opposites attracted, a proposition I suddenly found it necessary to contradict, and which I did with an unintentionally abrupt, blurted denial.

"Opposites don't attract," I said sharply.

Lola Faye's lips sealed, and she stared at me silently.

"People say that," I added. "But I don't think it's true."

"What do you think *is* true, Luke?" Lola Faye asked softly.

"Well, for example, you said that my father liked Debbie," I answered. "Well, sure he did. Because Debbie didn't have much ambition. She was happy where she was. That's what my father liked about Debbie. That she was easily satisfied. Just like he was easily satisfied and didn't care if he never accomplished anything. He liked Debbie because she was like him, simple."

"Simple," Lola Faye repeated. "Is that why he liked me?"

She didn't appear to find what I'd said either offensive or inoffensive. There was, instead, a sense of her not being sure what she should feel in the wake of my last remark, whether I'd been speaking philosophically or more personally when I'd said it, the latter making it a veiled insult.

"I don't know you well enough to answer that question," I said quickly. "I just meant that my father liked down-to-earth people."

Lola Faye offered no argument to this. "So, would he have liked Julia?" she asked. "Your wife."

I couldn't recall having mentioned my wife by name and immediately wondered how Lola Faye had come by this particular bit of information.

"How did you know her name was Julia?" I asked. "I don't remember saying it."

"I saw it in a write-up about you," Lola Faye answered. "It said you were married, and that your wife's name was Julia. Was that your first job, Luke? The one at Clarkston?"

"Yes."

"So you're still at that same college," Lola Faye said expansively. "That's great, Luke. Keeping a job that long. Woody couldn't hold down any job for more than a year. That's why he went into trucking."

I stared at her silently.

"And you're on the website too," Lola Faye informed me. "The college website. It has your picture and the courses you teach." She looked at me admiringly. "They trust you with the kids who're just coming in."

"I have several freshman classes, yes," I said.

"That's a lot of responsibility, Luke," Lola Faye said. "Young blood." She winked playfully. "See how I've been keeping up with you?"

"Yes," I said coolly.

"Now it's easier to do," Lola Faye went on. "I can just Google you and know exactly where you are. That's how I knew you were going to be in Saint Louis." Her second wink seemed less playful. "I Google you a lot."

"Why?" I asked.

"I guess just because of it all," Lola Faye answered casually. "Because we went through this big experience together." She released a long, dramatic sigh. "A lot of blood on the kitchen floor."

I stared at her, stunned by the brutal reference she'd just made, since it was there on the kitchen floor that he'd been found, my father, lying in a wide swath of blood.

Even so, I assumed that Lola Faye had simply made a ghastly choice of words. But her next question made it clear that her mention of the kitchen floor had been anything but unintended.

"You didn't see him, did you, Luke?" she asked. "Your daddy, I mean?"

She meant my father in his bloody sprawl, of course, a bullet hole in his chest, lying flat on his back with his arms spread out, his mouth open, eyes open, caught in dread surprise.

"No, I never saw him," I told Lola Faye. "But I saw a police photo. Sheriff Tomlinson showed it to me." I released a bitter chuckle. "Maybe I should have gotten it and put it in that scrapbook my mother kept."

"*Luke's Journey*," Lola said almost to herself. For a moment she seemed lost in thought, then she said, "Why would the sheriff have shown you a picture like that, Luke?"

"I don't know," I answered. "I just know that at one point he took it out and put it on a table so he knew I'd see it." I recalled the way the photograph had slithered out from the file folder and onto the table, face-up and in full view, the sheriff talking on and on as if unaware.

"At the time, I thought he'd just done it without thinking," I added. "But, who knows, maybe he did it on purpose, for the shock value."

Lola Faye's gaze became very still. "Why would he have wanted to shock you, Luke?" she asked.

"I don't know," I answered.

"I mean, your father, dead on the floor like that, with blood all around him, that's not right, him letting you see that." She paused a moment, then added, "So it was only your mother saw him that way in real life?"

"That's right," I said.

"She was upstairs when she heard the shot."

"How did you know that?"

"Sheriff Tomlinson told me."

"Why would he have told you where my mother was?"

"He was eliminating suspects, I guess."

"My mother was a suspect?"

"The spouse is always a suspect," Lola Faye informed me quite matter-of-factly.

"Is that according to those crime magazines you read?" I asked playfully.

"No, it's what Sheriff Tomlinson told me," Lola Faye replied. "He read all kinds of how-to-investigate books. He even went down to Montgomery and took courses with the state police. He was smart. At least he seemed smart." She laughed. "I mean, he had country ways, I guess, but he was smart. He asked good questions." At which point, she clicked them off. "Where I was. What I was doing. Questions like that. Shrinking the ring. Cops use that term. Shrinking the ring, like a boxer

98

does. Always tightening up the space the other boxer can maneuver in. Shrinking the ring until you box the other guy into a corner." She took a quick sip of her drink. "Questions like that."

"That must have made you pretty nervous."

"Nobody likes talking to cops," Lola Faye admitted. "Even innocent people don't like cops asking them questions."

I abruptly leaned forward and rested my arms on the table. "By the way, where were you?" I asked. "When it happened."

"At home," Lola Faye answered casually, as if I'd asked her to name her favorite flavor of ice cream. "With Cubby. My cat."

"Your cat?" I laughed. "A cat couldn't corroborate your story."

"I never had a story," Lola Faye returned quite seriously. She seemed surprised by my comment. "I just told the truth, Luke." She smiled. "And you?"

"Me?"

"Where were you? You said your mother was alone. Except for Doug, I mean. Just her and Doug at home."

"That's right."

"So, where were you?"

"Out," I said. "Driving."

"Up on the mountain? Visiting Debbie?"

"No, just driving around. Decatur Road. I didn't get home until close to midnight. My father's body had already been taken away by then, but the sheriff was still there." I took a quick, decisive sip of wine and set down my glass louder than I normally would have.

"How long did Sheriff Tomlinson question you, by the way? Was it one of those all-night things, like you see in the movies? Or did he keep coming over day after day?"

"He came to my house several times," Lola Faye answered with little sense of discomfort in responding to such a question. "And once he brought me to the police station."

"That must have been disturbing," I said absently.

"Why would it be disturbing, Luke?" Lola Faye asked with an innocent shrug, then added in a voice that struck me as a little bit harder, "I didn't kill anybody."

"But you broke down, didn't you?" I asked. "Those drugs you mentioned. They must have given them to you because you —"

"That didn't have anything to do with your father, or even with Woody," Lola Faye declared. "That has to do with life, Luke. The way it is." She looked toward the window, where, as if on cue, a gust of wind sent a spray of rain crackling against the glass. "Life can be depressing, don't you think?" She turned back to me suddenly. "But you have to keep going, right? I mean, look at the way you kept going, Luke. Look at what you became despite everything. A professor. A writer." Her eyes glistened. "I get so emotional, Luke." She brushed at her eyes, and let her smile wind around me as delicately as a silken cord. "I was always an emotional girl."

CHAPTER
NINE

This was certainly true, I thought. Lola Faye Gilroy no doubt was, and had always been, an emotional girl, though she'd not seemed so at my first sighting of her.

Still, this self-description returned me to the only time I'd seen her before she'd been hired by my father and which I would never have remembered had he not later hired her. It was one of those quickly passing moments during one's youth, something one sees or hears, notes with little interest, then largely forgets.

I'd been at the Qwik Burger, Glenville's sole, and profoundly unsanitary, teenage hang-out. A pervasive sense of grease hovered around the place, not just an odor, which was strong, but a physical presence in the air, like an oily mist.

I'd become something of a professional observer by then. I'd even come to think of myself as an Invisible Eye, forever watching, making notes on just about everything I saw. In my room each evening, I'd transcribe my latest observations concerning various townspeople and schoolmates, then try to fit them into some larger narrative, all of it practice, I considered, for the great work ahead. I also wrote sketches of whatever little scenes caught my interest during the day, along with bits of dialogue and *ruminations*, a word I'd only recently discovered.

All of this was done secretly, the practice shared with no one but my mother, primarily because, although I loved being considered smart, I didn't want to be considered peculiar or, worse, a nerd.

At the Qwik Burger, the Invisible Eye had taken up a position at a booth in the far corner, where the greasy atmosphere seemed slightly less suffocating and from which I could watch the older kids of Glenville come and go, alone or with dates, and the employees of Qwik Burger, wipers of tables and haulers of garbage, along with a few fry cooks bent over sizzling baskets of French fries and onion rings.

One of these was Lola Faye.

I didn't know her name at that time, of course. Nor did I know that she was twenty-two, from the mountain town of Plain Bluff, that her father had deserted her family years before, leaving her mother to work the dreaded night shift at Glenville's staggeringly malodorous dog-food factory. I didn't know that Lola'd had to go to work at sixteen to help support her younger brother, a victim of cerebral palsy. But most of all, I didn't know that several years before, Lola Faye had already done something unthinkable to me.

Nor would I have ever known any of this had not Eddie Whitmeyer slid into the booth opposite me and slyly indicated the rather bosomy young woman who was at that moment toiling in a cloud of steam at the rear of Qwik Burger.

"See that girl?" Eddie said.

102

I looked over to where a girl I'd vaguely noticed before but whose name I didn't know was drawing a metal basketful of French fries from unknown depths of grease.

"She's a catfighter," Eddie said.

Catfighter? I had never heard the term and would later learn that Eddie had made it up.

"She stabbed a guy," Eddie informed me with a knowing wink. "She's been on probation since she was fifteen."

"Who'd she stab?" I asked.

"Colin Brisbane," Eddie answered. "He likes mountain berries." He snickered. "You know . . . redneck girls. But that one there. He screwed up when he got on the wrong side of her." He laughed. "She didn't take it." He lit a cigarette and sat back in the self-satisfied way of a spy who'd just delivered secret information. "That's her boyfriend in that booth there."

I looked toward the rear of Qwik Burger, the back booth Eddie had indicated, where, bathed in bright light, a pudgy, red-faced young man hunched over his burger and fries, his tiny round eyes glittering.

"Woody Gilroy," Eddie said. "He works at Ray McFadden's." Eddie plucked the cigarette from his lips and flicked ash on the floor. "He better take out a big life insurance, 'cause crossing Lola Faye Maddox can get a fella killed."

Eddie left a few minutes later, but I remained in my booth for a while, my attention moving from person to person, until it was time for me to show up at Variety

Store for the daily sweeping of the aisle and restocking of goods.

It was only a short walk from Qwik Burger to my father's store, a dreary stroll down Main Street that seemed to take longer each time I made it, so even at that early point, it was clear that the sheer boredom of the place, its relentless sameness, had begun to eat at me.

I reached Variety Store in a few minutes. My father was in the back, mangling a box as he labored to remove the parts of a backyard grill. Each piece seemed to fight him; he looked more like a zookeeper attempting to restrain a wild animal than a small-town merchant working to assemble a scattering of inert metal parts.

"The front windows could use a wash," he said when he saw me watching him.

A few minutes later the task was done, and pail and mop in hand, I turned from the freshly washed windows of Variety Store and saw a dark green pickup truck crawl by, the girl from the Qwik Burger sitting silently in the passenger seat, unemotional, as she listened to the boy at the wheel, Woody Wayne Gilroy, a boy from Plain Bluff, I supposed, Lola Faye Maddox no longer in the thrall of Colin Brisbane, a rich mill owner's son, but now decidedly with a redneck like herself.

"An emotional girl," I whispered, as that green pickup truck cruised through my mind. "So I guess it's not just opposites that attract."

Lola Faye clearly failed to understand this remark.

"For example, you and Woody weren't opposites," I said. His round face surfaced in my mind, the watery gaze that had lifted from the uneaten burger and fries. "Because he was, well, an emotional boy."

Lola Faye looked at me intently. "He was emotional, sure, but I would never have thought he'd do what he did," she said, her voice and manner now quite calm, her earlier emotion no more than a distant rumble somewhere deep within her. "Shooting your daddy that way. Doug just sitting there. Woody shooting him from far away, through a window." She looked genuinely baffled by the fact that a human act could so surprise her, that a harmless figure like her former husband had morphed into a cold-blooded murderer. "Just a regular guy. Nothing special about him." She squinted slightly, as if looking into a bright light, or trying to look beyond that same brightness, glimpse what lay behind it. "Not smart like you."

"An ordinary guy, yes," I agreed. "He seemed that way."

After that first sighting, I'd seen Woody occasionally, as anyone might run into another person in a town so small there was practically no one with whom one was not at least marginally acquainted. Now I recalled only what was most obvious about him: that he was a short, round fellow with one of those gap-toothed grins, not at all the broad-shouldered farm boy I would have thought likely to win blond, well-bosomed Lola Faye Maddox. But then, I wouldn't have thought my father capable of turning her head either, though I'd always imagined that he must have promised her something, money or a ticket out of a life she couldn't bear anymore.

"Seemed that way?" Lola Faye asked. A hook appeared to catch in her mind. "But you didn't know Woody, did you, Luke?"

It was a simple question. Lola Faye's expression betrayed a combination of both doubt and possibility.

"Not really," I replied. "I knew who he was. I took that old blue Ford of mine into McFadden's Auto Repair once in a while."

"McFadden's," Lola Faye snapped with what seemed a long-smoldering resentment. "That Ray McFadden never treated Woody right. He was always taking advantage of him, working him overtime. I could have killed Ray McFadden."

The volatile and careening nature of Lola Faye's mind, the way she skidded off on tangents, sent an uneasy quiver through me, a renewed and more urgent yearning to end it now, this last talk with Lola Faye, make some excuse, head up to my room.

"But we weren't talking about Ray," Lola Faye said, returning to her previous calm, as if she'd gotten a whiff of my secret urge, knew that I was considering a deft exit.

"No, we were talking about Woody," I said, reluctantly settling in for what appeared to be another round of conversation.

"Not just Woody," Lola Faye reminded me. "Everything."

She lowered her head, and held it there a moment. I thought she might be crying, but no more than a blink later she lifted her face and a smile broke over it like a ray of light, a smile that offered a glimpse of what had always been perfectly shaped teeth, and which still were, so that I imagined the first smile they must have flashed my father, how bright it must have seemed, how open and welcoming and . . .

"You should tell me about Julia," Lola Faye said happily. "I like stories of true love."

I took a sip from my glass. "Well, as Shakespeare says, 'True love never did run smooth.'"

Lola Faye stared at me expectantly, like a child waiting for a bedtime story. "I bet yours did," she said.

"We're divorced, remember?" I reminded her.

"Yeah, but I bet it was great at the beginning," Lola Faye said. She seemed determined to hear a cheery story, something in keeping with what she appeared to consider the fairy tale of my life. "I bet it was love at first sight."

In my mind Julia came running across the college green, as young and vibrant as some girl in a toothpaste commercial. "She had long brown hair," I said, almost to myself.

"Like your mother's?" Lola Faye asked.

Now it was my mother who rose into my mind, standing at the fence, surrounded by her garden.

"Not quite that dark," I said.

"And I bet you met her when you were at Harvard," Lola Faye said with the enthusiasm of a little girl at a guessing game.

"Actually, Julia went to Bunker Hill," I said.

Lola Faye looked at me quizzically.

"It's a community college," I explained, though I had no idea whether Lola Faye knew enough about the structure of higher learning in America to discern the difference. "On Bunker Hill. You know, where the battle was."

A childlike awe suffused Lola Faye's face. "What a great thing," she said. "To go to school where something great happened." Her eyes twinkled. "So, you met and married."

"Met, married, and then" — I stopped and thought of our last moment together, the final words she'd offered, *I never knew you* — "we parted." I felt a heavy world of partings in the memory of her going, like the sea in Matthew Arnold's poem, a long, withdrawing roar.

"Julia was very . . . knowing," I said.

"Knowing," Lola Faye repeated, the word rolling slowly off her tongue as if she found it moving or beautiful, not just a word but a favored line of poetry.

She leaned back in her chair, clearly reassured that I was not about to flee, that although our talk had already continued longer than I'd expected, it was not about to end.

"Go on, Luke," she said. "Please go on." Her smile struck me as curiously satisfied, like a boatman who'd shrewdly maneuvered some tricky water and who could now relax a bit, drift along a less perilous part of the river. "Tell me all about you and Julia."

108

CHAPTER
TEN

Julia?

What did I know about her really, this woman who'd managed to remain my wife for a little over five years and who, despite the divorce, I thought of fifty times a day. Our marriage had been short, Julia growing more and more aware that she'd married a man mysteriously driven to achieve some great thing, who worked hours and hours and hours and even when at leisure appeared under the lash of an invisible whip, a man whose research notes filled box after box, but finally a man whose great effort and grand ambition had produced works of startling mediocrity.

But there'd been more to her leaving me than my uninspired work, for Julia had seen my descending moods, the way I often retreated into some interior castle, hauled up the drawbridge, and let no one follow me inside. To these withdrawals I'd added the winning attribute of sleeplessness, a chronic insomnia that made me seem like a man on the run. "You act like some criminal the cops are still hunting," she told me once, "like a man who's waiting for the knock at the door."

Even so, I knew that it was none of these things that had ultimately caused Julia to give up on me. The breaking point for her, the one thing she had not been able to bear, was my absolute refusal to have children, an aversion to parenthood she'd found inexplicable until the moment of clarity came, and after which nothing had been the same.

We'd been sitting in our town's small park watching a gaggle of suburban moms make their way toward its swings and seesaws, their yelping children in tow.

"Did you ever see *The Bad Seed?*" I asked.

Julia held her attention on the parade of mothers and children, her expression entirely admiring, perhaps even envious.

"You mean that movie about the little girl who murders people?" she asked absently.

"Yeah, that's the one."

"What about it?" Julia asked.

"We could have a kid like that," I said. "Some little sociopath."

Julia faced me with a sudden, almost violent movement. "Is that what you think, Luke? That our child would be a murderer?"

"Anyone's could be," I said quickly, though not quickly enough to dispel her correct reading that I'd been talking specifically of our child.

"You really believe that?" Julia asked.

"I know it," I said.

"How do you know it, Luke?"

Julia's expression was quite intense. I knew that much rested on my answer, and for that reason, I hesitated.

"I just do," I said.

"But how?" Julia asked insistently.

I shrugged and said nothing else, so that she saw the wall in all its impenetrable thickness and knew that there would be no breaching it.

She looked at me for a long moment, then said, "I don't know you, Luke. I don't think I ever will."

That had been the instant when it had all come apart, the fibers that, however frayed, had held us together until then. True, we'd gone to a few sessions of marriage counseling after that, sat stiffly and listened as the therapist droned on about openness and acceptance, but it was too late, because Julia had discovered the core truth: if she lived with me, she would always live with a stranger.

And so, in the end, she'd left me, moved to Chicago, gotten the degree in nursing she'd started at Bunker Hill, and now worked as a nurse on the city's northern fringes.

So what did I have to tell Lola Faye about Julia? Not much, really. But she had asked about her in the most expectant terms, and so I began my answer by telling her that I'd met Julia while I was still a graduate student, and by that means avoided the personal and painful, the actual beating heart of love and life.

"You know what a graduate student is, right?" I asked Lola Faye.

She looked a tad embarrassed. "Not exactly," she admitted.

Perfect, I thought, and immediately launched into a brief description of how academic advancement worked. First you went to the right college, and from there, after graduation, you sought to continue your studies either at the same place or at one renowned in your chosen field of study. It would be best if both these places were Ivy League, I explained, because the status of your graduate degree would certainly help your future prospects. Once in graduate school, you studied with the professor most well known in your field, preferably the one who had written the most books, was the most revered within the academic establishment. Then you helped this same professor in his research and thereby garnered an acknowledgment in whatever that effort produced, be it a talk, a paper, or, best of all, a book. You chose this professor to chair your PhD orals and to supervise your PhD dissertation. Once that was done and it was time to seek a faculty position, you got this professor to pull whatever strings he could on your behalf.

Through all of this admittedly dull recitation, Lola Faye remained in quite a rapture of attention, nodding her head as I proceeded and even, once, rather comically, giving her chin a thoughtful stroke, as if she were transforming herself into some white-bearded stereotype of a professor, which, I suspected, was the only image she had of such a person.

At last I returned to Julia and at that instant found it necessary to gird myself before going on, a pause that elicited a subtle look of concern in Lola Faye's eyes, though she said nothing at all, but only watched me, waiting, very still, like a student might watch a lecturer.

As I began, it struck me in a particularly poignant way that some people are last chances and that Julia had been mine. We'd met by chance, I told Lola Faye, met on the steps of a museum. I'd noticed one of my professors, a man of around forty, approach a woman from some distance, the woman quite obviously reading one of the books he'd written and which she closed softly as he neared her then all but let slip from her fingers as she rushed into his arms.

It was one of those moments when your own loneliness comes crashing through whatever barriers you had previously erected to keep it out. My wall had been constructed chiefly of academic work, along with extended bouts of solitariness, self-imposed confinements. I'd only that morning crawled out of my cell, and no doubt because of this, I'd been more open than usual to a casual aside.

"There's something sweet about it," a voice to my right said. "A May-December thing."

I turned to see a young woman sitting a few feet from me.

"Of course, those two look more like June-October," she added.

I nodded dryly. "Yes, they do."

"You're Southern," Julia said. "Where from?"

"Alabama."

"I'm Southern too, in a way. I was born in Florida. Or don't you hard-core Rebel boys count Floridians as Southern?"

"We count them," I said, but found nothing witty to add, so I simply stared at her, at a loss as to how to go on.

She clearly saw how bereft and clueless I felt at that moment, and so she stretched her hand toward me. "Julia Bates," she said. "I'm in nursing school."

"So she was smart, like you," Lola Faye said when I reached this part of the story. "I bet she was really pretty too. Was she as pretty as Debbie?"

"I guess she was," I said. "But of course, beauty is in the eye of the beholder."

"Beauty is in the eye of the beholder," Lola Faye repeated thoughtfully. "Well . . . not really, Luke."

I was surprised that for the first time Lola Faye had actually found it within herself to express an opinion contrary to my own.

"You don't think so?" I asked. "Why not?"

"Well, for example, you take Debbie," Lola Faye began. "Anybody looking at Debbie would have thought she was awful pretty. You must have known how pretty she was, right?"

"Of course I did."

"And her being pretty, you must have known that any man would think that," Lola Faye surged on. "And so you'd know that other boys were thinking how pretty Debbie was, right?"

"I'm sure they thought Debbie was pretty, yes," I said.

"Well, that's what I'm getting at," Lola Faye said. "That it wasn't just you who thought Debbie was pretty, Luke. It wasn't just 'the eye of the beholder,' meaning your eye, that made Debbie pretty. All those boys' eyes saw that she was pretty. That's why you could show her off, because you knew it wasn't just you, it was everybody thought Debbie was pretty."

"Showed her off?" I asked. "Did I show Debbie off?"

Lola Faye seemed surprised by my question. "Sure you did, Luke. Just like some farmer would show off his prize heifer."

I looked at her doubtfully.

"Oh, come on, Luke," Lola Faye said with a small laugh. "It was real obvious how proud you were of Debbie. Why, you even waltzed her down to Variety Store. You did that probably once a week." She laughed again, as if this whole business were a joke we shared. "One time, you even brought her into the store when she was wearing her majorette uniform. Remember that skimpy little thing?"

It was white with gold epaulets, I recalled, skimpy and short enough to display Debbie's long white legs.

"And tight too," Lola Faye added with a big grin. "You could see every little ripple of that body Debbie had." She laughed once more, this time with a kind of fraternal rowdiness, as if we were two men in a locker room, free to be ourselves in the absence of women. "You do remember bringing her into Variety Store wearing that thing, don't you, Luke?"

"Yes," I answered. "But that was only because she'd just marched in the parade that afternoon."

"Showing Debbie off in that majorette uniform," Lola Faye said, still chuckling lightly. "Showing her off" — she stopped and took a quick sip of her appletini — "to your daddy."

The sudden mention of my father in this context hit me like cold water in the face, so that I saw, like images on parade, all the times during my early boyhood when I'd presented to my father my all-A's report card only to have him push it away with an indifferent shrug; all the times I'd strutted and performed for him, even tried to play sports, hunt, be what he called "a regular boy"; all the times I'd reduced myself to this pathetic, needful son until I'd finally recognized the futility of it and sullenly accepted that I would never please him, earn his respect, or distinguish myself in his eyes, and at that point finally turned away from him to where my mother waited, had always waited, with wide-open arms.

"But that's just normal, I guess," Lola Faye went on as if she'd seen no sign of this dark cavalcade of memory, no pained constriction of my eyes or change in my features.

But was it normal?

I recalled the afternoon I'd brought Debbie into Variety Store after the parade, her white legs still moist with sweat from her heavy-duty prancing down Glenville's bedraggled Main Street. Her hair had radiated a golden light, and to my father's middle-aged eyes, she must have seemed a youthful goddess. *Surely now*, I remembered thinking as his gaze drank her in, *surely now he'll give me some goddamn credit.*

How, I asked myself now, *could any of that have been normal?*

"Maybe you're right," I said in a faint whisper. "Maybe I did bring Debbie to the store dressed that way to show her off to my father."

116

Lola Faye appeared neither surprised nor particularly impressed by what struck me as a rather painful admission.

Instead, she merely took another sip of her drink. "Thinking what you did about me and your daddy, I bet you thought that's what gave your daddy the idea," she said.

"What idea?"

"The idea of having a girlfriend too," Lola Faye replied as innocently as she might have asked if something else had given him the idea to pour salt on a slice of watermelon.

I wondered if Lola Faye was actually insinuating that it was I, rather than she, who'd somehow set events in motion.

"Are you saying it was my fault somehow?" I asked. "I mean, surely you're not saying that because my father saw me with Debbie he decided to get a pretty girl too. I mean, that he felt some sort of competition with me."

"Competition?" Lola Faye shook her head vigorously. "No, I don't think Doug felt that way," she said. "I don't think he felt a bit in competition with you."

Whether intentionally or not, Lola Faye was saying that it had always been one-sided, I wanting desperately to rise in my father's esteem, he utterly indifferent to his position in mine. It was a hard possibility to confront, the notion that had my father lived, it would not have mattered to him that I had gone on to college, gotten my cherished doctorate, even that I had written books; he would have cared not a whit for any of that but

117

instead would have noted only that I had failed in all the offices that by his lights took the measure of a man: failed at marriage, refused fatherhood, lived drearily alone. A hard possibility, yes, and one I found it necessary to question.

"So tell me, if it wasn't some sort of competition, why would seeing your son with a pretty girl suddenly make a man want a girl of his own?" I asked.

Lola Faye thought a moment, though it was unclear to me whether she was struggling to find an appropriate answer or merely searching for the right words to give an answer she'd found long ago.

"Loneliness," Lola Faye said. "A man can feel lonely."

A little spark of resentment fired in me at the notion that my father could ever have known the kind of loneliness that had been and still was my lot.

"My father wasn't lonely," I said flatly. "He had a wife, remember?"

Lola Faye nodded slowly. "Yeah, but you were married, Luke, you know that a married person can be lonely."

"I was never lonely when I was married," I protested.

"Was Julia?"

She'd asked the question in that casual, unoffending way of hers, and yet I suddenly saw Julia in her struggle to connect to me, the barrier she had confronted, how futilely she'd tried to overleap it, and with what finality she had at last admitted her failure to do so. *You're a suit of armor, Luke.*

118

But this thought was too painful for me to pursue, and so I quickly spun the topic of our talk back to Lola Faye.

"By the way, if seeing me with Debbie did give him the idea of getting his own girlfriend, I'm not saying it would have been just anybody he'd have chosen," I assured her. "I mean, even my father would have wanted a woman who had something that . . . spoke to him."

I'd meant this in some sense as a compliment, but it rolled off Lola Faye without impact.

"Something that spoke to him," Lola Faye repeated thoughtfully. "That's a nice way of putting it, Luke. Something that 'spoke' to your daddy." It seemed that the air darkened around us. "Did your mother have that?"

CHAPTER
ELEVEN

My mother?

Had my mother had anything that "spoke" to my father?

It was not a question I'd ever asked because the real question for me had always been what my mother had seen in him.

Her name was Joan Helen Pomeroy, and to me she was Joan of Arc; when I'd finally come to read about the life and sacrificial death of that fabled country girl, I'd thought of my mother, for she'd had the same nearly impossible blend of meekness and nobility.

Though she'd been born into a hardscrabble farm family, my mother had aspired to the more delicate things in life. She liked books, especially poetry. She read Emily Dickinson every day of her life, and she seemed to suffer from the same frail health — repeated colds, inexplicable fatigue — as this most favored of her authors. "Sick people know the most about life," she once told me. "Because they don't take it for granted."

If this was true, no one would have known better than my mother, who, in a stricken, soulful guise, moved through life like the heroine of a silent movie, Mary Pickford forever crossing the ice floe. As a girl, she'd been diagnosed with everything from anemia to pneumonia. Had she lived in the Middle Ages, she would have been classified as suffering from an imbalance of the humors, a diagnosis that, in its suggestion of inner disequilibrium, would have been most accurate. She was like a climber who never found purchase, the trail always too narrow and tricky for her to make much headway.

I often thought that had she been born after 1960, she probably never would have married at all. Instead, she'd have been one of those women who haunt the animal shelters, rescuing castaways from their dark fates. Had she been born Catholic, she would have become a nun, probably a great one, gentle, selfless, incapable of harsh judgment, the patron saint of the left behind. But my mother had been born into a hard-shell Baptist family, reared as a rural Alabama farm girl, and so marriage had been her lot.

But of all the men who'd come her way, why had she married my father? Why had my mother, so lofty in every respect, married so far down?

This was the reverse of Lola Faye's question, of course, and the only answer I'd ever had for it was that at some point my mother must have simply given up on better prospects and, in a drastic moment of resignation, chosen my father because he looked good in a uniform, or had a few fancy dance steps, or told good stories, or dressed well, or drove a shiny car, or made her laugh, or displayed any of a hundred other of those flashing qualities that briefly blind a woman's eyes to the otherwise ordinariness of a decidedly ordinary man.

Or perhaps my mother had merely grown tired of waiting to begin the next stage of her life, tired of sitting across from some boy who bored her or whom she bored, and knew it. Maybe my father was refreshingly different in some way, less talkative, rougher around the edges, muscled by the lowliness that had shaped him, a boy who looked away when she looked at him, whose smile was shy, and whose conversation held not one speck of sophistication. Perhaps she'd hoped that my father's very lack of worldliness might open him to her strangeness, allow him to look past her poor health and bookishness so that he might come to appreciate how quiet she was, and inward, how frail and charitable and tender, how kind, how selfless, to see all the shining characteristics of heart and mind and soul that she possessed, though ultimately none had proved sufficient to keep him from being enticed by a small-town shop girl from the wrong side of the tracks.

I might have mentioned any or all of this to Lola Faye, but instead I found myself following the grim thread of my family's tragic history all the way to the weedy cemetery in which my parents lay, though it was one incident along that dark route that returned to me most vividly.

Luke, c'mere.

My father had never been averse to some short delay between the moment he summoned me and the moment I responded to that summons, but on this occasion he yelled again immediately.

"Now, Luke!"

There was an urgency in his voice, so I knew something was wrong, though I suspected it was the sort of situation he was continually getting himself into, his hand caught in a sleeve he couldn't disentangle from or something equally the product of the awkwardness and general disorganization that relentlessly plagued him.

I headed down the stairs, though not hurriedly, fully expecting to find my father in the midst of struggling to maneuver a piece of furniture into place or adjust the television antenna.

At the bottom of the stairs, I turned to the right, toward the kitchen, since his voice seemed to have come from there. The kitchen was empty, however, and so I glanced to the left and there, in the middle of the dining room, found my father on his knees, his back curled forward over the body of my mother.

"She fell, Luke," my father cried. "C'mere."

I rushed to where my mother lay. She was conscious, but there was a confused look in her eyes, like that of a person who'd been struck on the head and was only now beginning to come to.

"Mom?" I said.

She seemed to be trying to bring my face into clearer focus. "Luke," she said softly. "Luke."

I turned to my father. "Call an ambulance," I said. "Hurry."

My mother tried several times to get to her feet before the ambulance arrived, but each time I pressed her back down. "Just wait," I said. "Don't move."

The ambulance showed up in only a few minutes, two beefy emergency workers in white uniforms, each with a stethoscope dangling around his neck. They asked my mother what had happened, and when she told them she wasn't quite sure, that she'd been on her feet at one moment and on her back the next, they'd taken her pulse and her blood pressure, then eased her onto a stretcher.

My father and I followed the ambulance, my father at the wheel of his dilapidated old delivery van. All the way to the hospital, he drove in that erratic way of his, pressing down on the accelerator, then the brake, so that we surged forward in fits and starts, a jerky progression that struck me as entirely suggestive of the way his brain fired and misfired, briefly sustained a thought, then let it go.

An hour or so after we arrived at the hospital, a young doctor came into the waiting room and spoke to us. My mother was going to stay overnight, he said, so that certain tests could be done. We shouldn't be alarmed by this, he told us, it was just a matter of trying to find out what had caused her to pass out. He said she might simply have been tired, or she might have experienced a sudden drop in her blood pressure. Many different things could cause a person to pass out suddenly, he said, nearly all of which would quickly resolve. He fully expected my mother to be released from the hospital the following day. If we wanted, we could visit her now, but we shouldn't stay too late, since after such an occurrence a patient was often in need of rest.

A few seconds later, my father and I walked into my mother's room. The light was quite subdued, and in that shadowiness, my mother looked truly ill, her skin pale, her eyes heavy-lidded.

"Luke," she said and lifted her hand toward me.

I took it and stood beside her bed for a long time, talking to her quietly, telling her what the doctor had said, reassuring her that everything was fine, that she would be back home with us very soon, probably within twenty-four hours.

She listened to all this but asked no questions.

"So," I said. "Dad and I will come back in the morning."

She gripped my hand with panic. "Don't go, Luke." Her eyes darted over to where my father stood pressed into a corner, head down, inexplicably shifting his dusty old cap from one hand to the other. "Don't leave me." Her voice lowered to a fearful whisper. "I'm afraid, Luke."

I attributed the terror in my mother's eyes to some brief derangement caused by her fall.

"The doctor told us not to stay with you too long," I explained. "He said you needed to rest. We're both going home now."

"They want me to spend the night here?" she asked, her voice still locked in a frightened whisper.

"Yes, Mom," I assured her. "They need to keep an eye on you until morning."

Her fingers tightened even more around my hand. "I want pajamas, Luke," she said.

"But they gave you a hospital gown," I said.

"I want pajamas," my mother said. "New pajamas." Again her gaze drifted over to where my father stood. "You got in some new ones, didn't you, Doug?"

My father nodded. "Yeah, I got in some new ones."

"Get them for me, Luke," my mother said.

"All right," I said, and with those words turned toward my father and stretched out my hand. "Give me the keys to the store," I said.

He seemed reluctant to hand over the keys. "I'll get them," he said.

I shook my head. "No, I'll go."

My father looked like a man trying to think his way out of a tight spot. "You don't know where they are."

I was sufficiently aware of the way my father scattered around the stock of Variety Store to know that women's pajamas might be stacked next to racks of garden tools or car parts or simply wherever my father had been standing when he'd decided to put them away.

"No, you stay with Mom," I told him. I pressed my hand farther toward him. "Give me the keys, I'll be right back."

At that moment, my father had no choice, I realized later, no way out, a man with only luck to rely on now, no other available resource.

He reached into the right pocket of his faded gray pants, fished about for the keys, then drew them out and placed them softly in my hand.

"They're inside the stockroom, right next to the door," he said. "A box of 'em. Just to the right when you go into the stockroom."

I found this an uncharacteristically detailed description of where I would find the pajamas my mother wanted, but I thought nothing of it until my father added, "You don't even have to turn on the light."

You don't even have to turn on the light.

Why would my father have said such a thing? I wondered. The backroom of Variety Store was a riot of disorder, boxes tossed willy-nilly, bicycles and lawn furniture lying in various states of assembly. Only a blind man wouldn't need to turn on the light to maneuver through such chaos.

At that moment, the thought occurred to me: *My father has something to hide.*

I gave no hint of this strange uneasiness, however, but simply closed my fingers around the keys and turned to my mother.

"Any particular color, Mom?" I asked.

She shook her head.

"Okay, I'll be right back."

A few minutes later, I opened the front door of Variety Store, flipped on the switch, and headed down the center aisle to the stockroom in the rear.

I walked quickly to the back, opened the stockroom door, and turned on the light.

At first I didn't see my father's secret. I glanced about, noting boxes of toys, small appliances, tableware, the usual items my father kept in the stockroom; it was only when I saw a large piece of plywood leaning in the back corner that something struck me as odd. It was perhaps six feet by six feet, this piece of plain, unpainted wood, and it leaned at roughly a forty-five-degree angle to the wall so that more than anything it resembled one side of a nearly collapsed tent.

What is that? I thought, and made my way through the stockroom's customary clutter. As I moved toward it, I saw a swath of lavender cloth dropping over the edge of what appeared to be a stack of broken-down cardboard boxes.

It would have been utterly like my father to secrete something in so obvious a way, and because of that, I felt quite sure that I'd found whatever he'd not wanted me to discover and which I suspected was some sort of bizarre purchase he'd made for Variety Store, something bought on impulse that he'd never be able to sell, an old radio or a miniature safe.

But what I found instead was a present wrapped in glossy pink paper, tied with a blue bow, and with an envelope taped to it, my father's scrawl easily recognizable: *For my dearest love.*

Now I took a good look at what lay before me, focused not only on my father's gift but on the carefully smoothed sheets that loosely covered the stack of cardboard; nearby was a little vase of plastic flowers.

I knew instantly that here, on a stack of cardboard boxes he'd dragged over to a dark corner of the stockroom and in his oddly chivalrous way had fashioned into a crude mattress, was where my father had his way with his "dearest love."

128

The strange thing was that I didn't gasp at the sight of my father's dreary little backroom boudoir. I didn't shudder at the thought of his betrayal. I wasn't even appalled by what I knew my father had done. What struck me instead was the artless and indelicate materials he'd used to construct his crude little love nest, and the haphazard and unskilled way in which he'd used them. Every element of this sordid tableau, from the ragged boxes to the threadbare sheets, confirmed the low opinion I'd always had of him.

And I thought, *Anything but this*. Anything but remaining in Glenville, inheriting this shabby store, ending up a middle-aged man in flannel pants whose only escape from such consuming drabness was a sordid fling with an ignorant shop girl in a make-shift bedroom with a plywood roof and cardboard for a bed.

Then, for the first time, I thought of my mother.

"Julia."

I returned to the present. "What?"

"She had something that spoke to you, I bet," Lola Faye prompted. Her eyes sparkled with anticipation. "So tell me more about her, Luke."

And to avoid the dark tale playing in my head, I took up the story of Julia and myself again, spinning out the narrative of my first date with her, Lola Faye taking it all in, offering not a single aside, asking not a single question, merely listening to my largely uneventful saga of courtship until I brought her around to the day Julia and I had married, how sunny it had been in that little chapel in Saint Augustine's.

"Julia's whole family was there," I said expansively, reveling in my memory of the festivities. "There must have been a hundred people." And suddenly I felt it again, the stark sense of how bereft I was, my life stripped down to the bare essentials of myself. "There was no one from my side, of course."

I couldn't tell to what degree Lola Faye felt responsible for the fact that I'd had neither father nor mother present on my wedding day, that they both lay buried in the dismal little cemetery on the outskirts of Glenville. But, of course, this was not a subject I had any desire to pursue, and so I shifted the focus of our conversation to less weighty considerations.

"But what about you?" I asked. "Tell me about your life after Glenville."

"I already have," Lola Faye answered. "At least a little, that I got married. Ollie, like I said."

It was obvious that Lola Faye did not want to discuss her unfortunate son, and so I didn't press her to elaborate on so painful a subject.

"A nice guy," Lola Faye added. "Ollie."

And he probably was exactly that, I thought, a nice guy. But then, wasn't everyone nice in Lola Faye Gilroy's book? Certainly my father had been nice. My mother too, for that matter. Even poor heartbroken Woody had been nice, though undeniably unstable as well, unstable and forlorn and crazed by betrayal.

"Ollie was already retired when I met him," Lola Faye added. "A retired cop."

"You married a cop?"

"A retired cop," Lola Faye answered.

I reached for my glass and rolled it slowly in my hands. "So, what does a retired cop do after he retires?" I asked.

"Whatever comes along, I guess," Lola Faye answered. "Hunting and fishing. Going to ball games. Guy things like that." She appeared to bask in the warm appreciation of her husband. "Going back over old cases." A smile flickered briefly. "I've learned a lot about that."

"Like what?" I asked.

"Oh, like how to investigate things," Lola Faye answered airily. "And law stuff too. Like the fact that there's no statute of limitations on murder, for example. It's because once you kill a person, they're dead. So the person who's the murderer, that person ought never to have a minute's rest. I mean, he should always know that he can be arrested at any moment. At least that's how the law sees it." She fingered the red rim of the coaster absently. "Is that the way you see it, Luke?"

I nodded. "I suppose so," I answered.

Lola Faye's smile seemed curiously painted on, a clown's smile. "And to think, I didn't even know about it until I met Ollie. Or how to look into old cases either. How to investigate. Questions to ask. How to shrink the ring, you know?"

I rolled the stem of my glass between my thumb and index finger. "So I guess you've gotten quite an education in law enforcement then," I said lightly.

"Yep," Lola Faye answered. "Smart, Ollie."

My eyes were drawn to a short, stocky man coming through the hotel's revolving door. He wore a dark brown ski jacket, and as he headed toward the bar he drew off a brown tweed cap with ear-flaps and slapped it against his sleeve, sending icy droplets onto the marble floor.

"Not smart the way you are," Lola Faye added. "He never wrote a book or anything like that. But smart anyway."

The man strolled to the entrance of the lounge, stripped off his jacket, and waited for the hostess to seat him.

"Smart like a fox, I mean," Lola Faye breezed on. "Like looking into a person's eyes and seeing the lies. Smart like that."

The hostess arrived and escorted the man to the shadowy corner he'd indicated, where he took a seat, his face obscured by the fronds of a potted fern.

"I can't believe the way I'm just running on at the mouth with you now," Lola Faye said, then put her fingers over her lips as if to hold back any further soul-freezing revelations. "It's like we're friends almost."

"Friends," I repeated as I returned my attention to her. "Yes."

"Just talking away," Lola Faye said expansively. "I don't usually do that. Ollie used to call me the Clam, because he said I held everything in. You know what I mean? All that frustration a person feels, all that anger."

"You don't seem angry," I told her.

132

"Well, that's the secret, isn't it, Luke, not to seem what you are?" Before I could answer, she laughed. "Anyway, I told Ollie, I said, 'Ollie, if I let go of all that's in me, I'd blow fire all through the world.'" She laughed again, this time a little less heartily. "After that, he called me Dragon Lady." She paused in this string of talk for a moment, then said, "Did you know that cops have a name for women who kill men?"

"No."

"Black widows," Lola Faye said. "There's a movie by that name, you know. With that actress in it. What's her name?" She threw her hand up. "Wait, don't tell me. Right. Yeah. Begins with a D. Debra. Debra Winger. She played the federal investigator."

"Did she?"

"Yep. And she was good in it too. You know what the name comes from, black widow?"

"It's a spider, isn't it?"

"A spider, right, but a particular kind of spider. The female bites off the head of the male right after they've mated. The male has no idea what's coming, of course, so he just climbs up and —" She stopped, like a child suddenly aware that she'd stepped out of line. "Talking away. It's not like me." She lifted her hand to her mouth again, briefly held it there, then let it fall. "Not like me at all." She drew her gaze down to the table. "It's this appletini. I bet that's what's making me blab on like I am." She nodded toward my glass. "Like that wine is making you talk, right? Because I get the feeling — and maybe I'm wrong, Luke — but I get the feeling you're not a big talker."

I smiled. "Oh well, you know what they say, *in vino veritas.*"

Lola Faye waited for the translation.

"In wine is truth," I said.

Lola Faye eased back slightly, rolled one shoulder, then cocked her head to the right, as if toward the lips of an invisible whisperer. "So smart," she said. "Smarter than everybody, Luke."

CHAPTER
TWELVE

And I had been too. Smarter than anybody, an intelligence I'd clearly inherited from my mother.

She'd remained in the hospital for two days after her fainting spell, wearing the red pajamas I'd retrieved from the madly disorganized stockroom of Variety Store and given to her, my father and I standing in the dimly lighted corridor outside her room while she put them on.

He'd looked at me warily as I'd come back into my mother's room, then seemed relieved when I said nothing to indicate that I'd seen his tawdry little boudoir.

"Find those pajamas without much trouble?" he asked a few minutes later as we stood in the corridor.

"Yeah."

There was a pause, during which the two of us faced each other silently, my faithless father on one side of the hallway, I on the other.

Finally he said, "Don't worry, Luke. Your mother's going to be fine."

The thought that came to me was razor sharp: *You know you want her dead*.

But another thought never occurred to me: *Tell her*.

We brought my mother home on a Wednesday afternoon. She was weak but as always made a brave, cheerful show. She had spent her life putting on a happy face, it seemed to me, and a sudden loss of equilibrium had done nothing to expose whatever regrets lay beneath all her many strengths and graces. Before leaving the hospital she'd changed into what she'd called "civilian clothes," though they were only the modest ones she always wore, a plain, solid blue dress, probably from some inexpensive lot my father had managed to procure. She'd combed her hair, powdered her nose, and applied a little lipstick, making me wonder darkly whether she intended to provide some sexual service to my father on this first night of her return to his bed.

When we got home, my father and I walked carefully beside her as she made her way, a little unsteadily, down the cracked concrete walk, up the chipped cement stairs, through the back door with its raggedly torn screen, and into the cramped little kitchen, where, a few months later, she would find my father lying on his back in a pool of blood.

"Do you want to go up to the bedroom?" I asked her.

"No," she answered. "The reading room."

It was hardly as grand as her name for it sounded; it was, in fact, no more than a little alcove where I'd often found her waiting for me when I came home from school, always with an open book in her lap and usually a dreamy look in her eye. Julia once said that my every description of my mother mythologized her, and I had to admit that yes, this was true, that I had rather idealized her, though I also knew that it was in comparison to my father that I had done this, the two of them so completely at different poles in my mind that they seemed scarcely able to occupy the same universe, my mother's learning and refinement the only counterweight I had to my father's unyielding ignorance and commonness.

Indeed, many times I'd imagined my mother with an entirely different man, someone elegant and well educated, the mate she deserved rather than the drab husband with whom she'd gotten stuck. I would sometimes see this other, ideal family sitting in an imagined parlor, the room lined with books, a perfect family, always only the three of us: myself, my mother, and this ideal man, tall, immaculately dressed, with impeccable manners, high culture emanating from his every word and gesture.

Perhaps my mother had had the same fantasy, or at least a similar one. For I'd sometimes caught the glimmer of some imagined life in the faraway look in her eyes. There'd been a wistful longing in the way she peered out the window on a rainy day, one of Mr. Klein's books held tight against her chest. In a certain light, she could have been dismissed as a Tennessee Williams caricature, which was how Julia once described her. But in the different light of my actual experience of her, my mother and her melancholy dreaminess struck me as the product of a long, private tragedy in whose aftermath she lived, one she could have escaped only by fleeing Glenville, so that a few days later, when I had my fateful meeting with Miss McDowell, my mother's life had come to provide a critical lesson, its concluding dictate insistently repeated in my mind: *Don't end up like her.*

"Read to me, Luke," my mother said once we'd settled her into the little alcove where a stack of books rested on a carefully dusted side table.

"Okay," I said. "What book would you like?"

She thought a moment, then said, "Dickens. The scene where Joe comes to visit Pip."

I knew *Great Expectations* was upstairs in the bookshelf that stood in the short hallway that led from her bedroom to the bathroom and that contained the few books she actually owned, all of them arranged alphabetically.

"I'll go get it," I said, and headed up the stairs, though not fast enough to avoid the low growl of my father's voice. "Well, I'll be getting back to Variety Store," he said.

Back to Variety Store, I thought angrily, *back to his little whore.*

He'd gone by the time I returned to my mother's reading room, and his going was a relief from the sharp pressure I felt each time I was forced to be in his presence.

"Just a few pages," my mother said as I drew up a chair beside her. "Then I'll take a little nap."

I read what still remains for me one of literature's most tender scenes, the lowly Joe Gargery in all his heartbreaking humbleness, the haughty Pip, embarrassed by Joe's uncouth manners and rural speech,

138

eager to be rid of him, relieved when Joe finally shambles down the stairs and into a bustling London he can scarcely comprehend.

The scene was only a few pages long, and once I'd finished it, I closed the book.

In the past, my mother and I had ended a reading with some brief discussion of what we'd read, but on this occasion, she remained silent for a moment, staring at me with what I saw as a deep regard.

"Mr. Klein says that I have a mind that's higher than my station in life, Luke," she said finally. "You do too." A trembling hand reached out to me. "Use it, Luke. Don't let anything stop you from using it."

And so it had always seemed to me that I'd been given two very important things by my mother, her intelligence and her tragedy, the former my only means of escaping the latter, a dark association that was playing in my mind when Lola Faye suddenly broke the silence that had briefly settled over us.

"How high is your IQ, Luke?"

Lola Faye's question hit me almost jarringly, out of the blue, like Julia's as I'd stared at those frontier blankets three months before.

"I have no idea," I answered quietly, the memory of my lost mother still pressing hard upon me.

"You never got tested?"

"No."

"Because you didn't need a test to know how smart you were, right?"

Something in this question snapped me fully back to the present. Was it a trick question, I wondered, a question meant to expose me somehow? One thing was certain: there was no way to answer it modestly. Because of that, evasion seemed the only available course.

"Well, it depends on what you mean by smart," I answered.

"Miss McDowell knew it too, right?" Lola Faye asked. "Your daddy said she did."

"How would he have known that?" I asked.

"Because she came by Variety Store one day," Lola Faye answered. "He said Miss McDowell had a real interest in you." She lifted her right hand, then drew the index and middle finger around each other in a pose that struck me as curiously erotic. "Close. He thought it was a little strange."

"Strange?" I asked. "Why would he have thought that?"

"Something about that talk they had, I guess," Lola Faye answered. "They stood at the front of the store for a long time. And when she left, Doug came back and said that it was one of your teachers. He said she was real interested in you, and was really pushing you. Then he said, 'Something strange there, Lola Faye.'"

"Miss McDowell believed I could get a scholarship to Harvard," I said, like one suddenly inspired to defend a fallen hero. "She encouraged me to apply for it. What's strange about that?"

"You're right, Luke. Nothing's strange about that. I don't know what your daddy saw that made him say that."

"Nothing, I'm sure," I said. "Besides, my father wouldn't have noticed anything strange about anybody. He wasn't a man for subtle signs."

"Signs?" Lola Faye asked. "Of what?"

"You know, anything strange," I said. "Miss McDowell was a teacher who was interested in helping a student, that's all."

In fact, she'd been the first teacher actually to notice me, to take an interest in my future, to mention the possibility of a college scholarship. *And I don't mean a scholarship to some cow college,* she'd added as we stood in her classroom that afternoon, *but a real university, maybe even the Ivy League, maybe even Harvard.*

Harvard.

I'd never thought of such a possibility before Miss McDowell brought it up, but it didn't take me long to see it as a goal, then to make the scholarship Miss McDowell had mentioned my first great achievement, one that I pursued as if it were the Holy Grail, since I knew that without it, I'd have no hope of attending.

"Miss McDowell thought I had potential," I told Lola Faye. "And she clearly thought that whatever my potential was, it could not be realized in Glenville."

"What can?" Lola Faye asked with a broad laugh. "Nothing, right?" She took a sip of her appletini and then set down the glass, her gaze focused on its dwindling contents. "I'm drinking too fast," she added. "I used to eat fast too." Her eyes settled upon me. "Like an animal, remember?"

"Remember? No."

"But you're the one who noticed it," Lola Faye said. "That I ate like an animal. Chewed like a cow."

"Did I say that?" I asked.

"You know you did," Lola Faye said, her tone rather steely, like a tough cop to a squirming liar. "You know you said that, Luke."

She was right, of course, and with that inward acknowledgment, I recalled the moment with startling vividness. It had come two weeks after I'd found my father's makeshift love nest in the backroom of Variety Store. I'd come to the store directly after school, Debbie on my arm, dressed in the tight clothes she knew I preferred. She'd lingered at the front of the store, in full view of my father, while I'd moved on down the center aisle to where he stood at the clattering old cash register whose money drawer, given the usual state of his business, I'd rarely seen open.

"Hi, Luke," he said. He looked toward the front of the store, where Debbie stood, backlit by the light that poured over her from the window, now idly turning the squeaky rack of books that all but blocked the entrance. "Debbie's a mighty nice girl," he said. "You should marry her."

I released an arid laugh, then suddenly, brutally, on the wings of a white-hot wind, I said, "You don't have to marry some girl just because you screw her."

My father's eyes hardened. "That's no way to talk, Luke," he said. " 'Some girl.' That's no way to talk about Debbie."

I was in no mood to take moral lessons from the man who was betraying my mother, going to work early and

142

coming home late, leaving her to lie alone all day in the upstairs bedroom reading her precious Emily Dickinson while her husband, my dear old dad, rolled around on a pile of broken-down cardboard boxes with Lola Faye Gilroy.

The object of my father's grimy desire abruptly swam into my view: blond, buxom Lola Faye, waltzing out of the backroom, straightening her skirt with one hand, a paper plate in the other, her mouth filled with whatever had been on that plate.

"She eats like an animal," I hissed. "Like a cow."

My father glared at me. "Watch your mouth, Luke," he warned. "You watch your mouth now, you hear me?"

With that I whirled around, marched back down the aisle, and with a great show of possession jerked Debbie, almost roughly, beneath my arm. All of this was done without my looking back until I stepped through the door, and then, with a sidelong glance, I saw Lola Faye out of the corner of my eye, standing next to my father, his arm lifting softly, sweetly, sadly, to draw her near.

Now, twenty years later, she faced me once again, her hair, what few sprigs I could see of it poking out from beneath her wool cap, considerably faded and with the strange hue of a bad dye job, wrinkles at her mouth, her once radiant skin almost completely without luster, all of her allure quite vanished, an object lesson in the brutality of time, although she still had the same wounded look in her eyes.

"I'm sorry," I said. "I shouldn't have said what I did. It was . . . cruel."

"No, no, you were right," Lola Faye said with a light, dismissive wave of the hand, no offense taken. "I did eat like that. Animal-like. Like a cow."

"Still, it wasn't a nice thing for me to have said."

"Well, you can't always be nice, can you?" Lola Faye asked sweetly. "And people need . . . correction, don't you think, Luke?"

Before I could answer, she picked up the glass again and gently swirled the electric green liquid inside it before she put it to her lips, took a slow sip, then brought the glass back down to the table. "People have to be taught a lesson, don't you think?" She opened her arms in the way of a Madonna, tender, forgiving. "Otherwise they never know what they did wrong."

There were still a few sips left in her glass, and for a moment Lola Faye stared into it as one might peer into a well, or a crystal ball, depths in which something either remained to be discovered or waited to emerge, an abyss that one was doomed to look into forever but from which no answer would ever come.

"So, Miss McDowell," she said with the clear intent of returning me to an earlier place in our conversation. "You were telling me that she had an interest in you, that she noticed you, that she told you about that scholarship to Harvard."

"That's right."

"And that she wasn't strange, which is what your daddy thought."

But what had my father actually seen, I wondered, that had given him a notion of the oddness of Miss McDowell? The subtle signs had been invisible to me, the signs so hidden, their revelations so sad and intimate, that even now I kept the knowledge to myself.

"Miss McDowell," I breathed softly, and on that breath again felt the dark energy that had come from her. "Yes."

CHAPTER
THIRTEEN

Despite her name, Miss Gertrude Jessica "Trudy" McDowell had not at all been the dowdy old spinster schoolteacher so familiar in stories of the small-town South. Rather, she'd been quite youthful in her look and manner, but oddly so, as if she considered age and maturity a hostile landscape where, waiting in the distance, there were surely dragons. In that way she seemed to see herself as part of the generation she taught, rather than of her own generation, or the one that had preceded her, a characteristic that could not have endeared her to her older colleagues at the school.

I remembered her best as a teacher who always attended the games and the dances and who seemed more comfortable in the teenage world upon whose periphery her chosen career had deposited her than in her own world. Occasionally at a game she would suddenly burst into a cheer so loud that she'd catch herself, glance about, and immediately rein in her own girlish enthusiasm, so that one sensed a self-imposed imprisonment, as if she were ever the groundskeeper of herself, forever checking fences and locking gates.

I'd gone to her classroom in a pleasant mood, expecting to hear more praise, but Miss McDowell had greeted me with more than the usual encouragement. In fact, there'd been an unsettling urgency about her, something dramatic in her every word and movement, a glancing toward me then away, sometimes moving around me in an ever-tightening circle. I'd actually thought her somewhat odd, at least insofar as the intensity of her enthusiasm for my intelligence and the ferocity of her drive to make sure I understood that I must, absolutely must, do whatever had to be done to advance myself.

"You don't get second chances, Luke," she declared at one point. "You have to take advantage of your gifts, because if you don't, you'll end up throwing them away. And you don't let anything get between you and what you want. Not even people. Parents, anybody. Rules. Not even the rules. What do rules understand anyway? Nothing, really. Not about people, that's for sure."

Everything she said to me that day was either odd or inappropriate. But more than anything, it was clear to me that Miss McDowell had taken it upon herself to alter the course of my life, to open its horizons, to expropriate, however briefly, the role of my parents, and that from then on, she seemed to suggest, it would be "us against the world."

"You can't be swayed by sentiment," she said, by which she meant that I couldn't allow myself to be strapped in place by any love I might have for my father or my mother.

"That will only tie you down," she said. "And, Luke, the point is to soar."

It was late in the afternoon, and the sun came though the tall windows of Miss McDowell's classroom in bright rays heavy with swirling bits of dust.

"Stupid people say you can't see the future," Miss McDowell declared. "But you can. All you have to do is look around you to see your future . . . unless you make something different for yourself."

She strode over to the window and pointed out to where, in the near distance, squat little buildings clustered around Main Street.

"There's your future, Luke, there's the future you can see," Miss McDowell said. "You'll work at your father's store. Then at some point, you'll inherit it."

As she continued, I saw the dreary trajectory of my days, a Variety Store stock boy, who would become a clerk, who would rise to have some place in management, a role that would expand as my father's diminished and that would come to full flower when he at last sank into his grave.

"You don't get what you deserve in life, Luke," Miss McDowell said. "You get what you settle for. And if you settle for Glenville, then Glenville is what you'll get."

She drew back from the window, made a quick turn, and came down the aisle in a kind of dramatic march, pressing forward until she stopped uncomfortably near to me, our bodies only a few inches apart.

"Most people don't have a choice," Miss McDowell said urgently, "but you do, Luke." She tapped her finger against the side of her head. "You have this!"

148

Then, in a strange transformation, her features softened, and in that softening she revealed a sad and vulnerable layer of herself.

"You're a good-looking boy, Luke," she said. "You can also use that."

For a moment we faced each other, something vaguely trembling in Miss McDowell's eyes, a jittery movement she blinked away, like someone coming out of a troubled dream. Then she stepped back from me sharply. "We won't do this again," she said in a voice that seemed once more in the grip of her own iron control. She stepped back a second time, and in a single fluid movement made an abrupt turn, marched to her desk, sat down, opened her roll book, and snapped up a red pencil. Her attention was now rigidly focused on her open roll book, her gaze moving in lockstep down its column of names. "We'll never have this talk again."

And we never had, so that I'd last seen her sitting in the football bleachers, gazing down at the field below, young men in combat, slamming into one another. She'd been curled over slightly, her arms around her knees, like one braced against the cold despite the warm spring air.

"Anyway, Miss McDowell noticed you," Lola Faye said, coaxing me out of my brief silence, returning me to the subject. "It's nice to be noticed."

I wondered if it had been this niceness about being noticed that had drawn her to my father. Separated from Woody, with no living relatives, friendless, living alone, would she not have found almost any kind word reassuring, almost any touch pleasurable? As I myself — I starkly realized at that moment — might find such attentions now.

"Nice that someone thinks you're smart," Lola Faye added. "Thinks you can do great things, go to a great school."

I recalled the letter from Harvard that had later trembled in my hand, the formal language, its expression of best wishes, how refined I'd found the ornate but quietly controlled red lettering, how magical the word: *Harvard*.

"Yes, it is nice to have someone like that in your life," I agreed. "I wonder what happened to her."

"She was murdered," Lola Faye answered with a startling bluntness. "Her husband killed her."

My mouth dropped open. "Miss McDowell was murdered? When?"

"Ten years ago," Lola Faye answered. "It was a big story in Glenville. The first murder since . . ."

"Since my father?" I asked.

Lola Faye nodded.

"You don't have to be shy about saying it," I told her. "We both know what happened."

Lola Faye stared at me silently, glanced away, then back. "Anyway, she was murdered by her husband."

I took a sip from my glass. "So, tell me. Why did he kill her?"

"Because she was having an affair," Lola Faye answered. There was a pause, during which she appeared genuinely reluctant to say more, in the same way that Julia had sometimes seemed hesitant to tell a dirty joke. "It was a shocking thing, Luke," she said at last. "What with it being with one of her students."

So it had been true, I thought, what my father saw.

"A senior at Glenville High," Lola Faye added. "He was eighteen, so it was legal, I guess, technically at least, but still."

"How . . . strange," I said.

"They call them cougars now," Lola Faye informed me. "Women who go with younger men. I read an article about them."

"Well, it shouldn't have been a student," I said casually. "But a little fling in middle age. With someone younger. What's the harm in it?"

Lola Faye stared at me darkly. "There could be a lot of harm in it," she said.

I saw every ghastly element of my father's murder in Lola Faye's eyes, his body flying out of the chair, a geyser of blood shooting from the hole in his chest, all the dreadful, murderous, irrevocable harm a little fling could do.

"So," I continued quietly. "What happened to the husband?"

"He got life," Lola Faye answered. "He never confessed, but the cops figured it was him. Because of that boy she was . . . you know . . . seeing. They figured it had to be the husband."

"Well, you said that's usually who the killer is in a case like that," I said.

"Someone in the family, that's for sure," Lola Faye told me. "It's like Ollie said to me once. 'Lola Faye,' he said, 'the danger is right beside you. Sitting across the table.'" Her features took on a cast of grim reality, as when a child discovers for the first time some dreadful truth of life. "And you don't even know it." Then a smile cracked that hardening mask. "Unless you're really smart." A shake of the head flung the few remaining aspects of this earlier grimness from her face. "Anyway, it was Miss McDowell that pointed the way out of Glenville, right?"

As if dropped out of one time and into another, I found myself staring at the envelope from Harvard, so thick it seemed bloated with fecundity, a great and beautiful flower about to bloom.

"You went off to a big Ivy League college just like Miss McDowell knew you would," Lola Faye declared triumphantly. "It's a pig in a poke, a dream like that, but you got yours, didn't you, Luke?"

Now I was in my bedroom about to open the envelope but then stopped by the sound of my father bursting into the house, bawling my name from downstairs, his voice locked in its regional twang, broad and nasal as a country singer's, endlessly stringing out the vowels, jettisoning the g's: *Luke, c'mere.*

"Things sure were never the same for you after that," Lola Faye added with what seemed undisguised delight.

"No, they weren't."

"And you never came back to Glenville," she added cheerily.

I felt the lurch of the bus, heard a dying wheeze in its groaning engine.

152

"No," I said, "I never came back."

"Or looked back either, I bet," Lola Faye continued with added exuberance, as if in full celebration of another's far more fortunate life. "'Cause, like you said, what would be the point?" Lola Faye's voice lifted exultantly as she raised her glass high above her head. "So here's to leaving Glenville, Luke."

I raised my glass somewhat hesitantly, not sure that Lola Faye's toast was entirely in celebration of myself.

"Dear old Glenville," Lola Faye said happily as she clinked her glass a tad sharply against mine. A smile tore across her lips, then lay there like a jagged crack in a sheet of ice as she repeated her toast, this time more slowly, and with what I took to be a vague, nostalgic sorrow. "Dear. Old. Glenville."

The scene of the crime, I thought.

PART III

CHAPTER
FOURTEEN

Perhaps she'd known it all along, Lola Faye, known all along that our greatest hope, the early dream we seize upon and follow, truly is, as she'd said, a pig in a poke, something we buy in a grab bag, not knowing if it's worth the price we pay.

Dear old Glenville.

Hearing those words, I instantly recalled the high spirits with which I'd headed toward Variety Store after my talk with Miss McDowell. With wings on my heels I'd flown down the walkway that led from Glenville High School to our town's far-from-bustling Main Street. The vision in my head was not just of going north and getting an education at a storied university. It was of writing those grand works I'd set my heart on, how I'd learn to get inside the experiences of the New England farmers who'd first broken that frozen soil, the slaves and tenant farmers who'd hoed the black earth of the South, the harvesters of grain in the great breadbasket of the Midwest, the steel- and ironworkers who'd welded together our towering cities. Breathless with the realization that I might actually attain this heady ambition, I'd strode with a wild energy toward the raggedly painted façade of my father's store.

"Hi, Luke," my father said as I came through the door.

"Hi," I said, and added nothing else, since it was clear to me that not a word of the momentous things Miss McDowell had said to me a few minutes before would have any impact on my father.

"Plenty to do today," my father said.

With that, he recited a mundane list of chores: sweep the floor, restock the small-appliances section, hang Christmas lights in the front window, break down the day's collection of cardboard boxes and drag them into the back alley, where they'd be picked up and carted away by the town garbage truck.

During the next couple of hours, I completed all these tasks, though it seemed to me that I was no longer doing them as if they were my fate, but with the inflamed certainty that my destiny lay elsewhere and that I was already on my way to that other life. There was Harvard, after all. There was that scholarship. There was the monumental life's work that now seemed within my reach. And so the work I did at Variety Store that afternoon was all done while Miss McDowell's words whistled through my brain, all that talk of my being so very smart, that a great future awaited me, that with an act of will, I could enter a larger arena. Suddenly I was no longer just the smartest kid at Glenville High. I was the smartest kid in Alabama, in the South, in America, in the world . . . the smartest kid ever.

By the end of that afternoon, I'd convinced myself of everything Miss McDowell had said to me. If I studied, applied myself, followed her passionate advice, then one day I would pen the great works I dreamed of writing.

There was only one problem, it seemed to me. I had a job. Each afternoon, I had to beat a path from school to Variety Store and, once there, spend the next two or three hours carrying out whatever menial tasks my father demanded.

The answer to this problem was simple: I had to be relieved of these trivial duties. I had to tell my mother what Miss McDowell had told me. She would then have to speak to my father and explain the importance of my studies, of my getting that precious scholarship, and by that means convince him to release me from all my after-school duties.

I had no doubt that my mother could do this, and so as the afternoon came to a close, I felt quite certain it would be my last day working at Variety Store.

And it was, as it turned out, but not because of anything I later said to my mother or that my mother said to my father.

Luke, c'mere.

The words couldn't have been simpler, and I'd heard them many times before. *Luke, c'mere and help me move this crate. Luke, c'mere and take this garbage out back. Luke, c'mere and do this. Luke, c'mere and do that.*

I could hardly remember a day when my father hadn't begun some trivial order with that banal summons. And each time I'd answered his call obediently, done whatever he asked.

"Luke, c'mere, I wanna tell you something."

He'd been at the back of the store and I at the front, shelving a bunch of Santa Claus dolls he'd priced so cheaply he wouldn't make a penny, a price he'd refused to raise even after I'd pointed this out.

"Just a minute," I called to him, then arranged the last of the dolls at the top of the little pyramid I'd created to show them off.

He'd almost finished whatever he'd been doing in the back by the time I turned to face him.

And that afternoon, what did I see? A tall, gawky man with legs so disproportionately long that the belt that held up his trousers seemed to circle just below the midpoint of his chest rather than at his waist. He was facing a spindly display table he'd built himself and that consisted of a series of vaguely square bins in which he'd placed, in utter randomness, the cheap detritus of the five-and-dime: miniature cars, fountain pens, hair curlers, plastic sewing kits.

"Luke, c'mere," he repeated, this time with a wave of his large, rough hand.

When I got there, I expected he'd turn from whatever he was doing long enough to issue another mundane order and then go back to work.

But instead he finished the little task he'd set himself, then shifted around and faced me squarely.

"You don't have to come here after school anymore, Luke," he said.

I actually thought I'd misheard him. "What?"

"I said you don't have to come to work here anymore," my father repeated. He started to turn away.

160

"But who's going to . . . do my job?"

"I hired a girl," my father said.

With this he offered a quick smile, and again turned to the back of the store.

"A girl?" I asked.

"So you can go straight home after school," my father said. "You don't have to come here anymore."

I stared at him, stunned. "How can you afford to hire a girl?" I asked.

"That's not your worry, Luke," my father answered. His tone was matter-of-fact yet evasive, and I sensed some secret motive in all this, though I had no idea what it might be nor, given the prospect of no longer working in the store's chaotic atmosphere, did I feel any desire to inquire further. My father's impulses had always been his own, disorganized as he was, and with little display of deliberate thought.

"This is your last day working here Luke," my father said firmly.

"Okay," I said with a dull shrug.

My father was clearly relieved by this response, by the fact that I had no further questions. He glanced toward the clock at the front of the store. "And I'm letting you off early," he added. "You can go home now."

"Now?" I asked. "But the dolls, I —"

"Don't worry about them dolls," my father said. "Tell your mother I'll be a little late for supper."

We'd always driven home together, my father and I, and it now struck me as quite odd that we'd not both be sitting in his old delivery van heading for 200 Peanut

Lane at the end of the day. There was nothing about this brief journey that had ever appealed to me, and most of the time it had been completed in utter silence. And yet, my solitary departure from Variety Store that afternoon struck me as a separation from my father that was in some way irrevocable, and so when I reached the door, I stopped and turned toward him.

"I could wait for you," I said.

"No, you go ahead."

"Are you sure?" I asked, like a judge offering a condemned prisoner one last chance to state his case.

My father shook his head and continued at his task. "No, you go on home, Luke," he said. "I have to wait for the new girl."

CHAPTER
FIFTEEN

That "new girl" was now sitting across from me, her face framed in the muted light of the hotel lounge. In that pose, Lola Faye still appeared rather ghostly, despite how utterly physical she was, the way her body rested heavily in the chair, the small hints of sagging skin beneath her eyes, time quite obviously no longer on her side. In some ways, she seemed as empty as her glass.

"How about another round?" I asked, rather expecting her to refuse, perhaps glance at the clock, decide it was too late for another drink.

"Okay," Lola Faye said.

I summoned the waitress and gave our orders.

After that we chatted about nothing in particular until the drinks came. This time we made no toast but simply tapped our glasses together.

"I've always wanted to ask you something," I said as I set my glass down. "Did he know you before? My father, I mean. Did he know you before he hired you?"

Lola Faye shook her head. "No," she answered. "Did you think he did?"

"I wasn't sure," I replied. "But it seemed so abrupt, the way he just hired you out of the blue. I'd worked at

163

the store for years. Then, all of a sudden, he didn't want me to work there anymore. So, naturally, after everything else, I wondered if maybe he'd known you before you came to work for him."

"Sheriff Tomlinson asked the same question," Lola Faye said. "I told him that your daddy and me had never met before the day he hired me. I just came in the store and mentioned that I was looking for a job. I guess he sort of felt sorry for me. I was separated from Woody, with no job."

I leaned forward slightly. "But he really couldn't afford to hire anyone," I told her. "The store wasn't making any money."

"Well, Doug didn't always think about money," Lola Faye said.

I released a slightly mocking laugh. "Well, that's true. Those fancy Christmas dolls he sold, for example. They were expensive, and he never figured out that when you added in the shipping, the storage, all those extra costs, he'd priced them way too low to make any money on them. I told him that every year, but he never seemed to get it."

"Oh, he got it, Luke," Lola Faye said. "He knew he was losing money on those dolls."

"So why didn't he raise the price?" I asked.

"Because he wanted lots of little girls in Glenville to have a really nice doll for Christmas," Lola Faye answered. "So he priced them real low so more people could buy them. Not just the bankers and the lawyers, but lots of people." She laughed. "Doug had a soft spot for kids, you know."

164

"Not for this kid," I said. "Not for his son."

Lola Faye said nothing, and in that silence I sensed that I'd touched upon a subject she was reluctant to pursue, and so I returned to the prior one.

"But hiring you," I said. "That really cost him money. An employee he didn't need. Why would he have done that?"

Lola Faye was clearly hesitant to answer this question, which only made me more persistent.

"Why?" I asked again. "If he didn't have designs on you, why would he have done that?"

"Maybe he just wanted someone else working with him," she said cautiously. "Someone else in the store." She glanced toward the nearest window. "It's getting colder. I bet that snow's coming in."

I was in no mood to discuss the weather.

"Why would my father have wanted someone else?" I continued stubbornly. "I did every little job he gave me. Washing windows, sweeping. I did everything he asked."

"I know," Lola Faye said softly. "You were a good worker, Luke. Doug always said that whatever he told you to do, you did it."

"So why replace me?"

Lola Faye shifted uneasily in her seat. "Well, maybe it was the *way* you did it, Luke," she said. "Maybe that's what your daddy didn't like."

"What do you mean, the *way* I did it?" I asked.

Lola Faye appeared trapped. She was quite obviously reluctant to answer, though she clearly recognized that

165

the determined nature of my questioning made any further evasion impossible.

"The way you made him feel," she said, as if she were giving up a bit of information she could no longer avoid revealing.

"Which was how?" I asked.

"Like he was sort of a pitiful guy," Lola Faye admitted. "A loser type of guy. A man doesn't like to *feel* that way, Luke. Dumb or clumsy or like he didn't know what he was doing. Your daddy didn't like being *looked* at that way. Especially by you."

And there they were, hanging like dark sketches in a museum, all the critical glances I'd offered my father during the years I'd worked at Variety Store, all the barely audible sighs of exasperation and all the barely visible shakes of the head that had conveyed in no uncertain terms how inept I thought him, how physically clumsy he was, how gross his manners, how unkempt his dress, how drab and tiresome and commonplace and unexceptional I found this only life he had.

The hard nature of my judgment, along with the sudden recognition of how my father had suffered under it, must have registered in my eyes, because I saw the reflection of it register in Lola Faye's.

"But I'm sure that would have changed," she said quickly, like a nurse stanching a bleeding wound, "if he'd lived."

If he'd lived.

Almost as if I'd been standing at his side that night, I heard the bullet crash through the kitchen window of the house on Peanut Lane, saw my father's body jerk backward and spill to the floor, saw a geyser of blood spurt up from his chest, shoot up and arc over with each dwindling beat of his heart.

"But he didn't," I said quietly, and with those words felt a peculiar sensation run through me, a subtle quickening, as if some slender, long-deadened nerve had suddenly sprung to life.

Lola Faye lowered her head slightly. "No," she said. "He didn't."

A silence enveloped us, longer than any before it, which I finally broke with a quick, almost lighthearted aside.

"I saw you, you know," I said. "The first afternoon you came to work at Variety Store."

To my surprise, my casual recollection of this first sighting gave every impression of delighting Lola Faye, so that for a moment she appeared to think of herself recalled in that distant and less troubled moment in her life, recalled perhaps as an old lover might have.

"It was late in the afternoon," I continued. "Around five. All the other stores were closing. That's probably why I noticed you, because there was really no foot traffic in Glenville at that hour."

"Where was I?" Lola Faye asked in a manner as guilelessly inquisitive as a child's.

"Up the street," I answered. "Around Sanford and Main."

"Sanford and Main," Lola Faye repeated, and appeared to be carrying out some sort of calculation.

167

"Wow. You have a good memory, Luke. And it was around five, you said?"

"That's right."

"In December, of course," Lola Faye said. "Mid-December, yep, because it was near my birthday." She thought a moment longer, then added, "Around five, so it would have been nearly dark in the middle of December. And Sanford Street is over a block away from Variety Store." She narrowed her eyes dramatically and her voice hardened. "So how do you know it was me, Luke?"

She posed the question like an attorney to a hostile witness, and with an unmistakable glint in her eyes, as if she were challenging me at every level, a change of mood that came at me like a flying object, and that I could only dodge awkwardly, with a brief loss of balance.

"Well, I —"

Suddenly Lola Faye laughed quite loudly, a kind of violent eruption, as a laugh might come from the barrel of a gun. "Did you ever see *Twelve Angry Men*?" she asked. "That movie with Henry Fonda? It all takes place in a jury room."

"I don't think so," I said warily, still recovering from the feeling of disequilibrium caused by her erratic change of tone.

"You don't like courtroom dramas?" Lola Faye asked.

"Not particularly," I answered, now working to determine why Lola Faye had injected so odd a subject into our conversation.

"Well, you should, Luke," Lola Faye told me. "You can learn a lot watching them."

"I guess I should watch them more often then," I said distantly.

"Anyway, that's the sort of question the jurors start to ask in that movie," Lola Faye informed me with all the innocent relish of a movie fan recalling a favorite scene. "And at the end of that movie, they didn't convict the guy. The guy everyone thought did it, that guy was innocent." She released a strangely jolly laugh, and I half expected her to poke me playfully in the ribs. "I was just acting like Henry Fonda does in that movie. You know, trying to find out how you knew it was me you saw on the street that afternoon."

"Well, who else could it have been?" I asked, slightly embarrassed that Lola Faye's sudden dramatic flair had briefly unsettled me and determined to regain lost ground. "Given the time of day, no one else would have been on the street, right? Oh, and this too: my father had already told me that he was expecting you."

"Expecting me?"

"That the new girl was coming in," I told her. "Coming to the store that same afternoon." I leaned back slowly and slightly more confidently, convinced that although earlier taken by surprise, I had now regained control in Lola Faye's little game of courtroom drama. "So who else could it have been but you?" I asked.

For a moment, our eyes locked. Then, in a slow pulling away, Lola Faye uncoupled her gaze from mine and shrank ever so slightly back into her seat.

"Of course it was me you saw, Luke," she admitted. "I was wearing a light blue skirt and a white blouse, and I'd taken a ribbon that matched the skirt and tied it around my neck." The hostile attorney shifted to intimate confidante. "I guess I thought that little touch of blue, that little ribbon, would make it seem like I knew things, like I had experience in business, something like that." Her smile was all sadness and disappointment, making her look in some way like a shattered dream. "Maybe even give your daddy the idea that I'd been to college, was smart, had some education."

I dismissed any such notion with a quick wave of my hand. "If my father had thought you were educated, he wouldn't have hired you."

"He wouldn't have?" Lola Faye asked in a tone of genuine wonder. "Why not?"

"Because he had no respect for education," I answered. "I don't think it had ever occurred to him that I might want to go to college just for the education, that I might want to go to a great school, not some local cow college. It never occurred to him that I might want to write a book or had big dreams or anything like that."

"Never occurred to him," Lola Faye repeated thoughtfully, with no indication of arguing the point. "Wow."

"As a matter of fact, nothing occurred to my father," I added, a hint of my old hard judgment of him returning once again, deep and ineradicable, like a stain that forever reappears. "Not even what would happen to my mother if something happened to him."

Lola Faye lowered her gaze and with that penitent gesture appeared to take full responsibility for everything she'd done. "I guess none of it would have happened," she said softly. "If it hadn't been for me." She seemed to consider the dreadful consequences of her having been hired to work at Variety Store, and then, quite abruptly, to see them in another light. "But when you look at it a different way, it's sort of funny, don't you think, Luke?"

Funny?

The word itself seemed ludicrous within the context of all our prior conversation, like a clown at a funeral.

"Funny like in how things can turn on you in a split second," Lola Faye said, as if she'd quite unexpectedly glimpsed the side-splitting humor at the core of all things tragic. "You go along and go along, and you think you know who you are and how things are going to turn out, and all of a sudden, everything changes."

I felt a dreadful jangling deep within me, like the rattle of a jailer's keys.

"Changes fast and forever," Lola Faye added pointedly. "Like a car going over a bridge."

CHAPTER
SIXTEEN

Like a car going over a bridge, I repeated in my mind.

Lola Faye's words tightened around me like a noose, and in that tightening, I thought of the shattered window, my father's dead body on the kitchen floor, all that had happened after that, everything from that first murder to Julia's departing words, *Call me, Luke, when your past is in the past*.

But where had it begun, *Luke's Journey*?

While Lola Faye talked on about the vicissitudes of chance, how lives could turn on a dime, in car accidents, for example, or airplane crashes, I considered the somewhat less subtle twists my own life had taken.

Surely a great one had been when Miss McDowell mentioned Harvard, but what if I had taken no notice of what she'd said? What if I had been like Buddy McPharland, practically devoid of either ability or ambition? What if I had not been inspired first by my mother's reading and later by my own? What if I'd never known that great men existed, or that there were men who wrote about great men, great events, who took the sweep of human life as their own lives' work?

And what if someone at some point had tried to stay my hand, cool my brain, put things in perspective, or

172

simply offer a word of caution? What if someone had said, *Luke, be careful?*

I wouldn't have listened. I knew that I wouldn't have listened even as Lola Faye droned on about the hairpin curves of life, now with other examples, the world's grotesque fortuities great and small, all of this flowing from her mouth in a steady stream: illness, sudden death, chance encounters, all the unforeseen twists and turns that can derail a life.

No, I would not have listened, because I'd been in a fever of dreamy ambition and riotous hope, both of which were still blazing away when I arrived home that same evening, now mercifully relieved of any further duties at Variety Store by my father's decision to hire a new girl.

My mother stopped washing dishes when I came storming through the door nearly breathless with anticipation.

"What is it, Luke?"

"Miss McDowell," I said. "I had a talk with Miss McDowell."

From there, I told my mother everything Miss McDowell had said to me, that I was gifted, that I could get into Harvard, maybe even get a scholarship, that there was a road I could take, and that this road would lead to the fulfillment of my dream. It had gushed from me, all of this, and it had flowed around and over my mother. I could see it in her eyes, how fully she absorbed every word I said, how she shared this dream, how united we were in the pursuit of it.

When I finally exhausted myself, she stepped away from the sink and drew me into her arms. "You're on your way, Luke," she said. She tightened her arms around me, as if sealing in my grand ambition, and while she had me locked in that embrace, she said the darkest thing she could have said to me: "Don't let anything stop you, Luke. Don't let anything stop you ever."

From there we talked on and on, the bus I would take to Boston, the dorm I might live in, the new friends I would have, and as we talked my future blossomed like a hothouse flower until, loud as a rifle shot, my father arrived, his lumbering figure easily visible as he made his way across the back porch, past the large window that looked out over the backyard, where, some weeks before, he'd stacked cement blocks into a ragged pile.

"Oh, Doug," my mother said when she released me and turned to him. "Luke's going to Harvard. One of his teachers says he can get a scholarship!"

"That's nice," my father said with a quick grin. Then the thought passed and he sniffed the air. "Potatoes," he said, the grin widening now. "How you making them, Ellie?"

"Did you hear me, Doug?" my mother asked emphatically. "Luke is going to Harvard."

My father clearly had little notion of what Harvard was. In fact, from what he said, it seemed that he thought my going there was in some way the result of chance, like drawing a fourth ace, rather than the product of my own high abilities.

"Well, that's a lucky break for you, I guess," he said to me.

"It's because Luke is so smart, Doug," my mother informed him. "It has nothing to do with luck."

With that, my father at least understood that he should react both differently and with considerably more enthusiasm to this news. Even so, it was quite obvious that he had no idea as to the nature of the reaction expected of him.

"Because Luke's so smart, right," he repeated. He turned to me and flashed his Variety Store smile. "That's right," he said. "Smart, Luke, not luck."

"And so you have to take luck into consideration when you think about life," Lola Faye declared at the end of her latest effusion concerning the stark hardships of life. "But you have to work too, of course," she added. "Remember what Arnold Palmer said." She stopped dead. "You know who that is, right, Luke? Arnold Palmer?"

"The golfer," I hazarded.

Lola Faye seemed to think that this shared bit of mutual knowledge formed a common bond between us, like two people interested in the same field of science. "The golfer, right," she said happily. "Ollie repeats this one famous thing he said. But in this case, other golfers may have said it too, so maybe it was Sam Snead or even Bobby Jones that really said it. Anyway, some famous golfer."

"And what is it exactly that one of these famous golfers said?" I asked.

"That golf is a game of luck, and that the more you practice, the luckier you get." She was clearly pleased to have this quotation — or a paraphrase of it — in her intellectual arsenal. "That's true, don't you think, Luke?"

"I suppose it is, yes."

Lola Faye took a sip of her drink. "But you never depended on luck at all, did you? And that's the best attitude to have. Because you can't depend on luck. You have to work for what you want."

She'd obviously come to the end of her discussion of fortune's slings and arrows, the good or ill that may come to a person by luck alone, and from there had shifted the focus of our talk from philosophy to biography, from the play of accident to the fruits of labor.

"You worked very hard for that scholarship, right, Luke?" Lola Faye asked. "Because getting it was the key to your whole future."

"Yes, I worked hard," I told her.

And I had.

There'd been high grades to maintain and essays to write and forms to fill out and references to secure. I'd even gotten the mayor of Glenville to write a letter on my behalf, naively thinking that the recommendation of so high a public official might matter to the acceptance and scholarship committees at Harvard.

"But my mother helped," I added.

She'd applied herself to this labor with all her power, sat through long nights of writing and rewriting. Through draft after draft, she'd maintained a fierce vigilance, her eye alert to the smallest points of grammar, suggesting that I add this detail or that one to my essay, making sure that my writing was crystal clear. She'd even suggested the title for my essay: "The Touch of Time: How History Is Felt."

"It was a ridiculously grandiose ambition," I admitted to Lola Faye. "Going to Harvard on a scholarship. Even my essay was grandiose. But it got the point across, I guess. How I wanted to make readers actually feel what it was like for people in the fields and on the plains, the way the wind whipped around them, that burning sun. The physical touch of history."

Lola Faye nodded. "You mean, what ordinary people feel," she said. "When they work, for example."

"Physically, yes," I said. "The lever of a machine. The handle of a hoe or a broom."

The foolish and impossible grandeur of my youthful ambition settled upon me like a weight. "It was a crazy idea," I confessed. "Poetry instead of history. But that's not my mother's fault. She did everything she could to help me write that essay. And then she went to the post office with me the day I sent it all out. My application for admission. My application for a scholarship. Everything."

"Your mother was your biggest supporter," Lola Faye declared.

"She was my only supporter," I said.

Lola Faye quite clearly saw the double-edged sword in my response, that I had efficiently eliminated my father from the ranks of those who had noticed me, believed in me, urged me to pursue my youthful dream.

"My mother worked as hard as I did," I added.

And it had all paid off.

For the first time in years, I recalled the heady lift of that wild success, the sparkle of a dream in the process of coming true.

The envelope had come in April. I'd been checking the mail for several weeks by then, had many times reached inside the dark mouth of the battered old mailbox on which my father had scrawled our last name in typically ill-formed and drippy letters. I'd flipped through all the many bills: light, gas, mortgage, along with numerous obscure creditors of Variety Store who, it seemed, were now writing to my father at home.

But suddenly, amid all these mundane demands for satisfaction, it was there, nestled between a letter bearing some lawyer's letterhead and a fourth-class-mail advertisement for lawn mowers: *Harvard University*.

It was not a thin envelope, and Miss McDowell had told me that only rejections were thin.

I'd made it, and I knew I'd made it.

Did I tremble? I don't think so. But I know that I felt a wave of fierce happiness sweep through me and carry me down the cracked cement walkway and into the house, where I found my mother toiling as ever, this time with a sewing kit, mending one of my father's impossibly stained flannel shirts.

"It's here," I said. I gave her the still-unopened envelope. "I think *you* should open it, Mom."

178

My father's shirt slipped from her hand, but she didn't take the envelope. "Why do you want me to open it, Luke?"

"Because it's as much yours as mine," I told her.

She drew the envelope from my hand, opened it, read its first line: *It is with great pleasure that . . .*

She never finished it but instead began to cry.

For a tingling moment in the hotel lounge, the memory of that shared victory, my mother's breaking voice, *Luke, I'm so proud of you,* all of it, all of it, seemed as real to me as anything that happened later. I felt the full exuberance of her pride in me, the awesome depth of her goodwill, how she would truly have taken her own advice and done anything, anything, to ensure that I would make it out of Glenville, go north, get educated, write great books.

As if still lifted on that remembered instant, I recalled how I'd floated through the rest of the day in a blissful reverie, dreaming of the bus ride to Boston, all the places I'd see on the way there: the National Mall of Washington and the fabled skyline of New York City. I'd fantasized about strolling the Harvard campus, always with a book under my arm, a budding sage, serious and determined. My professors all wore bow ties and spectacles in this absurd rendering, and all my fellow classmates were handsome men and beautiful women; all of us, professors and students, equally in pursuit of some shining excellence, we few, we happy few, we band of brothers.

Throughout that long day I'd practically soared above the drab streets of Glenville, my future no longer

179

subject to its downward pull, no longer crushed beneath its leaden weight. By the time I reached Debbie, I'd sprouted wings.

"So," she'd said as she drew the letter from my hand. She didn't have to read it to know the news I'd brought her. It was radiating from my face. "You got in," she added.

"Yes."

She read the letter, then looked at me. Her eyes were glistening. "That's so great, Luke," she said. "That's just so great."

She knew what it meant, of course, a reality that was also in those glistening eyes.

"When will you leave?" she asked.

"Well, I have to get that scholarship first," I told her.

She held the letter out to me. "You will, Luke," she said.

I suddenly glimpsed the impossible future she'd hoped for but never spoken of, that ours would not be just another high-school romance doomed to fall with the first leaf of autumn. She had wanted it to deepen and mature, wanted me to love her and somehow take her with me, or if not, then at least ask her to wait for my return. She had wanted me to leave for Harvard as other boys left for war; when the victory was won, I would return to claim her. She had hoped for this while I'd filled out my application and written my essay and applied for my scholarship, and during this time, her hope must have intensified even as the likelihood of its realization diminished, and finally disappeared.

180

"You'll get everything you want," she added. With my acceptance letter suspended motionlessly between us, she seemed like the last holdout in a doomed fortress, watching as the enemy massed in the distance, all hope now surely lost. "Everything you want, Luke."

Despite all Debbie must have been feeling at that moment, she asked nothing of me, and appeared to expect nothing. "I won't forget you, Luke" was all she said.

"I won't forget you either," I said as I drew her into my arms.

But I did.

CHAPTER
SEVENTEEN

I should have stayed in touch with Debbie," I said as I returned to the present. "She must have felt . . . forgotten."

My abrupt reversion to an earlier point in our talk did not seem to faze Lola Faye, so I guessed that she'd had many such wandering conversations.

"Debbie was a nice girl," she said. "A very sweet girl." She shrugged. "But people drift away from people, don't they, Luke?"

I thought of Julia, how I was drifting farther and farther away from her even as she labored to stay in touch, her letters still arriving with little bits of news: a piece of furniture added to her apartment, a patient for whom she'd developed a particular affection.

"But you know, with Debbie, people from Glenville, you couldn't have kept in touch with them," Lola Faye assured me. "Because you had to keep your focus, right, Luke?"

"Yes," I said. "I had to keep my focus."

And like a scroll, the days following my Harvard acceptance unspooled, the fact that I would soon be leaving Glenville so certain that I could think of nothing else. In the magical way that hope so often generates its own unreality, I saw my future bloom before me, the books I'd write, the praise I'd receive, the awards I'd win.

In anticipation of my leaving, I bought new clothes, mostly casual ones, but also a black suit and some white shirts and two sober, drab-colored ties. At Glenville's only consignment shop, I found an old leather suitcase with brass fittings. The leather was scarred and the brass was faded, but over the course of a long afternoon, I imagined all the places I would take it: to Gettysburg and Little Bighorn, the factories of Lowell, the farms of Iowa. And beyond America, it would see fjords and rainforests, this traveling case. It would see blue grottoes and desert wastes. It would know the world, and after I'd described that world in ways as yet unknown to me, it would be the symbol of that great journey, a precious artifact of my life's work. Ludicrously, I even imagined it on display, resting in some museum's glass case, an object imbued with history itself, like Lindbergh's empty flight suit.

"Motivation is the key," Lola Faye said. "Ollie said that once. You got to be motivated."

Her sudden interruption of my train of thought brought me up short, so I quickly stammered, "I'm s-sorry, what was that?"

"Motivation is the key," Lola Faye repeated matter-of-factly. "Ollie taught me that."

The man who'd come in earlier and was sitting behind the fern cleared his throat rather loudly. I glanced toward where he sat but could make out only the hint of a profile, his features broken up and rearranged by the green fronds that obscured him.

"The key to what?" I asked when I turned back to Lola Faye.

"To everything," Lola Faye said. "Of course, when Ollie said that, he was talking about murder."

"Murder?" A sharp current of uneasiness ran through me, as if I'd heard the rustle of something just outside my bedroom window.

"Murder, yep," Lola answered. "Ollie taught me that if you find the motive, chances are you'll find the murderer." She started to add something to this, but stopped and gazed at me quizzically. "What were you thinking about just before?" she asked. "You had that look you get when you think hard about something."

I was relieved that she'd returned to our earlier topic of discussion.

"I was thinking about how I'd kept my focus, I guess," I answered. "On going to Harvard, I mean. Getting that scholarship." I shrugged. "Which I didn't get, by the way."

"You didn't get the scholarship?" Lola Faye asked. She appeared both surprised and oddly enlightened by this information, like a person who'd just received news that was both unexpected and darkly illuminating. "That must have been a blow."

"It was, yes," I said. "Because a lot depended on it. Everything, really. My entire future. Without it, there was no way I could go to Harvard."

"Yeah, but you got to Harvard anyway," Lola Faye said, as if to remind me of my good fortune. She

184

yanked her LA coroner bag from the back of her chair, took out my book, and opened it to the brief biography below the small black-and-white photo of me Julia had taken some years before. "See?" She turned the book toward me so that I stared briefly into my own troubled eyes. "Undergraduate degree and PhD from Harvard University."

"Yes," I said. I turned the book back around. "But for a while it looked hopeless."

"Yep, I guess it must have," Lola Faye said. She snapped up the book, sank it in her bag, then returned the bag to the back of her chair, where it hung, lifeless as a pelt. "When did you find out, Luke? That you didn't get that scholarship, I mean."

I recalled the moment exactly.

The second letter had come two weeks after the first, this time with a very different greeting: *We regret to inform you . . .*

I'd read it with disbelief, unable to accept the dire truth it so clearly and succinctly stated. There would be no scholarship for Lucas Paige.

As I'd done only two weeks before, I went to my mother, bearing this far different news, and found her working in her garden.

She groaned slightly as she got to her feet, then turned to me, and at that instant saw the terrible distress in my face.

"What is it, Luke?"

I handed her the letter. "I didn't get a scholarship," I told her.

She took the letter and read it silently, a silence she held for a time even after she'd finished reading it so I knew she was desperately searching for the right thing to say, some little word of encouragement, a buttress, however frail, against the tidal wave of disappointment she saw in my eyes. Finally she said, "Oh, Luke," and sank down into a lawn chair.

Her tone was as tender as I'd ever heard, but it did nothing to quench the annihilating fire inside me, nothing to convince me that all hope wasn't lost, that there might be some other way to realize my grand ambition, that I was not at that searing instant doomed for all time.

My mother saw all this, then acted quickly to shore up the crumbling she glimpsed at the center of myself.

"Maybe there's a way, Luke," she said.

"A way?"

"A way you can still go."

"What way?"

"I don't know," my mother admitted. "Let's talk to your father."

No suggestion could have struck me as more absurd than this, but in the deep cavern of my despair, I would have grasped at anything.

He arrived home two hours later, carrying a sack of kindling he tossed willy-nilly into the garage before strolling inside to where my mother and I sat glumly at the kitchen table.

"What's for supper, Ellie?" he asked as he tromped over to the stove, yanked the lid from one of the pots he found there, and peered inside.

"I haven't made supper yet, Doug," my mother told him.

This clearly struck my father as a very curious development. He returned the lid to the pot. "Okay," he said in that befuddled way of his. Then he shifted around to my mother and me, saw the intensely troubled faces that greeted him.

"What's going on?" he asked.

"Luke didn't get a scholarship," my mother told him flatly.

"Oh, yeah?" my father asked. He looked at me. "Okay, well, you know what they say: when the going gets tough, the tough get going."

"What's that supposed to mean?" I asked.

"I guess it means you'll have to make other plans, Luke."

I released a dismal laugh. "Like what, Dad?"

"Like going somewhere else to school," my father said.

"Somewhere else?"

My father nodded. "Somewhere else, yeah. Somewhere around here maybe."

"Like where?"

"Well, like that junior college," he answered. "The one up on the mountain."

Miss McDowell's voice rang in my ears: *And I don't mean a scholarship to some cow college.*

"Mountain Community?" I burst out. "That's a cow college!"

"Cow college?" my father asked. He looked at my mother to explain the term he'd quite obviously never heard.

"I'm not going to Mountain Community!" I cried.

"What's the matter with it?" he asked. "Buddy McPharland's going there."

"Buddy McPharland?" I yelped.

"Okay, all r-right," my father stammered. "You could come back to work at Variety Store then." A broad smile lit his face. "We could change the name: Paige and Son's Variety Store."

And I thought, *That's what he wants. That's what he's always wanted. For me to give up on doing anything or being anything. He wants me to be nothing . . . like him.*

And at that moment, all the disdain I'd felt for my father, along with whatever remained of my secret need for his approval, turned to sheer, incinerating hatred.

"I'm getting out of here," I snapped. "I can't stand this."

I leaped from my chair and stormed out of the house, out into the night, toward where our ragtag old Ford sat in the gloom of our garage.

"Where are you going, Luke?" my mother called from the kitchen window.

"Just away," I shouted without looking back at her.

And that is what I wanted to do, simply go away, far, far away, fast and furiously away to someplace where no one would know me, or ever care what I thought or did, or entertain the slightest interest in my hopeless hope.

CHAPTER
EIGHTEEN

"Your Daddy never mentioned that you didn't get that scholarship," Lola Faye told me. She still appeared surprised by this fact, and somewhat thwarted by having been unaware of it, like an investigator who'd been denied a vital piece of evidence.

"That's because he never understood how important to me it was," I explained. I felt my resentment of him harden once again, encase me like a crust. "That I couldn't go to Harvard without it." I shrugged. "Of course, he never understood why I wanted to go there in the first place." I shook my head. "Or how could he have mentioned Mountain Community?"

It struck me as quite odd that I'd actually told Lola Faye all I'd just related to her — the lost scholarship, my father's reaction to it, even down to the rage that had overtaken me as I'd strode angrily to that old blue Ford. But I'd been careful to seal this part of my story within the strict confines of the incident itself, and by that means I'd given no hint that my rage had spilled over into the following weeks. In fact, after that I'd never again spoken to my father with affection or even kindness; our communication became little more than a language of shrugs and glances, most of them hostile on my part, and to which at last he grew indifferent, so that, in the final days, he hardly seemed to see me at all.

"You must have been pretty desperate," Lola Faye said. "Losing something you want that much could drive a person crazy."

"Yes, it could," I admitted.

"You have to watch out for that kind of thing," Lola Faye added. "I saw a *Dr. Phil* episode once, and the guy there, he said, you have to be proactive. You know that word, I bet."

I nodded.

"You have to be proactive when you feel like you're under too much strain," Lola Faye continued. "Like you're just going to blow up if you don't *do* something. That must have been the way you felt, right, Luke?"

"I suppose I did feel that way, yes."

This admission appeared to strike Lola Faye as confessional, one small piece of a puzzle she was assembling in her mind.

"So what happened after you left the house that night?" Lola Faye asked.

With this question, her tone shifted from the conversational to the interrogatory, as if she were trying to establish the sort of police timeline whose complexities and cross-references she'd quite possibly picked up from Ollie.

"I went for a drive," I answered with a great show of both fearlessness and forthrightness. "I ended up at Debbie's house."

190

She'd been surprised to see me, of course, and at her first glimpse of me she'd known that something was horribly wrong.

"What is it, Luke?" she asked.

"Get in," I said. "Just get in."

She had, and a few minutes later, on what remained of an old mining road, I'd taken her hard and brutally in the back seat of that ragtag Ford, driving into her deeper and more violently with each thrust, propelled by anger, lovelessly and without pleasure, a rapist's sex, blind to her feelings, and so it was only after I'd climbed off her that I'd noticed the disturbed look in her eyes.

"You scare me sometimes, Luke," she whispered.

I blinked the bleak nature of that memory away and looked steadily at Lola Faye. "We went for a drive," I told her. "Debbie and I. On Decatur Road."

"The same ride you took the night Doug was killed," Lola Faye said.

"How did you know that?"

"You told me before, I think. And I guess Sheriff Tomlinson mentioned it," Lola Faye answered casually. "You were driving fast, I bet. Being upset like you were."

I recalled making that same drive some weeks later, Debbie's eyes widening in terror as we closed in on the bridge at Dead Man's Curve.

"Yes, I was driving fast."

"But I bet Debbie calmed you down."

I wondered if Debbie had gone through all this with Lola Faye during their conversation and if Lola Faye was now in the process of cross-checking the facts.

"Yes, she did," I said, careful to keep as close as possible to the truth. I took a sip of wine. "Anyway, we drove around for a while, then I went back home."

Home to Glenville, a drive that took me past Variety Store, where I noticed, to my surprise, my father's delivery van was parked out front, all the lights off inside the store save for a single illuminated sliver that came from the back storeroom, a memory that prompted a question whose answer I could get nowhere else.

"Did you ever stay with my father at night?" I asked Lola Faye. "After the store closed, I mean."

Lola shook her head. "No." She seemed to think that I didn't believe her. "No, never, Luke." She became more emphatic. "It was only at the store." She leaned forward and lowered her voice. "And it was just work when we were together, Luke. It was only work. That's all we ever did together."

"What do you mean, only work?"

"I mean only work, Luke," Lola Faye answered firmly. "Not what Woody said in that note he wrote."

I felt something give way deep inside me, then resist the cracking and shore itself up again.

"Are you saying that you and my father never . . . ?" I asked.

"I mean there was never anything like that between your daddy and me," Lola Faye said decidedly. "No matter what Woody wrote in that note he left, or what Sheriff Tomlinson and everybody else in Glenville believed because he wrote it."

192

I stared at her, stunned not only by her denial but by the sincerity of it, and with that sincerity I realized the awesome fact that it might be true.

"I know Woody believed that stuff he wrote," Lola Faye told me. "But he got it wrong. Your daddy and me, we never did anything but work together."

I recalled the broken-down cardboard boxes with which my father had fashioned a bed, the plywood tent he'd dragged over to make a roof for his boudoir.

"But what about that little bedroom he made?" I asked cautiously. "Wasn't that where you and —"

"What bedroom?"

"The one in the storeroom," I answered. "Some boxes with a sheet over them. He put a piece of plywood over the whole thing, like a lean-to."

Lola Faye looked at me without the slightest suggestion that she had any idea what I was talking about.

"I came to the storeroom one night," I explained. "My mother had been taken to the hospital, and she wanted pajamas. I went into the storeroom at the back of Variety Store to get them, and that's where I saw this plywood leaning against the wall. There were boxes inside it. Broken-down boxes. And there was a sheet pulled over them."

Lola Faye stared at me intently, as if she were trying to see some figure in the clouds, a galloping horse or sailing ship, a formation she herself could not make out but that I could show her.

"A bed!" I said emphatically. "Or at least it was sort of a bed. Anyway, it was exactly the kind of thing I knew my father would make. Just a bunch of boxes and a sheet with an old piece of plywood that he'd —"

Suddenly, horrifyingly, Lola Faye released a shockingly hearty laugh. "Oh, that!" she cried. "I remember that now. Sort of looked like a tent." Another raucous laugh broke from her. "That wasn't a bed, Luke. A bed? You thought that was where . . ." She shook her head almost violently. "That's just the way your daddy put things away. He just scattered things around, you know that. Why, he probably just had some old boxes and threw a sheet down, and that's what you saw. Because he never made a bed for us." She abruptly reined in her laughter and looked at me quite pointedly. "Because we never went to bed, Luke," she declared evenly, like someone falsely accused and determined to convince the jury simply by telling the truth, the whole truth, and nothing but. "Never once," she added solemnly. "Ever."

I didn't believe her, couldn't believe her, and, at that instant, simply refused to believe that the single fiercest and most life-changing image of my youth had been little more than a mirage.

"Then who was that present for?" I demanded.

Lola Faye looked at me as if I'd suddenly begun to speak Latin.

"It was inside that . . . structure," I said. "A little box wrapped in pink paper and tied with a blue bow. There was a little card. It said, 'For my dearest love.' Wasn't that for you?"

Lola Faye's gaze became inexpressibly tender. "No, Luke," she said. "That was for your mother."

I stared at her incredulously, and when she saw this, she added a fact she must have considered proof.

"Your father bought her a little diamond ring," she told me. "She'd never had one when they got engaged. They were going to renew their vows, he said. He was going to take her to Trenton, where they'd gotten married. A second wedding. That was the plan. It was supposed to be a big secret. He showed me the ring and said he was going to hide it so your mother wouldn't find it when she brought his lunch that day."

"What day?"

"It was his birthday," Lola Faye said. "She made him a special lunch that day and brought it over to the store. He knew she was coming so he hid the box."

I saw the little pink box again, the absurd place where my father had tucked it away, typically haphazard. But even then I couldn't allow myself to believe that it had all been a lie I'd told myself, this tale of my father's grotesque infidelity.

"What happened to the ring?" I asked.

"When your mother got sick he took it back," Lola Faye answered. "He knew she wouldn't be up to a second honeymoon and I guess money was tight, so he took it back to Mr. Klein."

"Mr. Klein?"

"It was Mr. Klein that picked it out," Lola Faye said. "You know, Klein's Jewelry, over on Sanford."

I stared at her mutely.

"Mr. Klein was good about it," Lola Faye added quite casually. "He gave Doug his money back." With that, she took a sip from her glass, and with no show of having the slightest idea that any of these revelations were now rumbling over me like storm clouds across the plains, she said, "Anyway, tell me the rest of the story. You drove around, picked up Debbie. After that, you both went for a drive, then you dropped her back at her house."

I took a long restorative breath, though deep inside, I could feel the creak of supporting rafters, an old foundation crumbling. "Very good," I said. "Everything in sequence."

Lola Faye seemed pleased by the compliment. "Ollie taught me to put things in order like that," she said happily. She glanced toward the man who sat in ghostly stillness behind the fern, then, as if annoyed by her own distraction, snapped her gaze back to me. "Okay, then after you dropped off Debbie, you went home, right?"

"Yes."

I felt the night air hit me as it had through the open window of the Ford, saw the darkened front of Variety Store sweep by, my father's delivery van resting before it like a dusty old mule.

"My father wasn't home when I got back," I said. "I thought about going right to bed, but I was still too upset, all my hopes dashed."

Lola Faye watched me with what appeared to be a truly melancholy gravity.

"I figured my mother would be in that little alcove in the house where she liked to sit and read, but she wasn't there. So I knew she'd already gone to bed, and I would have too, but I knew I couldn't sleep. I was still too upset about not getting that scholarship."

196

I'd been reading Burke's *Reflections on the French Revolution*, I told Lola Faye, but given the utter hopelessness of my ever writing a similarly grand work, the thought of continuing to read it had been more than I could bear, and so I'd turned to one of the bookshelves that stood between my room and my mother's. I'd touched Austen and the Brontës, glided past Dickens and George Eliot, and finally decided on a book whose author I didn't know but whose title appealed to my current state of mind.

"It was called *The Ordeal of Richard Feverel*," I said. "And when I drew it from the bottom shelf, I heard a soft clank come from behind it."

Lola Faye watched me with a rapt attention that spurred me on, and for a moment I felt myself touch the hem of that great storyteller I'd once hoped to be, a writer whose narrative voice and drive could hold a reader spellbound.

"There was a little metal box behind that book," I said, now adding a hint of tension to my voice. "It wasn't locked, so naturally I looked inside." I allowed a brief, dramatic pause before I went on.

But just as I opened it, I told Lola Faye, I heard the door of my mother's bedroom open, and I turned to find her standing a few feet away, her eyes fixed on the box.

"Open it, Luke," she said.

I did, then watched as she came forward and drew out the stack of bills inside it. "It's yours, Luke," she said. "I've been saving it up for you since you were just a little boy." She waved the money gently in the shadowy air. "It comes from the grocery money your father gives me. I thought you'd need it if you ever left Glenville," she added as she dropped the money back into the box. "It's not much, but it would have helped, I guess." She looked infinitely weary, like some vital force had been drained from her. "I'm going back to bed now," she said.

"Okay."

She looked at me tenderly. "There has to be a way you can still go, Luke," she said.

I shook my head dolefully. "No, Mom," I said. "It's over."

Lola Faye's gaze was wonderfully engrossed as I finished my narrative of the events of that night, and I expected her to urge me on, beg me in that flattering way of hers to provide another captivating episode of *Luke's Journey*. But instead, she rocked back in her chair and said, "Cops call it Old Mother Hubbard fraud."

"What?"

"Mother Hubbard fraud," Lola Faye repeated. "That's what cops call it when wives steal from the money their husbands give them to buy groceries and stuff like that."

I unconsciously glanced toward the man behind the fern and was seized by an urgent need to defend my mother. "I wouldn't call what my mother did stealing," I said.

Lola Faye considered this. "No, I wouldn't either," she said. "Not exactly, anyway." She peered out toward the lobby of the hotel, increasingly unpopulated now, a

198

room filled mostly with empty chairs. "Ollie always called it getaway money because the women who did it, who took money like that, Ollie said they were planning to use it to get away."

"Get away from what?" I asked.

"From their husbands," Lola Faye answered. "From their families. From their whole lives."

I laughed, though somewhat self-consciously, the need to defend my mother from any such accusation still lingering in my mind. "My mother wasn't planning to run away," I said.

"You're right, Luke," Lola Faye said. "It was too late for her."

"Too late for what?"

"Too late for whatever her dream was," Lola Faye answered flatly.

I recalled my mother in those last days, how she'd shuffled forward uneasily, grabbed at whatever was nearby for support.

"Yes," I admitted sadly. "It was too late for her."

"But not for you," Lola Faye said brightly. "She knew it wasn't too late for you, Luke. At least according to what she said to you that night, how there had to be another way. I guess she meant another way you could get to Harvard, which you found, right?"

I nodded. "Yes," I answered softly. "There was another way."

With that admission, I saw the little metal box again, the document that had rested snugly beneath my mother's getaway money, and I suddenly thought of my mother on the night of my father's murder, how I'd found her standing in the backyard only a few feet from the garage, her rail-thin body pulsing in the light of Sheriff Tomlinson's cruiser. She was wrapped in a bloodstained terry-cloth bathrobe, and her long hair, usually tightly pinned, hung loose and disheveled down her back. Coming toward her, I'd thought she seemed less a woman than a character in some tragic romance, lost, bereft, one of life's grim pawns.

"Mom?" I'd said.

She turned, but for a moment seemed genuinely surprised to see me.

"Mom, are you okay?"

"Luke," she breathed. "You're here."

"What happened?"

She'd been upstairs, she said, reading as she often did in the early evening. She'd heard "a pop" followed by what she called "a hard thud, like something dropped on the floor." At that point she'd risen from her bed, gone down the stairs, glanced into the kitchen, and discovered my father lying face-up on the linoleum tile, his eyes open but unlighted, a hole in his chest, blood coming from his mouth.

At that moment, as we stood in the darkness, Sheriff Tomlinson watching from only a few yards away, the reality of my father's death appeared to strike her fully and powerfully, though something else struck her too.

"You don't look surprised, Luke," she said softly.

"Surprised?" I asked. "By what?"

"By this . . ." She stopped, paused, then let the word fall from her lips like a drop of poison. "Murder."

She'd said nothing else, only waited as Sheriff Tomlinson came toward us.

"I can't tell you how sorry I am about this," Tomlinson said. He let his large, relentlessly searching eyes drift from my mother to me, then back to my mother. "A terrible thing." He settled his gaze on my mother for a moment before drawing it over to me. "A terrible thing," he repeated.

"Yes, sir," I said.

He studied my mother and me for an added moment, and seemed to glimpse something unsettling in the grim tableau we made.

"I know that nothing can bring Doug back," he said. "But I want both of you to know that I won't stop until I find out who did this." He let this declaration settle in, then touched his hat. "Well, good night, folks."

And he was gone, leaving my mother and me alone in our backyard, and later alone in the little living room, where my mother's doilies lay on the old armchair, and where her knitted blanket was draped over the back of the worn sofa, and where my father's dusty work shoes rested, not surprisingly, in the middle of the floor, the thoughtless and inappropriate place he'd left them.

"You should go to bed, Mom," I said in a voice that was suddenly quite commanding, the man of the house at last.

My mother rose in that airy way of hers and slowly drifted up the stairs to her bed. I sat alone in our cramped little living room and thought of the night a few weeks before when I'd come home still locked in my simmering rage and disappointment, trudged up the stairs, drawn a book from my mother's shelf, found the money she'd secreted there, and, as she returned it to the box, glimpsed the document the money had concealed, the weight of this memory pressing down upon me on the very night of my father's murder, one more dark turning, as it had seemed to me, in *Luke's Journey*.

CHAPTER
NINETEEN

"Did you know about it?" I suddenly blurted to Lola Faye.

She looked startled by this abrupt explosion. "About what?"

I felt that I was once again in the dimly lighted corridor outside my mother's bedroom, the metal box in my hand, the letters of the very official-looking paper peeping out from beneath the cash my mother had set aside for my use: *Ward Life and Casualty*.

"The 'other way,'" I answered.

Lola Faye appeared genuinely at a loss.

"The insurance policy," I added.

Lola Faye still gave no indication that she had the slightest idea what I was talking about.

"The one on my father's life," I added, now abandoning the grim supposition that had suddenly overwhelmed me, a suspicion that it was perhaps she, Lola Faye Gilroy, rather than Mr. Ward or Mr. Klein who'd told Sheriff Tomlinson about the policy. "The one for two hundred thousand dollars."

Lola Faye shook her head. "No, Luke. How would I have known about that?"

"I thought my father might have told you," I said.

"Doug wouldn't have told me about anything like that," Lola Faye assured me. "He didn't even tell me that you didn't get your scholarship, remember?"

I had no way of contradicting her on this point, nor could I find a way to go deeper into the subject save by adding, "It was in that little metal box. The one where my mother kept that money she was going to give me when I left for Harvard. I saw it there the night I found the box."

Lola Faye looked as if a wildly entertaining thought had just crossed her mind. "Did you ever see *Double Indemnity*?" she asked excitedly.

I shook my head.

"It's a movie classic," Lola Faye informed me. "With Fred MacMurray and Barbara Stanwyck. They show it once in a while on Turner Classic Movies. It's about insurance. Well, not just insurance, but a clause in an insurance policy. Double indemnity. It means that the amount doubles in case of death by accident."

"I see," I said rather mordantly.

"You can even get it when the person is murdered," Lola Faye continued brightly. "The person who's insured, I mean."

"Really?" I asked coolly.

"But not the kind of murder it is in *Double Indemnity*," Lola Faye added, her demeanor quite cheerful, a movie fan warming up to a discussion of a favorite film. "If the insurance company finds out the beneficiary is the murderer, I mean. That changes everything."

"No doubt," I said dryly.

204

"Which Edward G. Robinson does find out," Lola Faye told me. "He's the insurance investigator in the movie." She shifted slightly, and her eyes sparkled. "You see, in *Double Indemnity*, the wife kills her husband," she continued. "With her lover's help."

"Did they get caught?" I asked.

"Oh, sure," Lola Faye answered. "Pretty fast too. But even if it had been years and years, they could still have gotten caught."

"Because there's no statute of limitations on murder," I said.

"Right, Luke," Lola Faye said. "Boy, you never forget anything, do you?"

"I'm sure I've forgotten a lot," I assured her.

She smiled, but coolly, something glimmering darkly in her eyes. "Who was the beneficiary of your father's policy, Luke?" she asked.

"My mother."

I'd half expected Lola Faye to find something suspicious in this, despite the fact that it would have been very strange indeed for there to have been a beneficiary other than my mother. But instead, she seemed to feel quite obviously moved by what my father had done.

"Well, it's good that your daddy had made arrangements for your mother," she said sweetly. "Otherwise it would have been even harder on her."

But of course it had been plenty hard, and on that thought I instantly returned to the day of my father's funeral, how my mother and I had stood beside his grave, both of us in the grip of terrible emotions.

At that point, Sheriff Tomlinson had known nothing of Lola Faye, or of Woody Gilroy's heart-rending telephone calls to his estranged wife, or of her finally telling him that she would never come back to him. This was told tearfully but in no uncertain terms as Woody frantically demanded to know why his adored wife continued to refuse his entreaties — wasn't he a good man, a good provider, wasn't he head over heels in love with her, wouldn't he do anything, anything, just to get her back? — Woody going on and on pathetically until Lola Faye finally hung up on him.

The fact that she'd done this had been told to my mother and me as we sat in our living room a few days after my father's funeral, Woody dead as well by then, Sheriff Tomlinson at that point fully aware of Woody's drunken, rambling three-page suicide note, the one in which he'd stated that his motive for killing my father was that he'd seduced Lola Faye.

My mother had sat quite rigidly in place during all this, so Sheriff Tomlinson, almost in an effort to elicit a response from her, had gone on to give enough detail for me to imagine the fateful final moments of Lola Faye's last phone conversation with poor, distraught Woody:

But why, Lola Faye? Why won't you come back to me?

I just can't, Woody.

But why?

I just can't.

But Lola Faye . . .

I just can't.

And with that, I'd imagined, Lola Faye had hung up.

I'd always assumed that there'd been many such conversations between Lola Faye and Woody, though perhaps they'd ended less abruptly, with Lola Faye attempting to soothe Woody's fraying nerves or talk him out of killing himself, which, according to Sheriff Tomlinson, Woody had on several occasions, and not always drunkenly, threatened to do.

"The thing is, Woody was pretty upset," Sheriff Tomlinson told my mother as we all sat in the gloom of our tiny living room on Peanut Lane. Then he released the bombshell. "With Doug."

My mother's eyes sprang into focus. "With Doug?"

"Yes, ma'am," Sheriff Tomlinson answered edgily.

"Why was he upset with Doug?" my mother asked.

"Well, I hate to tell you this, Mrs. Paige, but it's all going to come out in the inquest, so you'll hear about it anyway." Sheriff Tomlinson paused and in that pause became the Old South lawman, gentlemanly and reserved, particularly with regard to women. "The thing is, Woody wrote a long note before he shot himself, and it seems that Doug and Lola Faye Gilroy were having a . . . relationship."

My mother's body stiffened and one of her hands dropped from her lap and dangled, like a hanged man's, just inches from the floor.

"Relationship?" she asked.

"According to Woody it was a romantic relationship," Sheriff Tomlinson told her softly, his eyes regarding her closely, studying her reaction.

My mother peered at the sheriff stonily but never once glanced toward me. "I don't believe that," she said.

"Well, I don't blame you, Mrs. Paige," Sheriff Tomlinson said gently. "But, you know, a man doesn't usually kill another man for no reason at all."

The sheriff waited for my mother to respond to this, but she only stared at him mutely.

"Mrs. Paige," the sheriff said, "I have to ask you if you had any idea that something like this might have been going on between your husband and this girl."

"No," my mother said stiffly. "And as I just said to you, Sheriff, I don't believe a word of it."

"Yes, well, but —"

"I've told you everything I know, Sheriff," my mother interrupted curtly, the only time I ever saw her demonstrate the least hint of bad manners. "I am reticent to say more."

Reticent, I thought at the time, how entirely the right word, and how typical of my mother to have found it.

Sheriff Tomlinson offered the resigned look of one long acquainted with the crimes and misdemeanors of his fellow human beings. "Well, like the Bible says, it's a vale of tears, this life."

With that, he rose and headed for the door, though not, I noticed, before giving a final glance about the house, his gaze wandering around the front room, then over to the stairs, which led to my parents' bedroom. "You were upstairs when you heard that shot?" he asked, a question directed to my mother though he didn't look at her when he asked it. "And you came right down when you heard it?"

"Yes," my mother answered firmly.

The sheriff faced her and touched the brim of his hat. "Good night, then, Mrs. Paige."

By then a mere week had passed since my father's murder, and in the chill aftermath of so much blood, my mother had said nothing of the future, hers or mine. It was as if any such talk would have been disrespectful to my father's memory, perhaps even slightly disrespectful to Woody's also, at least in my mother's view.

But that night, her mind seemed to emerge from the cloud of violence and then scandal that had swept down on her, as had the stark reality that tomorrow would, in fact, come and had to be faced.

"You don't have to change your plans, Luke," she said.

She meant my earlier vaunted plan for Harvard, which the lost scholarship had dashed several weeks before.

"There's money now," she added. She looked at me pointedly. "Enough for you to get away from all this."

When I started to speak, she pressed a finger to my lips. "We should have a bite to eat," she said.

"We should have a bite to eat," I said, suddenly seized by hunger.

I noted Lola Faye's nearly empty glass.

"And refill our drinks too," I added.

I twisted around and called for the waitress, then returned my attention to Lola Faye. "So, what were we talking about?" I asked. "Movies?"

"*Double Indemnity*," Lola Faye answered. "But we don't have to talk about movies, Luke. You probably don't go to movies."

"I used to," I told her. "Julia liked to go. We went every weekend. But I haven't gone since Julia —"

I stopped in mid-sentence as Julia rose in my mind with all the force I'd once felt each time she entered the room, and on that vision, I recalled the day we'd first strolled the Harvard campus, an autumn day, with falling leaves brushing by, the way she'd slowed for a moment and watched them tumble, *So helpless*, she'd said, *like the Italian prisoners in* A Farewell to Arms. I'd recalled the scene instantly, those hapless soldiers marched out into the courtyard toward the wall where they would be executed, and all around them, swirling helplessly, a ragged army of fall leaves. It was then I'd looked at Julia, stopped and simply stared at her, amazed at the lovely and impossibly complicated way her mind connected things. And then and there, stunned by my own conclusion, I'd thought, *It's you*.

"— since Julia left me," I said.

Lola Faye smiled softly, now accustomed to the way I sometimes lapsed into memory, lingered there, then came back almost with a start, like a time traveler abruptly returned to the present. "It must have been hard, getting divorced," she said.

I nodded.

210

"I didn't even want to divorce Woody." Her gaze drifted toward the window. "You need someone with you at the end. I think that's the most important thing in life."

"Why is that the most important?" I asked.

"Because you need to feel like someone cared enough about you to be with you when you die," she said. "That you meant enough to someone for that person to stay with you all the way to that point."

"Yes, that's true," I said, and with that admission faced the hard fact that it was likely no one would be with me.

"So, I know it must have been hard for you, Luke," Lola Faye added. "Losing Julia." She offered what appeared to be a deeply sympathetic smile. "You should call her, Luke. I bet she still loves you. You know why? Because some people can only love one time, and I get the feeling Julia is like that. As matter of fact, I get the feeling you're like that too."

I feared Lola Faye would elaborate on this painful, as well as slightly saccharine, point, but she was thankfully stopped when the waitress appeared.

"We'd like another round of drinks, but also something to eat," I told the waitress. "What do you have?"

The waitress rattled off the usual bar offerings.

"Shall I order for us?" I asked Lola Faye when the waitress at last fell silent.

Lola Faye nodded with a sudden, unexpected heaviness, as if her head were bobbing in dense water.

I gave her an indulgent smile. "You just went somewhere, didn't you? Was it back into your past?"

She shook her head softly. "No," she said. "Into my future."

It was so bleak an answer, given with such sadness in her eyes and voice, that I immediately dodged away from that aspect of Lola Faye's life, whatever cheerless circumstance she'd glimpsed in her future, and fixed my attention on the waitress.

"We'll have fried calamari," I told her. "And the vegetables and dip." I looked across the table to where Lola Faye sat in a great stillness. "Does that sound like enough?" I asked.

The smile that flickered on Lola Faye's lips was quite devoid of either playfulness or enjoyment. "It sounds fine, Luke," she answered.

"Because if you'd rather have something else . . . ," I offered.

She shook her head.

I turned back to the waitress. "Okay," I told her. "I guess that's all for now."

The waitress vanished so quickly she seemed to have effervesced, the space she'd occupied now so empty it felt like a void, so that I had no alternative but to return my gaze to Lola Faye.

She'd shifted slightly to the left, I noticed, and was gazing at the LA coroner bag with what appeared to be a dark contemplation of the otherwise comic outline there.

I couldn't imagine what she was thinking. I knew only that I wanted to lift her spirits, if possible, and in

212

that way lift mine, and in so doing perhaps allow us to sail on a bright summer breeze safely to the end of this last talk.

"So," I said with as much cheerfulness as I could muster. "We'll have a little food."

CHAPTER
TWENTY

The food came a few minutes later, and I pushed the basket of calamari toward Lola Faye. "You should try these," I said with a hint of exuberance.

Lola Faye looked at them suspiciously, as if, like the young woman of the museum fountain had appeared to, I were offering her refreshment laced with poison. "What are they?"

"Calamari," I answered. "Squid."

Lola Faye made a face. "Squid? You mean like in *Twenty Thousand Leagues Under the Sea?*"

"Well, not exactly. Real squid are much smaller." I moved the basket a little closer to her. "Try one. The batter is really good."

"Try one," Lola Faye repeated with a sudden, unexpectedly jovial chuckle that cracked through her earlier gloom. "Goodness, Luke, I've already tried an appletini." Her mood grew even more jolly by a peg. "I'm trying all kinds of things tonight."

"Well, it's good to experiment, I suppose," I told her.

"Even with squid?" Lola Faye asked jokingly.

Her demeanor now seemed wholly cheerful, but it also appeared somewhat forced, as if this latest and rather inauthentic display of happiness were a weight it took all her inner strength to lift.

"Even with squid, yes."

Lola Faye took this as a more or less irresistible statement of encouragement, and with a slow, hesitant gesture, obviously reaching for something she found faintly disgusting but felt obligated to try, she picked up a single ring of calamari and slowly brought it to her mouth. "I don't know about this," she said.

"Come on," I said. "Throw caution to the wind."

Something in Lola's eyes glittered knowingly. "All right, I will," she said, and in a quick snap she plucked the calamari from her finger.

"Well, what do you think?" I asked as she chewed it slowly.

She appeared both surprised and genuinely delighted, the last of her earlier gloominess, along with her effort to conceal it, dropping from her like pieces of a shroud. "It tastes sort of like a French fry."

"Similar, yes."

"Only chewy; it's like a cross between a French fry and a rubber band."

"It has a rubbery texture, that's true," I agreed. "But it tastes quite good, don't you think?"

Lola Faye snapped up a second calamari and ate it. "Yep."

"Try it with the sauce," I said.

Without hesitation, she dipped a third calamari in the red sauce and popped it into her mouth, though a little awkwardly so that a single drop of red remained on her lips.

I pointed to it. "There's some sauce on your lips."

She drew the white napkin up to her mouth and wiped her lips, then glanced at the red stain, curiously transfixed for a moment, like a woman caught in a dark spell.

"What are you thinking about?" I asked.

Lola Faye didn't answer, but she was quite obviously distressed.

"What is it?" I asked.

"Doug," she whispered, and on the stark mention of my father's name, her eyes glistened. "I'm just so sorry about everything, Luke."

To my surprise, I found myself unexpectedly moved by what appeared to be Lola Faye's genuine sense of regret; touched, in fact, more deeply than I'd been touched by anything in a long time.

"It wasn't your fault," I said with a soft shrug. Then I snapped up a piece of calamari and bit into it with the violence of a black widow ripping off the head of its oblivious suitor. "I wish I'd loved him, but I didn't."

"Well, all that feeling probably went to your mother," Lola Faye said gently, as if it were now her turn to show concern for me. "Because she was so good to you."

It was one of those inadvertent remarks that set in motion a dark mental wheel, and I suddenly felt the turn of that wheel quite distinctly.

"I went numb when she died," I said quietly. "Inside, I mean. I went numb inside." Without meaning to do so, I lifted my hands and stared at my fingers. "I stopped *feeling* things."

216

"Froze up, yeah," Lola Faye said. "Sometimes you do that when someone dies."

The lonely sweep of that frozen field was not one I wished to traverse with Lola Faye, and so I fixed my mind on the immediate present, the gleaming Christmas lights that had bedecked the houses we'd passed in our walk from the museum to my hotel, elements coming together to offer an escape.

"You've just had a birthday, haven't you?" I asked.

Lola Faye was clearly amazed. "How did you know that?"

"Those Christmas dolls," I said. "The ones at Variety Store. I came in one day and you were looking at them. You said, 'It's my birthday soon. I hate having my birthday near Christmas.'"

"I still hate that," Lola Faye said; it seemed she'd never quite gotten over this injustice. "You don't get two different sets of presents if your birthday is too near Christmas." Her shrug seemed less a matter of harsh reality than her acceptance of it. "My brother was born in April, so he always got two completely different sets of presents. Birthday and Christmas. But December fifteenth is too close to Christmas, so I only always just got one set."

"How unfair," I said.

"Yeah, well, that's life, I guess," Lola Faye said. "You can't pick the day you're born."

"Or much of anything else," I said with mock fatalism.

"Oh, you don't really believe that, Luke," Lola Faye protested with a small laugh and a dismissive wave.

217

"You couldn't believe that. If you believed that, you wouldn't have taken matters into your own hands the way you did."

"In what way did I take matters into my own hands?" I asked.

"By studying hard and getting those grades," Lola Faye said. "My goodness, Luke, you took your life into your own hands. That's what your daddy admired about you."

I let the doubtful notion that my father had ever admired anything about me pass.

"He used to say to me, 'One thing about Luke, he knows what he wants,'" Lola Faye steamed on. "'He'll get it too, he won't let anything —'"

I felt a wave of revulsion pass over me, not only for my past but for the dreary future that inevitably lay ahead. I thought of all the mistakes I'd made, the hideous miscalculations, every pit into which I'd fallen, the empty degree, the lackluster teaching, the arid texts, Julia lost, my life utterly bereft without her, so that at last I had ended up here in Saint Louis, facing none other than Lola Faye Gilroy, evidently my one and only confidante.

"Oh, please!" I said sharply. "Spare me!"

Lola Faye stared at me as if struck mute, her eyes a weird combination of confusion and tension.

"I'm sorry," I said quickly. "It's just that I know full well what my father thought of me and that —" I stopped, unable to finish the sentence that had scorched my mind: *and that he was right.*

218

Lola Faye remained quite tense, like a little girl who thought she'd done something wrong.

I leaned forward. "I may not even have been reacting to my father. It may have been this idea that I had everything by the tail, all my ducks in a row, so to speak, everything lined up so that nothing would ever go wrong."

"But it didn't, did it, Luke?" Lola asked hesitantly. "Everything turned out just like you hoped it would."

"Not exactly," I admitted. "I mean, things go wrong. There are things you can't be sure of." A horrible weight fell on me. "Things that are out of your control, things that . . ."

In that pause I felt the wildly spinning chaos that surrounds us, the play of chance, the veil of the unknown, the smudged glass through which we strain to see our futures but never can.

"Things you can't envision, things that take you by surprise," I added. "It's both a gift and a curse."

"What is?" Lola Faye asked.

"Blindness to our fate," I answered.

Lola Faye's eyes brightened. "You got that line from Prometheus, right?" she asked.

I stared at her, astonished that Lola Faye had brought up such a reference, an astonishment she clearly saw in my amazed expression.

"It was on the History Channel," Lola Faye explained. "They did a whole series on Greece. The myths, I mean. He was the one that got tied to a rock and the birds pecked at him, right?"

"That's right."

"They had a great quote at the end," Lola Faye added with a sudden gusto, obviously proud of the knowledge she was demonstrating. "The quote said, 'Chance is the only hope of an unprepared mind.'"

"That's Pasteur, not Prometheus," I corrected. "Only the quotation is 'Chance favors the prepared mind.'"

Lola Faye shook her head. "I don't ever seem to get anything right." She laughed. "Ollie used to lecture me on that. 'You got to look closely, Lola Faye,' he'd say. 'You got to keep your focus on the details.'" Her eyes brightened cheerfully. "So you'd read that quote before, Luke, the one from . . . who was that?"

"Pasteur," I said. "You know, like on milk. Pasteurization. Louis Pasteur."

"Louis Pasteur," Lola Faye repeated. "Where did you read that quote?" Her gaze took on a slightly different cast. "*Bartlett's*?"

"No, not *Bartlett's*," I answered, as if I'd been challenged and had to defend myself. "I probably read it in a biography of Pasteur."

Now Lola Faye's mood shifted again, this time toward an incontestably cheerful eagerness. "Do you watch the Biography Channel?" she asked.

"No."

"I like it, but Ollie didn't," Lola Faye gushed on. "Ollie and the History Channel. Now that was a perfect match. Especially the war stuff. Battles. Weapons. Particularly handguns." She smiled with a childlike happiness. "He taught me to shoot, did I tell you that?"

I shook my head.

220

She lifted the LA coroner bag from the back of her chair and let it fall to the table with a clunk. "I even have a license to carry."

I jerked backward, like a man under fire. "You have a gun in there?"

Lola Faye laughed heartily, as if she'd played a scary little joke. "Oh, Luke," she scoffed. "Why would I bring a gun to Saint Louis?" She reached into the bag and brought out a metal pillbox. "Time for a med." She popped open the box, plucked a green capsule from it, and swallowed it without water.

"What's that for?" I asked.

"Depression," Lola Faye answered. "You know, keep Lola Faye under control. Keep Lola Faye from blowing up." She waved her hand. "Anyway, Ollie said I should pack. He said every woman should pack."

"Well, I don't think you should have taken that advice," I said. "Especially, I mean, what with the . . . depression."

The playfulness in Lola Faye's manner trailed off abruptly. "Yeah, but there really are some bad people in this world," she said pointedly as she returned the pillbox to her bag. "People you have to protect yourself from. They could be anywhere." She paused as her eyes lifted toward me. "Murderers."

A brief silence followed, one that seemed weighted, before a smile broke over her face once again. "Ollie said a nine-millimeter automatic was the best for getting the job done. There's a clip of sixteen in that baby." She stroked the bag absently, but her eyes never left mine. "That's a lot of firepower."

"It sounds it," I said grimly.

"What's the matter, Luke?" Lola Faye asked.

My chuckle was a trifle edgy. "I guess it's just that if this were a play — our talk, I mean — then you know what they say: if a gun is mentioned in the first act, it has to go off before the end of the play."

I found Lola Faye's smile anything but reassuring.

"Anyway," she said. "At the firing range, Ollie put that nine-millimeter auto in my hand and he said, 'Lola Faye, if a man ever hurts you, you just point this bad boy at him and pull the trigger and hold it down, and that little creep won't ever hurt anybody again.'" Her finger lightly traced the chalked body outline that adorned the canvas side of her LA coroner bag. "I guess you never did much shooting?"

"Not much, no."

I thought of the one time my father and I had gone hunting, how earnestly he'd tried to teach me the fundamentals of the toy-like, battered old .22 that constituted his arsenal. We'd gone into the woods, walked along the edges of a red-clay bluff, and finally stopped at the banks of a muddy little creek. Here, my father had taught me to draw back the bolt, insert the shell, close the bolt, aim, and fire. There'd been an abundance of small birds that day, and I'd fired and fired as they'd flittered about in the overhanging limbs. But for all the gunplay of that interminable afternoon, I'd never hit anything, and my father had finally drawn the rifle from my arms. "Huntin's not for you, Luke," he'd said, and with that he'd nodded toward the path that led out of the woods. "Better be getting back." All the way home, I'd felt a stinging inadequacy, although my father had done nothing to reinforce such a feeling, had, in fact, walked the whole way with his hand affectionately on my shoulder, pointing out this bird and that one, sometimes with a soft aside: "Who'd want to kill such a pretty thing?"

"Nothing to it," Lola Faye said when I failed to elaborate. "Shooting, I mean." She fell silent for a moment and seemed to make an effort to fathom the darkness that had settled over me. "Easy, really. Just a little pull, that's all. And after that . . ."

And I was there, abruptly and wrenchingly there, like a third eye in the void, an omniscient witness to the crime, watching as my father grabbed for the table even as his body shot back from it, the whole terrible scene playing in film noir, blood black as India ink soaking his shirt, spilling out across the floor, Sheriff Tomlinson no doubt later standing above this murderous sprawl, thinking it through, asking his questions.

"After that, a full investigation," I blurted.

Lola Faye looked at me quizzically.

"I suddenly thought of Sheriff Tomlinson," I explained. "All his questions."

"Oh, him," Lola Faye said as she twisted around and hung her bag once again from the back of her chair. "He was pretty thorough."

I recalled the detail with which the old sheriff later recited the events of that bloody night, the timeline he'd established, all Woody's movements down to the second, and how at the end of it he'd looked at me with a wary anticipation in his eyes, as if trying to discern if some small fact in his report had caught in my mind.

"He went at me pretty hard," Lola Faye added. "Questions about me and Woody and me and your daddy and your daddy and you."

"Me?"

Lola Faye nodded. "How y'all got along, stuff like that."

I remembered the way Sheriff Tomlinson had later found me busily doing an inventory at Variety Store. He'd pretended that it was just a social call, a way of checking on me, making sure I was okay, but there'd been a wily-old-lawman element in the question he asked me just before he left: *So tell me, Luke, how's it going with your scholarship?*

"I've always wondered how he found out as much as he did," I said to Lola Faye. "About us, I mean. My father and mother. Me."

Lola Faye glanced away and fingered her glass absently.

"For example, he knew that I'd applied for that scholarship," I added. "I always wondered how he knew that, because my mother never said anything about it, and I certainly didn't."

Lola Faye's right hand crawled into her left like a small, nesting crab.

"It was me," she confessed softly. "I told the sheriff that you were going to get a scholarship." She shook her head in a gesture I couldn't quite decipher. "He could be very tough, Sheriff Tomlinson. And he had this double killing on his hands, Luke. He wasn't going to

224

take 'I don't know' for an answer. He wanted to know all kinds of things. Like if your daddy had enemies. There was four whole days went by before Woody wrote that note and shot himself, so he was asking me about things at the store, figuring maybe it was a business problem, something like that. Maybe somebody your daddy owed money. He was looking for a motive. He was looking at lots of people."

"Like who?" I asked. "I mean, besides people my father did business with."

"Well, like you, Luke," Lola Faye answered. "Or your mother. I just told him what I knew. That your mother was a nice woman, and you were nice and smart and were going off to school on a scholarship. I didn't know you hadn't gotten it."

"So you were cooperative, I guess," I said. "You told him everything you knew."

Lola Faye gave a hesitant nod, clearly wary of the subject though helpless to escape it.

"I could tell that the sheriff had learned a lot about our family," I said. "I just didn't know he'd gotten his information from you."

Lola Faye shrugged. "Well, your daddy liked to talk, and we were always in that store together. So he'd just talk along while we worked."

"And evidently his favorite thing to talk about was his family," I said with a sharp pang of resentment that my father had shared the intimacies of our family life with anyone outside it.

Lola Faye's gaze fell to the seemingly bottomless green pool of her appletini. She held it there, nursing some thought or other, it seemed, until her eyes suddenly shot up, and something bright and almost playful sparkled in them. "Just the facts, ma'am," she said in a deep, no-nonsense voice.

"What?"

She cocked her head and looked at me sternly. "Just the facts, ma'am," she said again, now with a laugh. "That's Sergeant Friday. *Dragnet.* They play all the old reruns of it on one of the cable channels." She laughed again, this time a little raucously. "*DUM-da-dum-dum. Dum-da-dum-dum-DUM.* That's the theme song. Anytime I heard Ollie sing it out, I'd know the show was starting, so no matter where I was in the house, I'd come running."

I found this a ludicrous direction for our conversation to have gone, but not as ridiculous as the image of Lola Faye's being summoned with a television theme, then flying to that summons, bounding down a hallway or out of the kitchen just in time to land on the sofa before the final *dum.*

"I love police shows," Lola Faye declared. "Especially *Dragnet.* Ollie said it was more real when it came to the way cops really work."

"In what way?" I asked, since it was clear that the intricacies of *Dragnet* were to be the next topic of conversation.

"More real because it's boring," Lola Faye said. "Police work can be really boring, according to Ollie. You have to go through loads of false leads. And people lie to you all the time. You have to get good at figuring out who's telling you the truth and who's not. And

226

what you see in people, that can be pretty bad. When you look into the human heart, I mean. That's what Ollie said. 'Lola Faye,' he said, 'things aren't pretty in the human heart.'" She released a short laugh. "If Ollie was in *Bartlett's*, that would be his quote." She shrugged. "But like I say, the daily grind of police work, Ollie said that could get pretty boring."

"But you told me that he kept doing police work of a sort," I reminded her. "Even after he retired. Those cold cases you mentioned."

Lola Fay nodded. "Yeah, he kept doing it."

"Then he must have found it interesting, right?"

"He found one case interesting," Lola Faye answered softly.

"Just one?"

"Just one, yep." Lola Faye's expression dimmed slightly, as if a shadow had passed over her. "It haunted him." She glanced up as a man entered, obviously a hotel guest, in carefully creased pants and an open-collared shirt, then she looked back toward me, her eyes preternaturally still. "And something needs to haunt you, don't you think, Luke?"

"I suppose," I answered weakly.

Lola Faye's next question struck me as curiously pointed. "What haunts you?"

CHAPTER
TWENTY-ONE

Our minds are haunted houses.

That was the thought that came to me with Lola Faye's question.

My mind was a haunted house Julia had finally abandoned, dashing through its front door — to extend this metaphor to its natural breaking point — like a heroine in a horror movie.

At the first image of that haunted house, I might have thought of my father, recalled him in all his many shapes: threading me safely across a busy street; guiding me out of the woods, that battered old .22 slung carelessly over his shoulder; struggling to arrange the paperback books on the squeaky rack he'd absurdly placed at the front door of Variety Store; counting each day's dwindling receipts in that grindingly slow, distracted way of his, starting the count over again and again because some random thought had briefly intruded. At last, I might have seen him sprawled across the kitchen floor with a hole in his chest, eyes open, staring toward the back door whose awkwardly leaning frame was the result of his own poor workmanship.

It might also have been my mother's ghost that rose before me, the one person who'd understood my youthful dream, encouraged me to pursue it, warned in the starkest terms that I should let nothing stop me. I might have seen her reading in her alcove, or walking me toward the Confederate monument, or standing in the backyard on the night of my father's murder, or, later that same night, moving up the stairs to her bedroom, her pale right hand gripping the worn banister.

Moving away from the lead actors in the lethal drama of my youth, I might have recalled Miss McDowell, a solitary figure in the bleachers, watching all those handsome young boys in their basketball uniforms, tormented, as I now knew she must have been, by her own unsettling urges.

Or it might have been Debbie who came to mind, particularly on that spring day when it had been so clear to her that my dream of leaving Glenville was close to being realized, how softly she had said, "I won't forget you, Luke."

I might even have thought of poor, distraught Woody Wayne Gilroy, remembered a lonely, baffled figure sitting alone in a booth at Qwik Burger, noticing me as I noticed him, waving me over, asking that question when I slid opposite him in the booth: *Your daddy owns Variety Store, don't he?*

But none of these people had flamed into my mind at Lola Faye's haunting question.

Instead, it was Mr. Klein, tall, lean, forever set off and apart, as if, like Ruth, still in alien corn; gentlemanly Mr. Klein in his charcoal gray overcoat, hands clasped before him, his black eyes fiercely shining beneath his hat, dark, solitary, curiously forlorn, his voice solemn as an Old World bell: *We need to talk, Luke.*

On that memory, I glanced toward the right, where the man who'd come into the bar earlier in the evening remained at his table, still obscured by a potted plant. "Mystery man," I said, almost to myself.

"What?" Lola Faye asked.

"That man there," I answered. "Hidden behind the plant. I said he was a mystery man."

"Why do you think that?" Lola Faye asked.

"I don't know, just the way he looks, I guess," I answered. "Like a guy in a movie. A secret agent, a person like that. A mystery man."

Lola Faye's expression grew suddenly grave, but with a hint that something had caught in her mind. "Woody was mysterious," she said. "Well, not Woody, exactly. Just, you know, what he did." Her features were a question mark. "Something that didn't fit. Ollie said you always had to keep on the lookout for something that didn't fit. That's the mystery as far as Woody is concerned."

The old serpent coiled and I saw poor, desperate Woody as he'd last appeared to me, nursing a gigantic Coke, the hamburger and fries sitting uneaten on the table in front of him. Of all the people I'd ever known, he was surely the least mysterious.

"I was surprised that he believed what he did about your father and me," Lola Faye added. "But I was really surprised by what he did."

"You mean," I asked cautiously, like a man inching his fingers toward a burning coal, "the murder?"

Lola Faye shook her head. "Not exactly. Just something strange." She appeared suddenly more animated, like a dog once again on the scent. "I went over the whole thing with Ollie. Everything that happened that day. We'd go over all the little details again and again. Ollie said it was all in the details. The little things. That's what we looked at." She shifted in her seat with an unmistakable excitement, like a child about to open a Christmas gift. "So the thing is, Woody must have gone to the closet and fished out his cousin's old twenty-two rifle," she said, clearly turning over the events of that long-ago day in her mind. "Woody's cousin had been trying to kill this woodpecker that had been eating his toolshed. He shot and shot, but he never could hit it." She laughed. "But I'm digressing, right? That's the word, isn't it, Luke? To *digress*?"

She bounced ever so slightly in her seat, but I couldn't tell if this was a momentary girlish excitement or something more sinister, a dark relish, like a spider's delight at the moth's blind approach.

"Okay, so then Woody drove down the mountain and parked a few doors from your house," she continued. "Your daddy had just sat down to supper. Your mother was upstairs." Her eyes shifted toward the man behind the fern. "And you were out for a drive, right, Luke?" she asked. She snapped her attention back to me. "You told me that before. You said you were out on Decatur Road."

"That's right," I said. "I was."

I couldn't tell whether Lola Faye accepted this as a truth or if she thought she might recognize by some glimmer in my eyes that it was a lie.

"Okay, here's what I'm getting at," she said. "Two people saw Woody sitting in his car not far from your house. His head was down, they said. It was dropped forward and pressed against the steering wheel."

A vision of poor, broken Woody in this anguished posture appeared to settle into Lola Faye's mind, and as it did, it drained away her girl-detective enthusiasm, so that when she spoke again it was in an entirely sober tone.

"Then, at seven o'clock," she said, "at exactly seven — this is according to Sheriff Tomlinson — at seven o'clock exactly, Woody got out of the car."

"Seven on the dot?" I asked. "You said *exactly*. You said it twice. You know that for sure?"

"Seven on the dot," Lola Faye answered. "I know because the sheriff told me that one of your neighbors saw Woody get out of the car at the same time the news was just coming on TV, the seven o'clock news."

From there, Lola Faye went on to recount in quite careful order exactly the series of events Sheriff Tomlinson had related to my mother and me several days after my father's murder, the details pretty much revealed by Woody's suicide note along with his insistence, as the sheriff had said, that Lola Faye had had nothing to do with it beyond having the affair that had driven her estranged husband to murder my father.

There was no evidence that Woody had paused once he'd gotten out of his car, Lola Faye continued. This

232

meant that he'd walked directly to our house on Peanut Lane. Once there, he'd unlatched the gate of the storm fence that bordered our backyard, subsequently positioning himself behind the stack of cement blocks with which my father had planned to construct a storage shed but never did.

"And then he shot him," I said, in order to hasten Lola Faye through this grim narrative.

"Well, not exactly," Lola Faye said. "That's what's sort of strange, it seems to me. It was all in the crime-scene report."

She saw I had no idea what that was.

"You know, the form the cops write up when they investigate a crime scene," Lola Faye explained. "There are five different categories." She lifted her right hand and authoritatively ticked them all off, punctuating each with a raised finger. "Summary. Scene. Processing. Evidence collected. Pending." She seemed quite pleased that she'd been able to complete this recitation. "Scene is the most important one as far as Ollie was concerned. He knew all about how it was done, and how the report was written, so he called the sheriff's office, and you know how it is, one cop to another, they sent him a copy of the scene report, and we looked over it together."

"And Ollie noticed something?" I asked.

"No," Lola Faye answered. "I did." She appeared to relive that little moment of discovery, feel its eerie thrill. "A cigarette." She looked at me pointedly. "Woody smoked a cigarette. They found a cigarette butt on that stack of cement blocks he stood behind when he fired the shot. It was the same brand Woody smoked. Chesterfields. And your daddy didn't smoke at all, so it couldn't have been his, and you didn't smoke either, did you, Luke?"

"No."

"I didn't think you did," Lola Faye said. "Okay, so the cigarette butt the police found must have been Woody's."

"What's so strange about that?"

"That he only smoked one," Lola Faye said. "Because Woody was a chain smoker. He smoked one right after the other. Especially if he was nervous, which he must have been while he was waiting there behind those cement blocks."

"Maybe he was afraid to light a match," I said. "Afraid somebody would see him."

"But he'd already lit one match," Lola Faye said. "And he could have just ducked behind those cement blocks and lit one cigarette off the other." She shook her head. "No, he smoked just one cigarette during all the time he waited behind those blocks."

"Unless he didn't wait," I said. "Unless he just had a quick smoke, then fired."

Lola Faye's eyes gave off the witchy glitter of a cat's caught in a passing light. "But he couldn't have done that, Luke."

"Why not?"

"Because it would have been just after seven when your dad got shot if he did that," Lola Faye explained. "Remember? He got to your house at seven o'clock, just like the sheriff said."

234

"So?"

"Well, the thing is, your mother called the ambulance at seven twenty-four."

"Seven twenty-four?" I asked. "How do you know that?"

"It was in the police report," Lola Faye answered. "The one Ollie got from the sheriff's office. It was a nine-one-one call your mother made. They always record exactly when those calls come in, and it was seven twenty-four when your mother called, which was twenty-four minutes after Woody got out of his car and headed for your house." She offered a satisfied smile after this account. "The cops always do a timeline," she added. "A timeline for everyone involved, I mean. The victim. The witnesses. The suspects. Everybody."

"I see," I said quietly.

"And the thing is," Lola Faye continued, "the thing is, that nine-one-one call, the one your mother made, she didn't do that until seven twenty-four, like I said. That was twenty-four minutes after Woody got out of his car and headed for your daddy's house. That walk would have taken him less than a minute, so he'd have to have waited for at least twenty-two minutes before he shot your daddy." Her eyes rolled up in what appeared to be some form of mental calculation. "My guess is that Woody would have smoked at least five cigarettes by then. Maybe more, but at least five." She took a quick sip from her glass and seemed almost to hide behind it. "But there was just one butt at the crime scene, Luke. That's what's strange."

"But chain smoker or not, maybe Woody didn't smoke but one cigarette that night," I said. "Because maybe he only had one left in the pack when he got to our house."

"Woody always had a spare pack," Lola Faye said firmly. "I never saw him without a spare pack."

I recalled Woody as I'd last seen him, sitting alone at Qwik Burger, smoking one cigarette after another, one pack on the table in easy reach, a second winking from the pocket of his shirt.

"He was never without a spare pack," Lola Faye repeated with stony emphasis. She leaned forward slightly. "So I always wondered if your mother maybe didn't hear the shot, and so she didn't know Doug was dying, you know? On the kitchen floor, I mean. Maybe that's why she didn't call nine-one-one until twenty minutes had passed."

As if it were a film flickering in my head, I saw my mother repeat the movements she had several times described to me: lift from her bed at the sound of the shot, twist around in the bed, plant her feet on the floor, rise, and head for the stairs.

"No," I said. "She heard it."

"And she was able to get up, right?" Lola Faye asked. "She'd been sick, I know that. But she was able to get up and go down the stairs."

"She was getting weaker by the time of the murder, moving more slowly," I said. "But she could still get down the stairs in a couple of minutes."

I recalled the further details my mother had related to me the night of my father's murder, how she'd heard

236

the shot and rushed down the stairs and into the kitchen, where she'd found my father sprawled across the floor on his back, legs splayed open, arms stretched out more or less uniformly, fingers curled inward, as if he'd grabbed for an invisible bar.

"A couple of minutes," Lola Faye repeated quietly. "She heard the shot and went downstairs, and found Doug . . . in a couple of minutes."

I'd unspooled this rapid series of events in my mind many times, always in the same sequence and always ending in the same way: with my mother dashing over to my father's body, realizing the dreadful extent of his wound, bounding up and rushing to the phone, frantically calling for an ambulance.

Lola Faye took a quick sip from her glass, then set the glass down hard, like a gavel. "Then I'm sure that's what happened," she said. "Just like your mother told you." She released a short chuckle, which struck me as inappropriate. "I guess that for the first and only time in his life, Woody actually quit smoking."

But had he? I wondered.

Had Woody, who was reacting to the most bitter truth he'd ever known, Lola Faye's betrayal, and who was in the midst of making the most momentous decision he'd ever made, preparing to take a human life; had he, while concealed in darkness, armed with a .22 caliber rifle, and focused on my father as he gulped down his supper of corn bread and milk; had Woody at that moment, his mind and heart weighted down with dread and anguish, actually decided to quit smoking?

"Quit smoking," I repeated softly, almost to myself.

Lola Faye looked at me with what seemed an odd though vaguely tender challenge. "What else would explain it, Luke? What else could explain that there was only one cigarette?"

And I thought, *Only this:*

There is a shot.

My mother rises from her bed.

She listens for some innocent explanation, a car that backfired, some object my father might have dropped on the floor below.

Then she hears something else, something far more alarming: the thud of my father's body as it tumbles from the chair and slams onto the floor.

At this sound, she moves as quickly as she can, speeding up as she dashes down the short book-lined corridor, slowing somewhat as she heads down the stairs.

At the bottom of the stairs, she whirls to the left and rushes into the kitchen.

And there he is, my father, lying on his back, a geyser of blood spurting rhythmically with each breath.

It is 7:05 P.M.

What else could explain it, Luke?

Only this:

My father's eyes are open, staring. He sees the jets of blood that erupt from his chest, feels the pressure of his punctured lung, the lack of air, the ebbing of his life, how vital each second is.

He tries to move, but his body is deflated, a lead weight, without lift or buoyancy.

238

He tries to cry out, but his throat is clogged with blood. It flows in a torrent from his mouth each time he opens it. Blood and air combine as he struggles to speak, his communication now radically reduced to a burst of red bubbles.

Mutely, he raises his arms, stretches out his blood-lathered hands, every part of him, mind and flesh together, grasping desperately for help, reaching, frantic and terrified, for the lifeboat of his wife.

What could explain that there was only one cigarette?

Only this:

She stands at the entrance to the kitchen.

Momentarily frozen by the awful sight before her, she simply stares unbelievingly at her struggling husband.

Then she hurries toward him; drops to the slippery floor beside him; takes him into her arms; feels his blood warm her hands and arms and chest, soak into her robe, stain her fluffy pink house shoes.

She knows what she must do. He is dying, dying. Without help he will be dead very soon, a few minutes at the most, five, ten, twelve?

What could explain so much blood?

Only this:

She clutches him to her chest, tries not to see the wild question in her husband's eyes, his fierce but silent cry, *Why aren't you helping me?*

She hears and feels his animal need to live, sees his baffled anguish at her inaction, and in that final moment loves him as much as she once had, loves him

239

for his awkwardness, for all the fumbling ways he'd tried to please her, for the drudgery of his work, his dreary days spent in the fruitless light of Variety Store; she loves him for the old cash register and the creaking book rack, for his jumble and his mess, the hopeless disorder of his days, every failed effort he'd made to give her a better life; but most of all she loves him for the consideration that had brought him to Mr. Ward, caused him to take out insurance on his life, a policy still in effect and whose large sum could restore the lost dream . . .

Only this:

. . . to her son.

CHAPTER
TWENTY-TWO

But had she really done that for me? I asked myself. It was a question I didn't pose to Lola Faye any more than I'd conveyed the icy sensation I'd felt when she'd told me that my father had never betrayed my mother, that his death at Woody Gilroy's hands was entirely a mistake, that Woody himself was as much a victim as my father, that everyone in our story was somehow following a false lead.

And so, in a strangely urgent commitment to penetrate this bramble, and as Lola Faye sipped quietly at her appletini and dipped, with a comic show of daring, a piece of broccoli into what she seemed to regard as a suspicious white sauce, I asked myself again: Had my mother really done that for me? Had she gathered my father into her arms, said tender things to him, given him as much comfort as possible . . . and let him die?

And on that thought I recalled her actual grief, how deep it had seemed at the time, the pall that had fallen over her after my father's death and which had finally become what appeared to be a permanent spiritual and physical exhaustion.

I'd tried quite often to lift her from this darkness, of course. We'd gone for long rides, for example, the two of us rattling along dusty country roads in the old blue Ford.

On these occasions, we'd visited various places of my mother's youth, the farm where she'd grown up, the high school she'd attended, and finally the little house in which she and my father had lived during the first years of their marriage.

It was a ruin now, set upon a weedy lot, its roof badly worn, with a sagging front porch. Most of the exterior paint was gone, and what remained was peeling.

"Broken Pine," my mother whispered as she peered at its ramshackle remains from her place in the passenger seat. "That's what Doug called it." She smiled. "As if it were an estate. As if it were our castle."

"We should go home now," I said. "It's getting dark."

My mother held her gaze on the house. "I want to go in," she said.

"Why?"

"I want to go in, Luke," my mother repeated firmly.

She got out of the car and began to move toward the house as if she were responding to a call only she could hear; I imagined, with a wrenching pang, it was my father's voice, ghostly now but still with us, summoning her to his side: *C'mere, Ellie.*

I leaped out of the car and headed across the lawn, my mother almost halfway to the house by then.

"Wait," I said.

But she didn't wait, and she'd already made it to the door by the time I caught up with her.

"Here," my mother said. "Here is where your father picked me up in his arms."

It was that fabled threshold, of course, my father now quite visible to me, standing in his fancy duds, I imagined, drawing my mother into his arms.

I grabbed the rusty knob, turned it, and pushed at the door. It swung forward quite smoothly and stood as wide open as their future must have seemed to them at that moment.

My mother lifted her head slightly and stepped inside the house.

What greeted her was crumbling plaster and peeling wallpaper, a water-stained ceiling and splintery wooden floors. She saw broken windows with glistening shards of glass strewn beneath them, and a bedroom door that sagged from its hinges. She saw a sink with rust stains and everywhere, everywhere the limp remains of old torn screens.

"Heaven," she whispered. "This house was like heaven to us, Luke."

I couldn't have imagined a more unlikely word for my mother to have uttered at that moment in such a place, but stricken as I was by hearing it, I made no effort to challenge her.

"Shall we go now?" I asked.

"Not yet," my mother said.

Then, surprisingly, she said, "I want to visit him."

She meant my father's grave, and so a few minutes later we stood beside it, my mother peering down at his name on the modest gray stone she'd had erected: VERNON DOUGLAS PAIGE.

"I should have given him more," she said.

"You gave him everything," I told her.

She continued to stare at the stone. "He liked being touched." She looked at me, then returned her attention to my father's grave. "I should have touched him more."

I thought of all the times I'd seen my father sidle up to my mother while she was cooking or when he found her in the garden. From my bedroom window, or half hidden behind a tree, I watched as he came up beside her, his body very close to hers. He stood very still at those moments, and yet, even in that stillness, he'd seemed sadly beseeching, a figure bereft and needful toward whom my mother never reached.

"You need to find someone, Luke," she said. "Someone who'll love you all your life."

My mother clearly had found such a one in my father. But as I now recalled the ravages of her grief, I began to wonder if she had loved him just as powerfully, the estrangement I thought I'd observed no more than my own boyhood conjecture, supported by little actual evidence and perhaps no more real than the betrayal of which I had been so entirely certain before my talk with Lola Faye. And if she had loved him like that, would she have let him die?

Or had she perhaps simply frozen in place, dazed by the injury she saw, unable to act in any but the most nurturing of ways, as she had the day I'd gone flying off my bicycle and knocked myself out, coming to in my mother's arms as she rocked back and forth rigidly, muttering almost incoherently, *Luke, Luke, Luke.*

As I watched Lola Faye bring a final piece of calamari to her lips, I decided that I would never truly know what my mother had done on the night of my father's murder; whether my father had ever actually betrayed my mother; or what I might have done differently had I for a single, fleeting second doubted all the things I thought I'd known with such terrible certainty.

"Seven twenty-four," I whispered so softly I was surprised when Lola Faye repeated it.

"Seven twenty-four, yep," Lola Faye said, though she no longer appeared particularly interested in the exact time my mother had made her 911 call or in any other fact having to do with my mother. Instead, she drew in a deep breath and added, "That Woody, he was a strange one."

"You mean because of that cigarette?"

"No, not that," Lola Faye answered. "Something else."

Suddenly I wondered if all Lola Faye's prior talk about my mother had been nothing more than a ruse, a way of camouflaging the different approach to my father's death she was making now.

"I've thought it through plenty of times," she added, "but I just can't figure out what came over Woody."

Was *this* the dark thread Lola Faye was following? I asked myself. And was it her search for what lay at the end of that thread that had actually brought her to me, a detail so small, so inconsequential that it had escaped all other eyes . . . but mine?

"Woody?" I asked warily. "What 'came over' him?"

"Then all of a sudden, it came clear," Lola Faye said brightly.

I felt that strange tightening again.

"He was always smoking, right?" Lola Faye asked.

I recalled the few times I'd seen Woody Wayne Gilroy and that on every one of those occasions he'd been smoking a cigarette, a pack of Chesterfields winking out of his pocket, as it had been the day I'd found him slouched at a booth at Qwik Burger looking utterly bereft.

"Always eating too much, drinking too much, driving too fast," Lola Faye continued. "I could never figure out why he was always doing those things. Then I was watching *Oprah* one afternoon, and her whole show was about people like Woody. They're self-destructive, that's what the experts on her show said. And I listened to them, psychologists, smart people like that, like you, Luke, and they had Woody pegged. 'Self-destructive,' that's what they said. People like Woody are always trying to kill themselves." She glanced toward the window, the nearly impenetrable darkness beyond it. "But the thing is," she said, almost to herself, "why would he have killed someone else?"

She stared at me silently for a moment, her gaze as piercing as a laser beam, one I worked quickly to deflect.

"Well, people are complicated," I said with a shrug. "They're . . . unpredictable."

Lola Faye nodded slowly, like an old sage acknowledging the unsolvable mystery of life. "Unpredictable, yep." She took a sip, her eyes peering just over the rim of the glass in that penetrating way of hers. "You didn't know him, did you, Luke?"

246

Like a man stepping behind a shadowy column, I said, "Know Woody? No, not at all."

"Never even talked to him, I bet," Lola Faye said.

"Only once," I said. "We had a little talk."

It struck me at that moment that the truths we won't face are the ones that never stop pumping their slow poison into our blood, and at that searing instant, a grave and oddly galvanizing sense of the reality of life descended upon me, the awakening feeling that the ordinary rules of life are there simply to provide structure and that we live mostly outside those rules, doing what we wish, sacrificing whatever we must in pursuit of whatever we want, all our actions justified, none of them justifiable.

And with that darkly illuminating recognition, I suddenly saw Woody in a way that generated another, and surprisingly intense, quiver of true feeling. He had been a poor, sad, hard-working man, and as I recalled his melancholy fate, I felt vaguely, as if through gloved hands, all the objects his own hands had grasped: dusty seed bags and oily car parts, the steering wheel of his old pickup. In a flash of memory as unaccountably intense as any I'd had since leaving Glenville, I saw him hunched over his plate of greasy fries at Qwik Burger, baffled, wounded, dazed by pain, a doomed figure just as trapped within the dreary precincts of his hometown as a blind bull in an arena.

Lola Faye cocked her head to the left, quick and birdlike. "You and Woody had a little talk," she said. "Where was that, Luke?"

"At Qwik Burger."

Going there had been a form of study for me, part of my vast ambition, though in retrospect it was probably no more than a fancifully imagined way of honing my powers of observation. At the time I'd had the nascent idea of writing a powerful and poetic work on the quotidian, a word I'd recently discovered. It would be a study of ordinary conversation, of what people revealed about themselves in diners and hair salons and bus stops. I'd already come up with a grand title for it: *The Oral History of a Single Day.*

The lost scholarship had delivered a devastating blow to such hopes. But it was my father's ludicrously uncomprehending reaction to its loss that had injected a toxin into my veins, infused me with a sense of injury and grievance, fired not just contempt but spite. Since that annihilating moment, Qwik Burger had become my refuge, the place I went in order to avoid running into my father along Main Street or at home.

I'd been there for almost an hour when the glass door opened and there he was, Woody Wayne Gilroy, red-faced and red-haired, his overalls lightly daubed with traces of the hundred sacks of animal fodder he'd just unloaded next door at Glenville Feed and Farm Equipment.

It was a dreary afternoon, with a fog slowly descending, a gloom that added to my own and which spiked at the first sight of Woody, the way he shambled to the counter and gave his order, then, when it came, lumbered over to a booth in the corner. He stared at the mound of fries with a kind of mordant inattention, like a man who'd lost his appetite not just for food but for life itself. Then, with a shrug, he lit a cigarette.

Another casualty, I thought, of my father's tawdry backroom affair with Lola Faye Gilroy, the other wounded half of that betrayal.

It was at that moment that the resentment I bore my father flared in a way I'd not felt before and which seemed to boil away some previously untouched part of me, a searing I could feel physically, like a fire in my veins.

Mountain Community, I heard him say. *You can go to Mountain Community.*

And I thought, *Never!*

While that thought was still smoldering in my mind, Woody caught my eye and, with a hesitant movement, waved me over to his booth.

"You're Luke Paige, right?" he asked as I slid in opposite him. "Your daddy owns Variety Store, don't he?"

"Yes," I said.

"My wife works there," Woody said. "My wife, Lola Faye. Lola Faye Gilroy."

Even in his halting, somewhat broken speech, he still seemed proud that he, lowly Woody, had won such a lovely prize.

I nodded. "Yes, I know."

The glimmer of pride I'd seen in Woody's eyes now dimmed to disappointment. "We're not living together now," he added.

"Oh," I said quietly.

"We're separated, me and Lola Faye," Woody said. Now he appeared utterly crestfallen, like a man who'd lost a vastly treasured possession through his own negligence. "I been trying to get her back, but she won't come." He shook his head. "I don't know why, 'cause I been good to Lola Faye." He looked like a child lost in the woods, baffled by the thick undergrowth that pressed in from all sides, the gigantic trees, the labyrinth of trails.

"She wouldn't need no job if she'd come back to me," Woody added. "She never had to have no job when she was with me." He eyed me with the caution of a man who remained unsure of even his deepest convictions. "You think a woman oughtta have a job?"

"I guess it depends upon what that particular woman wants," I answered without answering, like a man hedging his bets.

Woody clearly found my response both baffling and unsatisfactory. He took a long pull from his cigarette, crushed the butt into the little tin ashtray to his right, and in a single motion lit another. "But what woman would wanna work if she didn't have to?" He shook his head at the confusion of it all. "When I asked Lola Faye, she said she just likes it at Variety Store. That she gits something out of it."

Before I could stop myself, I said, "I'm sure she does."

It was not the words themselves, I realized immediately, but the way I'd added something dark and veiled to them, the black seam of innuendo, then had punctuated that grim addition with an indecipherable sneer.

"What do you mean?" Woody asked tentatively, like a man who didn't want to hear an answer he already knew was true.

I glanced down at his untouched burger and fries.

"What do you mean?" Woody asked again.

His eyes glimmered with a trembling expectancy, making me see how many unbearable scenarios had already slithered through his mind, how many nights he'd paced the floor, sucking at one cigarette after another, fighting his way through pornographic images: his dear sweet Lola Faye in the back seat of another man's car, tangled in the sheets of another man's bed, the two of them laughing at poor, dumb, uncomprehending Woody in the sweaty minutes just after they'd screwed themselves into the fiery reaches of space.

"Nothing," I said.

Woody's gaze was gun-barrel cold. "She likes working at Variety Store, right?"

I nodded. "I guess she does. I don't go in there very much."

"Why's that?" Woody asked.

"I just don't," I answered.

"But Lola Faye, she likes your daddy, don't she?"

"I guess," I answered softly.

"'Cause he's good to her, right?" Woody asked.

"Sure," I said. "He's good to her."

"How good?"

What I saw was that combination of male pride, quick grievance, and the terror of humiliation that has always been the single most murderous element of manhood, the coiled snake at the core of masculinity that strikes the center of a man, sharp and stinging, before it strikes outside him.

"How good?" Woody repeated.

I knew absolutely what I should say. I knew because I was smart, and because a heart as simple as Woody's was not difficult to read. I knew the fundamental elements that drove him, and they were astonishingly rudimentary. He wanted to eat and sleep and have sex with his wife. He wanted to be a father someday, and a grandfather after that. He wanted to drink with his buddies, and play the roustabout, and yell for the home team, and have someone slap him on the back and say, *Good job, Woody.* But more than any of these things, he wanted to know absolutely that his wife had not cheated on him, played him for a fool, that she had not waited excitedly at the dark end of some midnight street, yearning for her first glimpse, and later the thrilling touch, of another man.

Because I understood all this so clearly, I knew what I should say: *My father treats Lola Faye very well. She's like a daughter to him.*

That would have been enough, those thirteen words, and had I said them, Woody, grasping for any relief from the nightly terrors that plagued him, would have believed me without doubt, believed me and left Qwik Burger reassured, left me and gone home and called Lola Faye and renewed his effort to get her back, secure in the knowledge that he'd been wrong in the brief suspicion my words had strengthened, sweetly certain, as he'd devoutly wished to be, that his wife was not sleeping with her boss.

I knew exactly what I should have said, but I thought of the tawdry little plywood bedchamber my father had erected, the cracked cardboard and rumpled sheet of its makeshift bed, the cheaply wrapped present to his "dearest love," and finally of the way my father had stood in the dim corner of my mother's hospital room, beside the bed of the woman he was supposed to love, the dark truth in his eyes that I'd pronounced in my mind: *You know you want her dead.*

And so, save with the fatal glimmer of my eyes, I told him nothing.

"Qwik Burger," Lola Faye said. "You and Woody had a little talk at Qwik Burger?"

Her eyes gave off their subtle flash, though I couldn't tell if it was because of a dark notion she'd always had or if she'd heard some small beat of my own telltale heart.

"What did y'all talk about?" she asked.

"We talked about you," I answered. "He mentioned that you'd left him, and he was trying to figure out why that was."

"And he was suspicious, right?" Lola Faye asked intently. "That something was going on between your daddy and me."

Before I could answer, Lola Faye raced ahead.

"Because he'd figured what you already figured. What a lot of people in Glenville were thinking, maybe." She stared at me evenly. "That bed you thought your daddy made, you didn't tell him about that, did you, Luke?"

I shook my head. "No," I answered, then stopped, considered the crimes of my youth, and decided without further thought to throw off some part of their long burden. "But I wanted to hurt my father, to strike back at him," I added. "And so when the subject came up, I didn't assure Woody that his suspicions were unfounded." I shrugged. "I wanted to take something away from my father the way he'd taken something away from me. Something important to him. Something he cared about and took pleasure in." I gazed at Lola Faye softly. "You."

I half expected this confession to light a terrible fire in Lola Faye, but she seemed not in the least inflamed by it.

"He was nice, your daddy," she said quietly.

I glanced toward the window as if expecting to see my father standing just beyond it, peering at me through its streaked glass. "Anyway, I didn't tell Woody that he was wrong in what he was thinking about you and my father," I said when I drew my eyes back to Lola Faye.

"Well, you had the same suspicions, right?" Lola Faye asked casually. "I mean, you and Woody had the same idea."

"Yes," I answered. "But if I'd just told Woody that there was no basis for him thinking that my father and you were —"

"Then you'd have been lying to him, Luke," Lola Faye interrupted.

254

I wondered if she'd always suspected that I'd alerted Woody and in that way, however inadvertently, had set him on his disastrous course. Perhaps it was to clear up this very point that Lola Faye had arranged this last talk, and with that point now behind us, she might simply go on chatting for a moment, and then take her leave.

"So it doesn't bother you," I asked cautiously, "that I may have contributed to . . . all that death?"

"No. Does it bother you?" Lola Faye asked.

"It once did," I admitted. "Particularly right after it happened. I thought about it a great deal during that time. Because I had a lot of . . . feeling then."

Lola Faye assumed what appeared to be her notion of a therapist's pose. "Tell me about that," she said.

And so I did.

As I spoke, I recalled the terrible recriminations I'd felt after my father's murder and Woody's suicide, how my guilt had been deepened by the curious affection I'd later felt for them both. I'd look out the kitchen window and notice the cement blocks my father had placed there, or see the bag of kindling he'd tossed into the corner of the garage, and think, with an actual note of sorrow, that Vernon Douglas Paige would never build his little toolshed or make a winter fire. At those moments, and living now with my mother's grief, I'd made an effort to see him as I thought she had, and thus to recognize that my late father, despite his infidelity, had had a certain battered charm. He had, after all, cared enough to take out an insurance policy, and in doing this, he had inadvertently provided for the glorious education that awaited me.

I'd felt the same guilt and offered the same affection to Woody Gilroy. He'd been one of life's poor souls, after all, the sort of man whose existence was essentially a long fist fight against invisible foes. I knew that the hapless rarely recognized their own haplessness, of course, and that Woody had certainly never guessed that he'd been doomed to live and die as one of those creatures forever pushed aside.

"And so I wasn't beyond feeling, if you know what I mean," I told Lola Faye. "Because I did feel for my father and Woody."

"I'm sure you did," Lola Faye said.

But was she?

I couldn't be sure, and so I offered her proof.

"It's silly to think about it now," I told her. "But in the days immediately following all this terrible stuff, I began to think about a great book. It would be about how in all of life's tragedies, all its ill fortune and sickness and death, there might be something embedded in the spark itself that promoted . . ." I stopped and released a brittle laugh. "Who knows what? I didn't know, but so what? I was young, with a world of discovery before me. It would come, whatever it was, this philosophical insight, and I had time to wait for it."

I'd expected Lola Faye to share in my ludicrous evaluation of this moment in my journey, but she seemed to take my great book quite seriously.

"So at that point, you were still going to write those great books?" Lola Faye asked.

"Yes," I said.

Lola Faye considered my answer briefly, then appeared to file it in some remote cabinet of her mind.

"Well, the bottom line is that you didn't mean for any of it to happen, right, Luke?" she asked. "That Woody would do what he did to your daddy and then to himself, you didn't intend any of that, did you?"

"No," I said truthfully. "No, I didn't."

"Then you shouldn't beat yourself up about it," Lola Faye told me. She drew in a deep, apparently restful breath. "It's the bad stuff you *mean* to do that matters," she added. "That's the stuff you can't get rid of."

I was quite surprised that Lola Faye had so easily let me off the hook, and yet I wondered if, by allowing me to escape from one trap, she was luring me into another.

"Right, Luke?" she asked lightly.

"Right," I answered warily.

She shook her head; then, as if suddenly returned to a brighter day, she said, "You'd have probably liked Woody. He was a nice guy."

I saw the nice guy Woody had been in the way he'd looked at that last meeting, a round, red-faced baby of a man, and as if driven forward by that final image, I leaned over, reached out, and for the first time in my life actually touched Lola Faye Gilroy. "I'm truly sorry about Woody," I said.

Lola Faye looked at my fingers on her hand. "A person can really miss that," she said. "Touch." She

257

looked me dead in the eye. "A person needs to touch, don't you think, Luke?"

I slowly drew back my hand. "It's important, yes," I said. "The feel of things."

"You miss Julia, I bet," she said.

I nodded but said nothing.

Lola Faye peered at me with what seemed quite deep sympathy. "It's sort of a sad story, the one we've been going over."

"It's Southern gothic, that's for sure," I told her. "Families with dark secrets. The war between fathers and sons. Selfishness. Greed. Violence. The debts of the past. Old bills too high to pay, but which keep coming in."

Lola Faye offered me a small, admiring smile. "So smart, Luke, the way you see things."

"Smart," I said, and with that word saw my life yet again as a long string of profoundly stupid choices: hopes and dreams whose wild rush had washed over my father, my mother, Debbie, Woody, Julia, and finally even over the very intensity of mind and heart by which I actually might have written some great book.

"Smart," I repeated dryly. "Yep."

Lola Faye let her eyes drift down to the few drops that remained of her appletini.

"Would you like another one?" I asked.

She looked at me with an uncertainty in her eyes I couldn't quite read. "One for the road, Luke?"

"Sure," I said. "Why not?"

Lola Faye's gaze now became at once more distant and more penetrating than any before it, so that I felt

258

like a man observed though a high-intensity lens, his every tiny move recorded by eyes he himself cannot see.

"So, I guess we're finished with *Luke's Journey*," I said with an entirely false lightness in my voice.

Lola Faye said nothing, but I could see her mind turning, as if she were going back over all those details Ollie had taught her to study and retain and put together in different ways until the crime scene was complete.

"We can talk about the future now," I added expansively, using a tone that I hoped would free our conversation from the bloody world of Glenville once and for all. "We can talk about your future, for example."

Lola Faye's body slumped quite visibly, like a suddenly punctured tire, and with that movement, she gave off a piercing sadness that gripped me with unexpected force, like a dead hand at my throat.

"No," she said. "Not mine."

"Why not?" I asked.

She covered her momentary descent with a sudden, radiant smile. "Because I want to hear more about your story, Luke," she said jovially.

"There's not much left to tell," I said.

"Yes, there is," Lola Faye said with an assurance that both surprised and troubled me, giving me the sense that everything before had been plotted, every word of our talk so far. "I'm sure there is."

I felt another quivering in my insensate core, a subtle charge whose movements quavered through me in a soft seismic rush but whose visible effects I acted quickly to contain.

"So, I guess we're not done with Glenville yet?" I asked in a tone that labored to be light, humorous, almost mocking of the gray web that still enshrouded my life.

Lola Faye's blue eyes radiated a shadowy intensity, as if she sensed a dark kernel she could not stop digging for. "No," she said. "Not yet."

PART IV

CHAPTER
TWENTY-THREE

Not yet.

So it would not end as it had begun, I thought, my last talk with Lola Faye. It would not end lightly, casually, with a handshake and a smile, both of us pleased that we'd spent a little time "catching up."

Not yet.

No, not yet, because there was something else she sought, as I could tell by the look in her eyes, something else she had come to find and that she would not leave without.

And on that thought he surfaced for the first time, strode into my mind like an actor whose moment had come to appear upon the stage, assume the role fate had assigned to him in the little play called *Luke's Journey*.

He'd waited until almost everyone else had offered condolences on my father's death before walking up to me and offering his own.

"I'm so sorry about your father, Luke," Mr. Ward had said softly when he reached me.

I nodded coolly. "Thank you."

Mr. Ward glanced about, clearly making sure that he could speak to me without being overheard. "Luke, we need to have a talk. I was your father's insurance agent, and he had a life insurance policy we need to discuss. I mentioned it to your mother, but she's rather upset at the moment, so she asked me to speak to you instead."

"All right."

"Just come by my office as soon as you think you're up to it."

I nodded.

"Good, thank you."

With that, Mr. Ward made his way over to where my mother stood a short distance from the grave, Debbie at her side, and toward whom, I saw with a quick glance, Lola Faye Gilroy was also making her tense, unsteady way.

But I wasn't thinking of Lola Faye or Debbie or even of my mother at that particular moment. With the lost scholarship, I'd faced a dreadful setback. My father's death, violent though it had been, had now reversed that downward course, and I could once again imagine a brilliant future for myself.

And so it was with a certain renewed hope that I went to Mr. Ward's office a few days later, sat down in the chair before his desk, and waited to hear about my father's insurance policy, perhaps even receive the check. While I sat, I felt my energy returning to me, my earlier sense of purpose charging through me, a charge that was visible and audible in the steady light tapping of my toe against the office floor. After a long dark period, I felt that my hope had been restored, the fire that had flared in me after my talk with Miss McDowell had come to life again. I would leave Glenville, get my education, write my tactile histories of America.

"Ah, Luke," Mr. Ward said as he came into his office. "You're very punctual."

"Thank you, sir."

"Not like your father," Mr. Ward added with a soft laugh.

"No," I agreed.

Harry Ward was a sophisticated man by Glenville standards, at least in the sense that he wore a suit that actually fit and a tie that matched it. He'd been born to one of the town's most fortunate families. There was something solid about him, and even a little worldly, so that the man who took his place behind the desk that afternoon, folded his hands, and leaned forward gave an impression of immense assurance and gravity.

"Your father worked for my father when he was a boy," Mr. Ward began. "We had a farm out on the mountain. Doug did whatever needed to be done around the place. He had his mother to support. Along with Wendell."

"Wendell?"

"His brother," Mr. Ward said.

"Oh, yes. I think I may have heard something about him, but I don't remember what it was."

"Well, Wendell didn't live very long," Mr. Ward informed me. "He had some sort of congenital heart condition. It ran in the family, evidently. They were never long livers, the Paiges. Doug was just a boy when his father died at, I think, forty-nine. Wendell, of course, was much younger, around six when he died."

"I see."

"Anyway, your father had to support his mother and Wendell," Mr. Ward went on. "Which is why he left school when he did." His smile was admiring, the small but visible honor the privileged often quite sincerely tender to those who've had to toil in less forgiving fields. "Your father worked awfully hard, Luke. He never let up."

This was true, and I would not have denied it, though at the same time I also had to admit that my father's work had come to precious little, save for the insurance policy he'd unaccountably taken out and that, though by no plan of his own, had restored my hope for the brightest and most achieving future any boy from Glenville had ever had.

"He did his best," Mr. Ward added. "What more can be asked of a man?"

Mr. Ward waited for me to respond to this, no doubt expecting that I would add some nugget of praise for my hardscrabble father, which is precisely what I did.

"He wasn't lazy, that's true," I said.

Mr. Ward leaned back slightly. "Of course, Doug wasn't very — how should I put this? — he wasn't very —"

"Smart," I interjected crisply.

Mr. Ward smiled. "Not in the same way you are, no," he said pointedly, then seemed suddenly afraid that he'd said something inappropriate. "Not to speak ill of the dead, of course, but truth is truth, and Doug was not a good manager. As far as Variety Store was concerned, at least."

"It barely got by, I know," I said by way of moving on to the subject at hand.

266

"Frankly, Luke, it didn't get by at all," Mr. Ward informed me. He drew in the deep breath of a swimmer before the plunge. "Your father never bothered to make a will," he added. "So by the law of survivorship, everything goes to your mother."

This was hardly news, but even had it been, I'd have found nothing disturbing in it. My mother, after all, was a river that flowed directly to me.

"Which brings me back to Variety Store," Mr. Ward continued with a grim look. "I'm afraid your father was badly behind in the store's rent. He also had quite a few bills that had remained unpaid for some time. As a result, there are several liens on the store's assets and inventory. In fact, Luke, the store's entire contents will have to be sold to pay them, and my guess is that it will be a wash, that there'll be nothing left over for your mother."

"I see," I said quietly.

Mr. Ward drew a folder from a stack of folders to his right and opened it. "Doug also had an insurance policy," he said. "Your mother was the beneficiary."

I nodded.

"The policy was for two hundred thousand dollars," Mr. Ward added. "He took it out the day after he married your mother."

Harvard Yard spread before me, shimmering and bright, like a fairyland.

"He seemed to feel that he might die at an early age, like his father," Mr. Ward continued. "That was why he took out the policy, because he felt that your mother would certainly outlive him, and he wanted to provide for her."

There would be long hours in the great library, I thought, long walks with professors, long nights of fervent discussion in the student lounge.

"So he never failed to pay the premium," Mr. Ward went on. "He paid it right on time for almost twenty years." He shifted uncomfortably in his chair. "Obviously he intended for your mother to be very well taken care of."

It was here Mr. Ward's tone suddenly darkened, a change that sent a ripple of dread through me.

"Intended?" I asked.

"Intended, yes," Mr. Ward said. His expression was grim. "Because I'm afraid that your father recently cashed out that policy, Luke."

"Cashed it out?" I asked.

"He cashed in its value, which was far less than the face value of the policy."

"How much less?"

"He cashed it out for thirty thousand dollars," Mr. Ward said. "I tried to talk him out of it, but he said he needed the money. That he was expecting some big bills."

"When did he do this?" I asked.

"About two months ago," Mr. Ward answered. "I checked with a friend of mine at First Federal. I know Doug deposited the money, but then he withdrew it."

"In cash?" I asked.

"Yes," Mr. Ward answered. "I have no idea what he did with it."

"So there's . . . nothing?"

"Not unless you can find the money your father withdrew from First Federal," Mr. Ward said.

The solid ground upon which my hope had briefly rested suddenly became a pit.

"Nothing at all?" I muttered unbelievingly. "We have nothing at all?"

The stricken look on my face must have roused Mr. Ward to a gesture of empty optimism. "Well, you have your house, of course," he said. "No one can take the house."

The house, I thought bitterly, what did I care about that drab little house on Peanut Lane? For a moment, I found myself drifting dolefully through its suffocating rooms, taking dreary note of all I'd hope to flee: the impossibly cluttered basement where my father hammered together some forever misshapen shelf, the tiny room where my mother endlessly mended the sleeve or pants leg he'd carelessly snagged on a nail. I thought of the cramped little kitchen where he'd spooned down his supper, then the musty living room to which he'd trudged after that and where he'd sat like a zombie for the rest of the evening, watching the flickering screen of the boxy old black-and-white television he'd never traded in for color. I saw him in our one tiny bathroom, the door wide open, pissing loudly into the toilet.

All this, according to Mr. Ward, I would never lose; 200 Peanut Lane in all its drab majesty was forever mine.

269

"The house?" I asked in the shock of this grim recognition. "That's all?"

"I'm afraid so."

"Does my mother know about this?"

Mr. Ward shook his head. "No, Luke, she doesn't. She wanted me to talk to you. She said you were in charge now."

It was just after four in the afternoon when I left Mr. Ward's office, the streets of Glenville already beginning to clear, the town's shopkeepers gathering up whatever wares they'd placed on the sidewalks and returning them inside their stores. I thought of all the many times I'd done the same, usually while my father counted the day's receipts, such as they were, then placed the cash in a plain manila envelope and headed for the bank to make his daily deposit. Now I knew just how completely useless all that work had been, that my father had accumulated nothing but debt, save for the thirty thousand he'd gotten for his insurance policy, briefly deposited, then withdrawn.

But why had he done that? I wondered.

Then suddenly, I knew.

For that woman! I thought.

My father was going to run away, leave my mother and me behind, find a better place to live with his shop-girl paramour; in another town, no doubt, or another state. He had taken the money that would otherwise have funded my vast dream, and in doing that he'd canceled my hope, exploded my ambition, and ripped to shreds the great books I would have written, and he had done it all for Lola Faye.

CHAPTER
TWENTY-FOUR

"What are you thinking about, Luke?"

I suddenly wondered if all my failures, the coldly academic tone and passionless subjects of my books, had first been a failure to understand that I could never tell another's story without disclosing my own, that every book is first of all a confession.

"Thinking about?" I stammered. "I'm . . . well . . . the past."

Lola Faye seemed to grasp that I'd turned a corner in the lengthening road of our conversation.

"I guess I was thinking about the books I'd hoped to write," I told her. "The big hopes I had."

"But you have written books, Luke," Lola Faye reminded me.

"Little books," I said with a dismissive shrug. "Dull books. Not at all what I had in mind when I left Glenville."

"Why do you think that is?" Lola Faye asked in a manner that made me sense the approach, cautious and yet insistently proceeding, of a grave inquiry.

"I lost the passion that would have made me do it," I said. "And the feeling for things that would have let me do it."

"Numb," Lola Faye said softly, but pointedly as well, as if she were reminding me of a thread of conversation that had been lost or avoided and that she was determined to take up again. "You went numb."

"That's right," I said.

"Why do you think that happened?"

"Oh, I've had plenty of excuses along the way," I answered as casually as I could. "Everything that happened in Glenville, mostly. I even laid the blame at your doorstep for a while."

"Because you thought I'd been sleeping with your daddy," Lola Faye said.

"Not just that," I answered.

I couldn't tell exactly what Lola Faye was expecting to hear, though it was clear she expected to hear something, a solemn anticipation I could find no way to deflect.

"I thought you were a thief," I told her bluntly.

Lola Faye appeared genuinely surprised to hear this.

"When you came to my father's funeral, do you remember seeing Harry Ward?" I asked.

Lola Faye nodded.

"Well, he came over to me at one point," I told her. "He said, 'Luke, we need to have a talk.'"

With that introduction, I told her about the later conversation I'd had with Mr. Ward, the cashed-in insurance policy, the thirty thousand dollars my father had briefly deposited in the local bank then mysteriously withdrawn, my certainty that he'd done all of this because he'd planned to run away with her.

272

"But it wasn't for you, that money," I added softly when I came to the end of this narration, now quite thoroughly convinced that I'd misjudged Lola Faye not only in thinking of her as an adulteress for all these many years but also in my later conviction that she'd secretly pocketed the only money my father had provided for my mother at his death. "I know that now."

Lola Faye had listened patiently to this latest episode of *Luke's Journey*, her face pretty much expressionless, so it was hard for me to tell exactly how she'd received it.

"Of course, I can see why you'd have thought that, Luke," Lola Faye said in a tone that was quite pleasant, as if she'd just heard some tale of vaguely eventful travel. "And it would make a good movie, don't you think? I mean, it would give things a twist, right?"

I wondered if Lola Faye had decided that all of what I'd just told her was pure fiction, a twist I'd made up.

"What do you mean, a twist?" I asked.

"Well, it would provide a motive for Woody killing Doug," Lola Faye said matter-of-factly. "Not just that he thought I was cheating on him with your daddy, but a money motive. Like in *Double Indemnity*."

"But Woody didn't know about my father's insurance policy," I reminded her.

"Yes, but suppose I'd known about it?" Lola Faye asked cheerily. "What a plot that would be."

She'd used the word *plot* rather ambiguously, I thought. Did she mean a plot in a movie, I wondered, or a plot she'd hatched herself?

"I'm afraid I'm not following you," I admitted.

"Okay, so it would go like this," she said eagerly and energetically, like how I imagined a screenwriter would pitch a script to a producer. "This girl gets a job at Variety Store. She gets involved with the owner of the store. She gets him to cash in his insurance policy and give her the money." Her smile was a twisted little thing. "Then she puts her jealous husband up to killing the owner of the store so she can keep the money. The owner is dead and the husband kills himself . . . or goes to prison. In a movie, it would work either way."

"But to make this work, the husband would have to know that his wife was having an affair, wouldn't he?" I asked.

Lola Faye nodded.

"So the problem is that the jealous husband might just as easily kill the wife as the owner of the store," I continued. "He might even kill them both."

"Well, it would depend on what the girl told her husband, right?" Lola Faye answered brightly. She narrowed her eyes in sly imitation of some B-movie femme fatale. "Suppose I told him that your daddy raped me."

"Raped?" I asked. "You?"

"The girl," Lola Faye answered quickly. "In the movie."

The complexities of this plot suddenly seemed all too intricate to have occurred to Lola Faye out of the blue.

"Are you sure you didn't get all this from one of Ollie's crime magazines?" I asked.

274

Lola Faye took a quick sip from her appletini, then wiped her mouth with the white napkin. "I wouldn't need a magazine to come up with that twist, Luke. Because people already thought I was behind it all. That I'd pulled off this scheme, killed two men, and got away with it."

"Who thought that?" I asked.

"People in Glenville," Lola Faye said. "That's why I left. You might say I was run out of town. You left because you wanted to, Luke. You had Harvard waiting for you, a great education, big hopes. But I got run out of Glenville. I didn't want to go. I liked Glenville, but I had no choice but to leave. No one wanted me there. Because I was a black widow." She drew in a quick, taut breath. "A pariah, that's what I was." She released a brittle laugh. "You know what a pariah is, Luke?"

"An outcast."

"I learned that from the History Channel too," Lola Faye said. "A program about lepers. It said lepers were pariahs back in biblical times. They were driven away and kept away. They could never go back to the place they came from."

It was clear that Lola Faye still bore the stigma of crimes she had not committed but with which she had been charged by her neighbors, tried and convicted in the silent courtrooms of their minds.

"You've thought a lot about what happened, haven't you?" I asked. "The acts, their consequences, everything."

"Yes, I have," Lola Faye said. "And sometimes, I had to wonder if maybe you believed all that bad stuff too. You know, that I was a black widow."

So was this why Lola Faye had come to Saint Louis? I asked myself now. Had she, all these years, felt a need to cleanse my mind of the grim and false suspicions she feared that I, along with the people of her own hometown, had harbored in regard to her? Not just that she had carried on an affair with my father, but that she had conspired to have him murdered?

"I never thought that," I answered truthfully. "I never thought you had anything to do with my father's death. That it was all a plot, I mean."

Lola Faye peered at me doubtfully.

"Of course, when I left Mr. Ward's office, I was thinking that my father had probably cashed in the policy so that he could run away with you," I added. "It was sort of Mr. Hubbard getaway money, you might say."

Lola Faye's expression turned quite serious. "I didn't know about any insurance policy," she told me firmly. "You know that now, right?"

"Yes."

I said nothing further, and in the silence, Lola Faye appeared unsure as to whether she should believe what I'd just told her, and so I quickly added, "I know you didn't have anything to do with my father's death."

She seemed to think over all the events we'd previously discussed, everything that had been said and done, the things she knew for sure, the things that remained in doubt, putting all of that in some kind of larger framework. Finally she said, "It's about bad luck, isn't it, Luke? Life's about how bad luck can just take over and change everything."

I hadn't considered that my particular life had been determined by bad luck, but the way Lola Faye had immediately homed in on that notion as life's central theme suggested that she thought her own life had been pretty much determined by it.

"Have you had a lot of bad luck?" I asked.

She drew her hands from the table and let them drop into her lap. "Everybody does," she said. "But you have to go on. You have to think of the future the way those pioneers did. The ones who went west. You have to be like them and just bull on through. That's one of the reasons I came to Saint Louis. I wanted to see where they started. To see the Gateway to the West."

"You came to see the arch?" I asked.

She nodded fiercely. "I always wanted to see it. Ollie told me I should do it. 'Lola,' he said, 'before you die, you should see that thing. You always talk about it, so you should go see it.' " She smiled proudly, like one who'd achieved a long-dreamed-of success. "So I'm here."

"So you didn't come to Saint Louis just to have a talk with me?" I asked with incalculable relief, as if a dark motive had been removed from an increasingly disturbing script.

"Nope," Lola Faye said. "At least, that's not the only reason. But I knew you were going to be here in Saint Louis tonight, and I thought, I can kill two birds with one stone. I can see the Gateway and have a last talk with you."

"Last talk?" I asked.

"Yep," Lola Faye said. "Last talk."

"You seem very sure of that."

"Well, there's no way I could do this again, Luke," Lola Faye said. "Kill two birds, I mean."

"Kill?" I asked, because the word, along with the curious way she'd said it, hit me icily, in the way of a sudden intruder, armed and dangerous, so that all one's other problems are instantly and radically reduced to the simple question of survival.

"Yep," Lola Faye answered. She lifted her hand and popped up two fingers. "Two birds. Kill."

I glanced at the man who sat behind the distant fern, utterly still, it seemed to me, like a dead bird. He'd draped his jacket over the back of a chair across from him, so that it faced him emptily, like a headless ghost.

"Tell me about Ollie," I said when I looked back at Lola Faye. "You said he was a cop."

"Retired cop," Lola Faye corrected. "A hard worker, that's what I'd say about him. Nothing special beyond that. You go to work and do your job and hope for the best. An ordinary guy, Ollie." She paused, then added with what I took to be a pointed significance, "Like your daddy."

It struck me that it was precisely such people I'd hoped to portray in my histories, the spinners of life's timeless fabric, the bakers and winners of its daily bread.

Lost in the mists of that thought, I lifted a long-belated toast to my father. "To my old man," I whispered.

Lola Faye looked at me, utterly puzzled in the face of such a cryptic salute.

278

"I was just thinking that one of the great books I was going to write would have been about people exactly like my father," I explained. "In a way, I can't ever get away from him."

"Like in *Blade Runner*," Lola Faye chirped happily.

This mental hairpin turn was sharper and more radical than any Lola Faye had made before it, and in its wild shift I felt myself hurled toward the edge of a precipice.

"That movie with Harrison Ford," Lola Faye went on. "The replicants, which are sort of robots but really almost human. They come back to Earth to find the guy who created them."

"Do they find him?" I asked.

"Yep."

"What happens then?"

"They kill him," Lola Faye answered flatly. "They gouge out his eyes. Really, just one of them does that. It's pretty gruesome."

"It sounds it," I said.

"Blood everywhere," Lola Faye added, her eyes now in that sparkly state I'd noticed before, piercing but at the same time turned inward. "Blood all over the place."

She seemed to go to some distant location, then slowly, like a building light, return to me.

"I was thinking of Danny," she said. "He got really sick before he died. He puked blood all the time. It was all over everything, Luke. The sheets. The bed. We had shag carpet. I had it all pulled up."

"I'm sorry," I told her.

Lola Faye waved her hand dismissingly. "Oh, don't be sorry. I never liked shag carpet."

"No," I said, "I meant about Danny."

Lola Faye burst out laughing at the ludicrousness of this misunderstanding, and both relaxed and spurred by her laughter, I joined her in it, so that for a time we laughed rather hysterically together, the laughter of one igniting the laughter of the other, laughter that died down then, with our shared glance, exploded again until we finally were made breathless by it and at last settled into silence.

The odd thing is that this silence lasted longer than any other before it, and during it, we seemed to drift closer to each other, so that when the silence ended, it didn't surprise me that Lola Faye's voice had taken on a far more intimate tone.

"Ollie thought maybe he should kill Danny," she said. Her eyes added something dark and weighty to the natural order of life. "Because Danny was in so much pain, you know." She shook her head. "But he couldn't do it, Luke." She looked at me as if she were still unsure whether such a murder might not have been better for her son. "To kill someone you love, that's hard to do."

I nodded.

Lola Faye abruptly emerged from the cloud of brutal memory that had momentarily engulfed her. "But kill someone I hate? That wouldn't be hard at all."

"No, I suppose not," I said.

"But not Danny," Lola Faye added. "After he died, I went a little nuts. I kept thinking how he was just a nice boy. Not smart like you, Luke, not a boy with big ambitions. But a nice, ordinary boy. And I thought to myself, Why did he have to die when there're all these really rotten boys out there? Selfish boys who don't care about anyone but themselves." A bitter, anguished edge came into her voice. "Why did these rotten, selfish boys get to live and live and live, and Danny have to die?" She looked at her drink, settled herself by an inward method of return, let some thought run through her mind, then looked back up at me. "Do you drink a lot, Luke?"

"Yes," I said. "Too much, really."

"Ollie said that a person should never drink alone."

"I do that too, I'm afraid."

"Why?"

"It makes the hands on the clock move," I answered. "Especially at night."

"At night, I bet that's when you think of Julia," she said.

She was right, of course. Night always returned Julia to me, sometimes recollections of the few good times we'd had, sometimes memories of how long she'd stuck out the bad ones, which had given me the notion that life had provided a reprieve, a commutation of the sentence I had imposed upon myself, mercy I had in the end rejected, instead returning to my solitary cell.

Lola Faye appeared quite relaxed now, her manner entirely peaceful, a quiet smile playing on her lips. "It'll be nice, seeing the Gateway."

"You haven't seen it yet?"

She shook her head. "Tonight I will. I'm going to walk there."

"That's a long way from here."

"I don't care how long it is," Lola Faye said. "It's one of the reasons I came, so I'm going to do it." Two fingers popped into the shadowy air. "Two birds, remember?"

"Two birds," I repeated darkly. "Yes."

Lola Faye smiled, but something in her eyes didn't. "I have a toast you'll understand, Luke." She lifted her glass. "Here's to doing what you plan."

CHAPTER
TWENTY-FIVE

We clinked our glasses in our fifth toast, and, as if responding to a signal, the man behind the fern reached for his wallet, paid his check, and rose.

I watched silently as he pulled on his jacket, careful to bring its collar up over the back of his neck before he headed for the door, sweeping past our table then turning and making his way to the hotel's front lobby and finally out into the night.

Lola Faye had noticed none of this, as far as I could tell, but had simply and in what seemed an effort at distraction launched into a discussion of her favorite songs, most of them country titles of the usual sort, some from Patsy Cline, but others that were contemporary, by Faith Hill and the like. Judging from the titles, she appeared partial to weepy ballads of lost love and betrayal, all of them unknown to me until she mentioned one from Bonnie Raitt.

"Yes, I like that one too," I said when she brought up "I Can't Make You Love Me." Then, rather reluctantly, I added, "It was Julia's favorite."

"Because it was about you," Lola Faye said.

She seemed so certain of this, I wondered if she'd been in touch with Julia the way she'd been in touch with Debbie, my ex-wife a part of her research.

"Maybe," I admitted. Then, to escape any further inquiry on this subject, I nodded toward Lola Faye's nearly empty glass.

"I guess you like appletinis," I said.

"Yep," Lola Faye said. "They go down easy."

"Care for another?"

She shook her head. "I got to keep my mind clear." She looked at my glass. "Pinot noir, that's French, right?"

"Yes," I said. "It's a kind of grape."

"*Noir* means detective story, right?" Lola Faye asked. "On TCM they show noir movies. They're always about detectives or crime, something like that. Ollie thought they gave good lessons, those actors. He said you could learn a lot by looking at the actor's eyes. When the bad guy was lying, stuff like that. He'd say, 'Right there, Lola Faye, right there's where you see he's trying to be deceitful.'"

I glanced toward a far window. The rain had stopped, the window fogging now, a sign that the air outside was quickly turning colder. "The snow will be here soon."

Lola Faye appeared to have no concern for the changing weather. "You didn't answer my question, Luke."

"What question was that?"

"If *noir* means detective story. You're so smart, I bet you know the answer."

"Actually, *noir* is French for 'black,'" I said when I faced Lola Faye again. "In those movies you mentioned, *noir* refers to the way the lighting was done."

"You sound like a teacher when you answer like that," Lola Faye said.

"I am a teacher."

"But like a . . . boring teacher."

"Well, I am a boring teacher," I admitted. "Like I told you before, my students call me that." This ripple of truth felt oddly relieving, like a knot in the belly suddenly unloosed. "And like I also said, I'm a boring writer too."

"Why is that, Luke?"

"We've already talked about this," I reminded her.

"But you really didn't say why," Lola Faye said. "You just told me that you went numb."

"Numb, that's right," I said.

"After Julia?"

"No, before that."

"After you left Glenville?"

"No," I answered. "Before that." I again peered out into the night. "Anyway, noir movies have lots of shadows in them. They're shot in alleys, that sort of thing." When I looked back at Lola Faye, her eyes were dead on me. "And somebody's always being chased too." I felt a jangling in my nerves. "Chased through alleys. Deserted streets. Like in a nightmare."

Time to shut up, I thought, which is what I did.

"And there's always a dangerous woman in those movies," Lola Faye said, as if she were coaxing information from a reluctant witness.

285

"Is there?" I asked.

"A dangerous woman, yep," Lola Faye said. "Do you watch a lot of noir movies, Luke? It sounds like you do."

"I've seen a few of them," I said. "Julia liked them. And they would sometimes play them at the college. Movie night on Friday. We went to a few of them together."

"How about TV?" Lola Faye asked. "I bet you don't watch much TV."

"Not much, no."

"TV shows about cops aren't realistic, according to Ollie," Lola Faye said. "The cops in those shows don't conduct real investigations, not like real people would."

"No doubt," I said.

"Take that money you thought Doug gave me," Lola Faye said. "Did you investigate that?"

That Lola Faye had returned to this subject surprised me, but then, what other subject was possible for us besides Glenville, my father, those old dark times?

"Yes," I said.

"You said Mr. Ward told you that Doug had deposited the money, then taken it out," Lola Faye said. "You checked that out, I bet."

"Yes, I did," I said. "I went to First Federal just to make sure. The people there knew me. I sometimes took the day's receipts to that bank just before my father closed the store."

"The First Federal, right," Lola Faye said. "I took over that job. I did it every day."

I had a vision of Lola Faye in the midst of this lowly task, strolling down the twilight streets of Glenville, caught in its falling gloom, thinking of Woody or of her mundane chores, wondering, as I myself had no doubt wondered during this walk, how life had brought her to such a pass and if there might still be a way to escape it.

"I could have been like Janet Leigh in *Psycho*," Lola Faye said. "You know that movie, don't you?"

"Of course."

"She just takes the money instead of depositing it," Lola Faye went on. "And you think she got away with it. But then she runs into this guy who killed his mother, and that's the end of her."

The terror of that famous murder in the shower ran through my mind so powerfully I all but shuddered.

"So, you must have talked to Mr. Carroll," Lola Faye added in a much lighter tone. "The bank manager."

"Yes, I did," I told her. "He said my father had made a deposit of thirty thousand dollars two months before his death. Then he'd taken it out in cash. On April eighteenth, as a matter of fact."

I imagined this moment in my father's financial history, my father's rough hands, forever punctured by metal staples or slashed by paper cuts, clutching a sack that had more money in it than he'd ever seen in his life, leaving the bank with it, heading back to Variety Store, I assumed, which was where I'd gone immediately following my talk with Mr. Ward.

It had been late in the afternoon when I'd unlocked the front door and stepped inside Variety Store for the first time since my father's death. The interior had always been a chaos of leaning shelves and teetering stacks. I'd often thought this disorder a physical rendering of my father's brain, the bramble of thoughts and impulses that were forever in collision there. But now it also seemed emblematic of a confusion that might serve my own vital interests. For of all the people I'd ever known, my father had seemed the least capable of forward thinking. That he had concocted some sort of plan with regard to the cash he'd taken from First Federal struck me as very nearly impossible. He had not been able to run away with Lola Faye before being murdered by her husband. This meant that the money had not yet been spent, and if he had not yet handed it over to his tawdry little mistress, then I could think of no other place for him to have hidden it than within the daunting confines of Variety Store.

I started in the storeroom, where I'd first learned of my father's affair. I pried open crates, probed behind plasterboard, peeled back bits of linoleum, shouldered my way through a tower of cardboard boxes. But I found nothing other than the awesome mess he'd left behind. The front of the store was only a little less disorganized than the back, but the floor space involved was considerably greater, so it took me several hours of going through innumerable cluttered bins and boxes before I finally reached the little rack of paperbacks beside the front door. Surely not there, I thought, where anyone could pluck a book from the rack. It was insane, but in that moment of complete desperation, I seized on even that absurd possibility and flipped through each and every book.

288

Nothing, of course. Absolutely nothing.

I was exhausted by the time I finally departed Variety Store that evening, now carrying with me the added burden of having to break Mr. Ward's news to my mother.

She was sitting in the living room when I arrived at home.

And she was not alone.

To my surprise, Mr. Klein was sitting on a chair in that dim little room, his dark Semitic features illuminated by the small lamp that rested on the table beside him.

"Hello, Luke," he said as I came into the room.

I looked at where Mr. Klein lounged in what had once been my father's chair and that now seemed as threadbare as my future.

"Mr. Klein brought me one of his favorites," my mother said.

I turned toward her and glanced at the book in her lap.

"*Anna Karenina*," she said.

"That's about an adulteress, isn't it?" I asked.

Mr. Klein, rather than my mother, answered my question.

"Yes, it is," he said. "You might want to read it one day, Luke. It's full of understanding."

My eyes slid over to him. "Maybe I will," I said without interest.

Mr. Klein nodded sharply. "Good."

I would later learn that the mind and eyes of Abraham Klein had been schooled in treachery and betrayal and worlds upon worlds of cruelty. He and his father and brothers and sister had been rounded up by people they'd thought friends and neighbors, rounded up and herded into the village square, where for days, with no food and very little water, they had waited for the train to the death camp at which all but he would perish. While in the camp, he'd seen men lie and cheat and steal in order to gain a crust of bread or a few more hours of life. He had seen his world fall over him like ash, and he knew as much as one human being's experience could teach about the evil that lies coiled in every human heart.

And at that moment, I sensed, he seemed to glimpse an evil coiled in mine.

"Well, I should be going now, Miss Ellie," Mr. Klein said softly. With those words he got to his feet, walked over to my mother, took her hand gently in his own. "I'll drop by again tomorrow." He smiled. "Doug asked that I keep an eye on you, you know."

"He was a dear man," my mother said in a voice that nearly broke in grief. "A dear, dear man."

"Yes, he was," Mr. Klein agreed. "Well, good night," he said.

Then, like a figure on a music box, he smoothly turned to me and offered his hand.

"Good to see you, Luke," he said.

"Good to see you too, Mr. Klein," I returned.

His gaze showed a piercingly dark understanding. "The man in charge now," he said.

"I am, yes," I replied stiffly.

His smile could not have been more distant had it been offered from Mars. "Take care then," he said.

And with that, he shifted to my left and made his way through the kitchen and out the back door.

"Strange man," I said, almost to myself.

"Not so strange," my mother said. "Just lonely."

She rose shakily, and with a soft groan. "Mr. Klein says I should see a different doctor," she said. "Dr. Philbert."

I turned to her. "But you've always gone to Dr. Blalock."

My mother moved forward, but without the grace she'd had only a month before, her motion now unsteady. "Mr. Klein says that Dr. Blalock isn't . . . well . . . isn't all he should be." She took my arm and urged me toward the kitchen. "But you won't have to interrupt school or your studies for me, Luke," she said. "Mr. Klein will look in on me."

"So it seems."

She stopped and faced me. "Doug asked him to do that if anything happened to him." Her face paled. "Poor Doug," she whispered.

With that, she moved forward again, her feet padding softly across the floor until she reached the kitchen.

Once there, she lowered herself into one of the chairs and released a long breath. "Would you mind making us sandwiches for supper, Luke? I'm a little tired."

I made the sandwiches, poured the tea, and joined my mother at the table before I approached the subject that was smoldering in my mind.

"I talked to Mr. Ward this afternoon," I said.

My mother seemed hardly to hear me. "I've decided to send you a copy of the Glenville paper every week," she said. "You don't want to forget that we exist down here. And Boston is a —"

"I won't be going to Boston," I interrupted sharply.

My mother's gaze snapped over to me. "What are you talking about, Luke? Of course you're going to —"

"There's nothing, Mom," I interrupted again. "That's what Mr. Ward told me this afternoon. The store is drowning in debt. Everything in it will have to be sold to pay those debts. There's nothing."

"Nothing?" my mother asked.

"Nothing at all," I told her. "Except the house. Which is free and clear, according to Mr. Ward."

My mother sank beneath the weight of this grim news; she gripped the arms of her chair and eased herself back as if she'd received a fierce but invisible blow.

"But what about the insurance policy?" she asked finally.

"He cashed it in," I told her. "He took a payout. Thirty thousand dollars. He did it two months ago."

My mother's hope quite visibly revived. "Well, that's enough for the first year, Luke. Thirty thousand dollars. Enough to pay for all your —"

"Except that it doesn't exist," I told her. "He deposited it in the bank, then withdrew it all in cash. I have no idea what he did with it."

"But why would he want so much cash?" my mother asked.

292

"I don't know," I muttered, though of course I did, and I imagined Lola Faye in a sultry pose, offering my father the lush fruit of herself.

My mother appeared utterly dazed. "What would Doug want with so much money?" she repeated. "What would have made him cash in that policy? He never mentioned doing that. Why would he have done it, Luke?"

"I don't know," I repeated, since there was little to be gained by bringing up Lola Faye, particularly in light of the fact that my mother still so emphatically denied that my father had ever had an affair with her. "But he took it and now it's gone." I glanced around at the little room with its flowery wallpaper and water-stained ceiling. "This house is all that's left."

My mother sat very still and said nothing for quite some time, like an animal stunned by a blow to the head, reeling, but still on its feet.

"He had to have a reason, Luke," she whispered after a while. "He wouldn't have done it for no reason." She seemed utterly exposed, as if I'd glimpsed her through an inadvertently parted curtain. "Nothing?" she asked brokenly. "Nothing at all?" She took my hand and folded it in hers, so that we appeared like people huddled on a lifeboat, the sea steadily building around us, storm brewing on all sides. "He had to have a reason, Luke," she repeated.

I thought of the crude boudoir my father had constructed in the stockroom of Variety Store, the little vase of plastic flowers, the small box wrapped ham-handedly in pink paper.

"He had to have a reason," my mother said yet again. "He was a good man and so he had to have —"

The dam broke, and I spewed out my long-suppressed venom.

"He cashed in that policy because he was going to run away with her," I burst out angrily. "With Lola Faye Gilroy."

And with those words, and even in the face of a crisis that had destroyed my deepest hope, a wave of delicious satisfaction passed over me, so entirely certain was I at that moment that my father had fully deserved the hot bullet that had pierced his chest; had deserved to see the geyser of blood shoot up into his face and feel his body tumble as his chair exploded backward; had deserved to sense his own dead weight fall to the floor; had deserved in every way to be murdered.

"No," my mother said firmly. "No, Doug wouldn't have done that."

"That's exactly what he did, Mom," I told her brutally. "I looked all over the store. I looked for hours!" I grabbed her shoulders and squeezed hard. "Face it, Mom! That's exactly what he did! He took out that money so he could run away with that little whore."

"No!" my mother said. "No, Luke. He would never have done that."

"How do you know that, Mom?" I asked hotly.

She didn't answer but instead turned away, as if she couldn't face the sheer horror of what she saw in my eyes.

294

"How do you know he didn't give that money to Lola Faye Gilroy?" I demanded, even more loudly.

"I just know," my mother said. Her voice broke and something deep within her seemed to crack at the same time. "I just know he wouldn't have done that to me, Luke."

But even as she shattered beneath my accusation, I added weight.

"He cheated on you, Mom," I reminded her cruelly. "He screwed a shop girl in the backroom of the store."

"Stop it, Luke!" my mother cried.

"A little hayseed tramp."

"No!"

"He did that, so why wouldn't he take that money and give it to her?" I shouted. "He loved her, didn't he?"

"No!" my mother cried. "He loved me!"

I bored into her with all my angry force. "How do you even know that, Mom?"

My question struck her like a blow to the face, and she seemed to reel away inwardly. "I know. Believe me, I know."

"How do you know?" I demanded.

Her eyes filled with tears and every part of her began to tremble. "Because he tried to touch me, Luke!" she cried. "Because the last thing he did was reach up and try to touch my face, my eyes."

So that was my mother's ludicrous reason for refusing to accept what my father had done, I thought grimly: he couldn't have done it because he'd loved her truly, madly, deeply, just like in the books she read.

Once I had felt lifted by my mother's romantic idealization of people — everyone nice, everyone honest, everyone ready to sacrifice him- or herself for others — but now I felt it as a veil that had blocked me from seeing life as it really was.

"You have to face the facts," I told her. "You have to face the fact of what he did and what he was."

She shook her head violently and in that exertion seemed to exhaust herself. "I want to go upstairs, Luke," she said. "I need to lie down."

She struggled to her feet, made her way to the stairs and then up them. From my place in the kitchen, I heard her briefly padding about in her room before she sank into her bed.

I sat alone in the kitchen for a long time after that. The window through which a bullet had struck down my father had been replaced, but that single hole with its starburst of cracked glass had been so seared into my mind that I knew where its exact location had been. For a moment, I imagined that fatal shot, my father tumbling backward and spilling onto the ground, my mother rushing to his rescue, cradling him in her arms, my father reaching up to touch her face as she'd claimed he had.

The last thing he did was reach up and try to touch my face, my eyes.

I heard my mother's voice in my mind, sounding so certain that my father in his last moments had thought only of her.

But alone in the kitchen, sitting in the very chair from which my father had fallen, peering at the place

296

on the floor where he'd lain, I imagined my father still in the grip of the tawdry little passion that had consumed him over the last few months, reliving it even as he died, his hand reaching up tremblingly as blood spouted from his chest, his mind fogging as he bled to death, and in that fog stretching his glistening red fingers toward the woman he'd wanted to be with him at that moment, younger than my mother, more passionate. I saw my father blearily reaching for one last touch not of my mother, whom his dying mind had erased, but of Lola Faye Gilroy, peering up and up, straining every last particle of his waning strength to get one final glimpse of her sky blue eyes.

CHAPTER
TWENTY-SIX

Those eyes were still blue, but they had lost their sparkle.

"You know what seems strange to me, Luke?" Lola Faye asked.

Was that a soft slur I heard in her voice? I asked myself. Was she actually getting drunk now, at the end of our talk? I heard her earlier pronouncement — *I'm a mean drunk* — and wondered if it might be a warning I should heed.

But try as I might, I couldn't decide if I'd heard a slur, and so I listened more closely as she continued.

"It seems strange that, thinking what you did, you never came to me," Lola Faye said. "I mean, if you thought I had thirty thousand dollars from Doug's insurance policy, why didn't you just ask me?"

No, I decided, no slur.

"Why didn't you do that, Luke?" Lola Faye asked. "Just ask me?"

"I didn't do it because I thought you'd lie," I answered frankly. "Most people do. Especially when it comes to money." I shrugged. "Or maybe something in me just gave up. Because it all seemed lost then, my hope of going to a great college, writing great books." I

298

shook my head, weary of the price I'd paid, made others pay. "Pursuing a dream is never cheap, after all."

"But pursuing most dreams has to be cheap, don't you think?" Lola Faye asked pointedly.

Uneducated though it was, uninformed by the sort of arid research to which I'd dedicated my life, Lola Faye's question was poignant, and I instantly thought of the West, the Gateway Arch Lola Faye claimed she'd traveled to Saint Louis to see. How cheap it had been for those first pioneers to begin their epic journeys. What had they needed, after all, but a few tools, some clothes, and the dauntless energy of the dream that fired them? With these, and nothing more, removed from everything but hope, they had proceeded on.

"You're right," I said. "A dream should be cheap." I glanced toward the empty table where the mystery man had sat and with a terrible certainty accepted the bleak fact that this was the only future that awaited me: to be a lonely man, arriving alone, sitting alone, leaving alone. "At least at the beginning."

Lola Faye took a sip of the last drops of her appletini. "So, you thought I'd lie."

I snapped my attention back to Lola Faye. "What?"

"You said you thought that if you'd asked me about the money, I'd have lied," Lola Faye said.

"Yes, but there was nothing I could do about anything, anyway," I said. "The money was gone, and without the money, I stopped studying, stopped reading, stopped . . . everything."

At times I'd felt that I was being held in an unlighted, airless, and ferociously hot room. It was almost summer by then, my arrival at Harvard scheduled for September, an acceptance I had to confirm by August 1, as a letter had sternly informed me, or *your place in our freshman class will be forfeited*.

"I gave up," I said. "People do that when they just can't see a future for themselves."

Lola Faye nodded slowly, and in the quiet sadness that swam into her face, I saw a lost hope in her as well.

"Yes, I do," she said.

She added nothing to this, and I saw that perhaps in some things, she displayed the "reticence" my mother had so long ago admired, though in a wildly different form.

"Anyway," I said, now returning to the prior subject of our conversation, "I knew there was no hope of my getting to Harvard in September. There wasn't a dime for that, not a nickel, not a —"

I stopped when Lola Faye suddenly glanced toward the window. "We should go out, Luke," she said. She nodded toward the window, where I saw that a light snow had begun to fall. "It's started snowing. It must be beautiful in the park." She turned to me and smiled brightly. "Don't you think that it would be nice to take a walk in the snow, Luke?"

"But it's rather cold for a walk, don't you think?" I asked. "And the park is deserted. It could be dangerous."

Lola Faye offered a playful little wink. "Well, you said you'd take a risk."

300

"I meant a risk with regard to our talk," I reminded her.

Lola Faye returned her gaze to the window and seemed to view the softly falling snow and shadowy park as a winter wonderland. "I want to take a walk in the snow," she said. "I may not get the chance again." She turned to me. "There's not much snow where I live."

"Which is where, by the way?"

"Glenville," Lola Faye answered. "I moved back after Ollie died."

"Ollie . . . died?" I asked.

"Just last year," Lola Faye said. "Real sudden."

"I'm sorry to hear it."

Lola Faye gave a quick nod. "So I'm all alone now," she said.

"Like me," I said with a soft shrug. "I guess we're two peas in a pod." I offered the mocking consolation of a withered smile.

"But tomorrow is another day, right? And so on, as long as there's something to live for."

A terrible look flashed in Lola Faye's eyes, one so violently lost that I found myself unable to speak. It was the look of an animal driven into a final corner, a dark, no-exit look, making her seem for a moment set apart from all the living world, drawn away and locked into the solitary confinement of her life.

Then she reached for her black bag and, like a doomed general determined to redraw the lines of battle, released a short though oddly labored breath. "Something to live for, right," she said. Her hand crawled to the bag's chalk outline of a corpse. "Some unfinished business, I mean."

Unfinished business?

Did that phrase seem ominous to me? Did I hear a hint — maybe considerably more than a hint — of warning in Lola Faye's words?

Yes, absolutely.

Then why did I agree to this walk in the park, agree to extend this last talk with Lola Faye?

I don't know, save that perhaps there comes a time when you are simply ready to let go, ready to be released from the terrors that have dogged you, a time when you are willing to face the stark facts, ready, truly ready, for the knock at the door.

And so I'd paid the bill, risen, and put on my overcoat, then watched as Lola Faye put on hers, her movements slower than mine as well as somewhat more encumbered by the weighty contents of her bag.

"You want me to hold that?" I'd asked her as she heaved the bag's strap over her arm.

"Nope," Lola Faye said, and added nothing else.

The snow had begun to settle thinly on the sidewalk as we stepped out into the night.

"It's so pretty, Luke," Lola Faye said.

I glanced across the street as we waited for the light to change, the park's bare trees now outlined in ghostly white. "Also a little spooky," I said.

"Do you get a lot of snow in Boston?" Lola Faye asked.

"Yes, we do."

"And in Chicago?"

"Chicago?"

"Where Julia lives."

"How do you know where Julia lives?" I asked.

Lola Faye drew the strap of her bag more securely over her arm. "I looked her up on the Internet, you know, the way I do a lot of people."

"You look up a lot of people?"

"Yep," Lola Faye answered. "Mostly people from the old days. Debbie, for example. Miss McDowell. That's how I found out about her being murdered. I looked up Ray McFadden. He's still alive, and probably still cheating people in that mechanic's shop of his. And I looked up Woody's cousin." The light turned and she stepped off the sidewalk, moving quickly now so that we'd almost made it to the other side when she added, "Sheriff Tomlinson. He died three years ago. And Mr. Klein."

"Mr. Klein?" I stopped dead. "Why Mr. Klein?"

A car honked, and in a nearly panicked gesture, Lola Faye grabbed my arm in just the way, it seemed to me, as my father had one busy afternoon in Glenville, and she yanked me up onto the curb. "You have to take care, Luke," she warned me. "You could get killed."

We walked briefly without speaking, just two people strolling deeper into the park, the snow increasing slightly as we walked. The darkness thickened as we moved farther from the street, away from streetlamps and the flickering beams of headlights.

"Why Mr. Klein?" I asked again.

"He died six years ago."

"But why did you look him up on the Internet?"

"Because he was close with your father," Lola Faye answered. She looked left and right into the park. "It's as quiet as a cemetery, don't you think, Luke?"

I thought of the cemetery in Glenville, its forever-silenced occupants, my mother and father, Woody Gilroy, Miss McDowell, Sheriff Tomlinson, Mr. Klein. Their stones were as silent as they were, and on that thought I felt for the first time, darkly and with a true sense of risk, that some abyss lay before me, devoid of hyperbolic foreshadowing but threatening in the distance, less a moment of wrenching self-discovery than a way of seeing more clearly than I had before. And Lola Faye Gilroy was improbably my guide, inching me farther and farther toward the precipice, talking about my father and mother, Debbie, and, finally, Julia, my forsaken wife's remembered question suddenly sounding in my mind: *So, Luke, what is the last best hope of life?*

On that thought, I stopped abruptly. "What do you want from life, Lola Faye?" I asked.

"Want?"

"What's your last best hope?"

She seemed honestly touched by the question, thought it over a moment, then said, "To know that I mattered to someone. To have that feeling at the end. That's what everyone wants, don't you think, Luke?"

"Yes, I do," I said. "I think everyone wants to matter to someone at the end."

"To know that for sure you made a good impression," Lola Faye added. "Like Danny knew it, because of the way I was with him and took care of him."

"Yes, to know it like that."

"Proof," Lola Faye said firmly.

I nodded. "Proof."

We started to walk again.

"Snow always looks so clean, don't you think, so pure," Lola Faye said after a moment.

I peered out into the dark reaches of the park and felt like a man in crumbling stage make-up, one part of the mask after another dropping away as the play progressed, here an eyebrow, there some hairs from a false mustache.

"Not like me," I said.

"What do you mean, 'not like me'?" Lola Faye asked in a voice that, for all its persistent probing, seemed quite casual.

"Well, we all have secrets," I answered with the same casualness. "Things other people don't know."

Lola Faye moved smoothly forward, her eyes on the snow. "Oh, I love secrets, Luke," she said. "Tell me one of yours."

If this was a game, I wasn't going to play it alone. "Only if you tell me one of yours," I said as lightly as I could.

"Okay," Lola Faye said, but this time in a voice that was less playful than before, something lurking inside it like a shark in the ocean depths. "But you go first."

This struck me as reasonable enough. "All right," I said.

"Good," Lola Faye said, as if she'd scored in some small but important game.

And I thought, *Only one, Martin Lucas Paige, you can tell her only one.*

Which is what I did.

In the weeks following my talk with Mr. Ward, I told her, the desperate state of affairs in which my father had left my mother and me became dreadfully clear. Variety Store was liquidated, the proceeds disbursed to my father's many creditors. A small sum had still been owed even after this sale, however, and to pay the last of his creditors, my mother turned to the getaway money she'd stashed in that little metal box. This final payment entirely exhausted that already meager fund, so even lowly Tompkins State was no longer an option for me.

But there'd been worse news to come, grim news about my mother's health.

She'd passed out a few months before my father's murder, although she was released from the hospital only a day later. After that, she'd seemed quite normal, though noticeably weaker. My father's murder had sapped considerably more of her strength, however, and I often found her in bed. I'd attributed this to depression, the residual effects of the death and the scandal with which she'd been forced to deal, and which, I thought, would eventually dissipate.

But her weakness had not gone away, and so I'd taken her once again to Dr. Blalock. He'd given her the usual examination but offered no actual diagnosis, and his only recommendation had been that my mother should rest and take a multivitamin.

But neither rest nor vitamins helped her, and by the time the last of Variety Store's assets was liquidated, my mother had become quite unsteady as she made her way about the house, most often to our cramped living room, where she talked with her only visitor, Mr. Klein.

His visits had become quite regular by then, almost always after he'd closed his jewelry store, gone to his own house, and had his solitary dinner. With nothing but the lonely night before him, he would drift up the walkway of 200 Peanut Lane, a strangely floating figure in the darkening air, often dressed in freshly pressed black pants and jacket, sometimes bearing flowers, so that I began to wonder if he might be courting my mother, a question that grew so large in my mind that I finally asked him, jokingly but somewhat seriously as well, if he had any designs on her.

His response chilled me: *We need to talk, Luke.*

"Talk?" I asked.

"About your mother."

With that grimly suggestive remark, he touched my arm and led me out into the backyard, where we stood by the little fence that had once bordered my mother's summer garden.

"Your mother is . . ." He paused a moment, then delivered the blow. "She has a very serious condition, Luke."

"Condition?" I asked. "What condition?"

"She's not just weak," Mr. Klein told me. "She's very gravely ill."

The moon and stars changed their courses, it seemed to me, and all the world grew still.

"She has multiple sclerosis," Mr. Klein continued. "I took her to see Dr. Philbert because I thought Dr. Blalock hadn't looked at her condition as closely as he should. He was just telling her she was overtired or stressed, that she needed to rest, take vitamins. Dr. Philbert did a much more thorough examination."

I'd entirely forgotten my mother's mentioning that Mr. Klein wanted her to see Dr. Philbert.

"Your mother isn't going to die," Mr. Klein assured me. "It's nothing like that. She could live for many years. But she won't be able to take care of herself, Luke. She's going to get weaker and weaker, and eventually she'll need full-time care."

"I see," I murmured.

Mr. Klein glanced toward the rear of the house as if making sure that we were not being observed. "Your father was afraid that there was something seriously wrong with your mother."

"I'm surprised he noticed anything about her," I said curtly. "Given what he was doing."

Mr. Klein let this pass. "Your father was always afraid that he might die at any moment," he said. "The way his father did. Suddenly. So he provided for your mother's care."

Nothing Mr. Klein could have said would have surprised me more.

"Provided for her care?" I said with a bitter laugh. "My father didn't leave her a dime."

Mr. Klein's eyes flickered with what seemed a curiously hostile regard. "Yes, he did, Luke," he told me in a voice that was more than a little scolding.

"How do you know that?"

"Because he entrusted it to me," Mr. Klein said. "Thirty thousand dollars. It was all he could raise, evidently."

"He gave you that money?" I stared at Mr. Klein, frozen with astonishment. "Why?"

"Well, as your father explained it, he had quite a few creditors," Mr. Klein told me. "He had to put this money beyond their reach. He asked if I might be his . . . private banker." He hazarded a sad smile. "So, what I'm saying is that you don't have to worry, Luke, the money is available for your mother's care when she needs it."

"When she needs it?" I asked. "So you're not turning the money over to my mother now?"

Mr. Klein shook his head. "It was your father's wish that I keep it safe."

"Safe from whom?" I asked.

Mr. Klein's eyes filled with the distrust of me my father had planted in his mind, so although he never answered, I knew what his answer would have been: *From you, Luke.*

CHAPTER
TWENTY-SEVEN

"That's my secret," I told Lola Faye at the end of this latest narration. "That my father thought that I was a bad son, that I wouldn't take care of my mother, that he had to keep what little money he had from me because he believed I'd take it and run away with it and leave my ailing mother with nothing."

"That's sad, Luke," Lola Faye said quietly.

We came to a halt beside a small playground, utterly deserted but with the swings moving slightly from time to time, shaken by little gusts of wind.

"But to tell you the truth, I've always thought that he may have had an even worse idea about me," I added. "A much worse idea."

Lola Faye's gaze struck me as quite tender, though by then I'd lost confidence in my ability to read the many expressions I'd seen in her face, some so intimate and genuine, some so cool and distant.

"That I was dangerous," I said. "That it was right, what Ollie told you. That the real peril is right next to you. Or sitting just across the table."

"How were you dangerous?" Lola Faye asked, though it seemed a question to which she already had the answer.

"Because I had a big dream," I said. "And would do anything to make it come true." The last words fell from my lips like scraps from a torn confession. "Even murder him for the insurance money, take all that money, and leave my mother flat."

I imagined the shot again, the cracked glass, my father's eyes widening in terror as he fell, his anguished mind drawing a terrible conclusion.

"So the minute Mr. Klein told me all this, it hit me that the last thought my father might have had was that it was me out there in the dark, me with the rifle."

Julia's words rang in my mind: *Your life is oedipal as hell.*

"That must have hurt," Lola Faye said. "Thinking something like that."

"Yes, but everything was hurting by the time I had that talk with Mr. Klein," I told her. "It's hard to explain, psychic pain. It's a gnawing ache. I was riddled with it."

Lola removed the strap of the LA coroner's office bag from her shoulder and nodded toward a nearby bench. "We could sit there," she said.

I glanced about, the night air so thick around us that we seemed to be enclosed, two people in a dark, windowless room.

"Okay," I said.

We walked to the bench, brushed off the light film of snow that covered it, and sat down together.

"Now it's time for you to tell me something I don't know," I reminded her. "One of your secrets."

She dropped her bag between us. It hit the seat with a heavy thud.

"What do you have in there?" I asked. "It's got to be more than my book."

"It's something for you," Lola Faye answered. "A parting gift. It's the other reason I came to Saint Louis. To give it to you."

"The second bird you came to kill," I said. "What is it?"

Lola Faye glanced toward the empty playground. "I saw you with your mother once," she said. "You were taking her into Dr. Philbert's office. She was leaning on you, like she couldn't have stood up without you."

"She was very unsteady, but she could have walked without me," I said.

"But she didn't have to," Lola Faye said. "That's the point. She had you with her at the end. Like Danny had me. Ollie too. Someone who loved her."

"Yes," I said softly. "I was there . . . to the end."

I remembered that last, dreadful evening, the torturous confrontation, the way I'd paced back and forth from the kitchen to the living room, and finally stormed out into the summer night, my mother standing in the doorway, utterly motionless, my words no doubt still ringing in her ears: *I am trapped!*

"But I could sometimes go out," I added.

"Yeah, I know," Lola Faye said. "Debbie said you still went out. You went out for long rides, the two of you." She paused briefly, as if waiting for a response, then continued. "Debbie told me you were pretty upset that last ride."

312

"Yes, I was upset," I admitted. I waved my hand. "But you don't need to hear another sob story."

"A sob story," Lola Faye said with a quick, inexplicable smile. "That's what you said to Debbie." She saw that I had no memory of this. "That last night, when you were driving so fast down Decatur Road," she reminded me. "And she told you about how she couldn't leave her mother alone that particular night. You said you didn't want to hear her sob story."

Suddenly the whole incident came back to me quite vividly. We'd been winding sharply down Decatur Road in the thick of night so that the beams from the headlights had seemed to slash ruthlessly at the darkness, as if in murderous attack. Debbie sat on the passenger side, stiffly, staring straight ahead, her body tense; she was fiercely unsettled, I knew, by the violent motion of the car, the way my foot remained heavy on the accelerator.

"You should slow down, Luke," she said fearfully. "Decatur Road is dangerous."

Very dangerous, in fact, with a perilous switchback predictably known as Dead Man's Curve. But at that moment, my own inward inferno was the only danger I was capable of feeling, a soaring discontent with my circumstances, the nefarious nature of my father's plot, how in a sense he'd crudely but decisively outmaneuvered me, and in doing so had successfully destroyed the only dream I'd ever had.

"Luke, please slow down," Debbie said.

But I did no such thing. Instead, I pressed down harder on the accelerator and with a bleak, suicidal thrill felt the old Ford surge forward, rattling loudly, the hot summer air whirling maniacally through the car's open windows, so that Debbie's long blond hair blew behind her in a sudden violent gust, like the mane of a horse at full gallop.

"Please, Luke, slow down!" she cried.

Her terror was like an exotic taste, something that only whetted my appetite for more, so I pressed down farther on the accelerator, the car now growling and rumbling and shaking, its old worn tires spinning hellishly over the rough pavement.

"Please, Luke!" Debbie shouted. She grabbed my arm and I felt her nails bite into my flesh, a pain that somehow managed to return me to my senses.

"Okay," I snarled. "Okay." I eased off the accelerator and, like an exhausted animal, the old Ford slowed and ceased its shaking.

"I thought you were going to kill us," Debbie breathed as she released my arm.

For a time we drifted on through the darkness, both silent, I nursing a fiery resentment that grew more anguished with each passing second.

"I'm trapped," I said bitterly.

Debbie peered at me fearfully, as if watching the slow burning of a fuse.

"I'm completely trapped," I repeated.

"No, Luke," Debbie said. "You'll find a way."

I shook my head. "I don't want to think about it anymore," I said. "Let's go to a movie."

"I can't," Debbie said. "I have to be home early tonight."

314

"Why?" I asked.

"My mother. I have to help her."

I faced the road, all my resentment and disappointment, all my shattered hope now seething in me again. "Fine," I said sullenly. "I don't need to hear another sob story."

I could feel Debbie watching me with the wary regard one has for a coiled serpent, but I simply stared straight ahead and clutched the wheel even more tightly, as if by that fatal grip I might hold on to the last wisps of my exploded dream.

"That wasn't a nice thing to say to Debbie," I admitted to Lola Faye when I finished my tale of that white-hot evening, the terrifying thrust of the car, Debbie's panic, my own fiery anguish.

Lola Faye's expression struck me as being like Debbie's was that night, unsure of the raging despair of the man who faced her, sensing the building storm but unable to forecast its direction or destructiveness.

"No, it wasn't nice," she said cautiously, in a voice quite clearly designed to convey a nearly maternal understanding. "But you were under a lot of pressure, Luke."

I wondered if Lola Faye was mocking me now, perhaps had been all along, her little gestures of sympathy and compassion merely a pose, maybe even a ruse, the velvet sheath that covered the knife.

"I didn't turn out to be very smart, if that's what you're saying." I told her.

Now, quite suddenly, that sheath came off.

"No, you haven't been, Luke," Lola Faye said. Her voice seemed to come from some arctic region of her mind, cold and isolated, where nothing lived. "In some ways you haven't been very smart."

"You sound like you've been investigating me," I said with a strained laugh.

"I have," Lola Faye told me bluntly.

A wave of anxiety shot through me. I stiffened reflexively, and like a small animal beneath the gaze of a looming predator, I felt my legs move, my body start to rise.

"You know," I said quickly, "it's probably time I got back to my hotel."

Lola Faye caught my sudden urge to flee, and in response she reached for the canvas bag. "Not yet, Luke." The smile she offered was so small it seemed hardly to exist at all. "Let's talk for just a little longer."

I eased back down in my seat and drew in a breath that seared my throat.

"All right," I said. "What should we talk about?"

Lola Faye's expression took on a weird radiance, like a translucent mask with a light behind it. "I could never figure it out," she said. She peered at me more intently, as if staring at the scattered pieces of a puzzle. "I mean, I never figured *you* out, Luke. Because back then, when we were in Glenville, I thought that nothing mattered to you but getting out of there, that you'd do anything to get out. Anything at all."

There was a brief pause. It was tense and charged, and during it I felt the unnerving sensation of standing on the gallows, the noose already drawn tight but the lever not yet pulled.

"But then I saw you, and that raised a question I couldn't ever answer," Lola Faye said finally. "I saw you on the bus the day you left Glenville. And I never forgot the way you looked."

"How did I look?"

"Like you were dead."

It was not difficult for me to recall that day, the bright sun and clear air, how the bus had moved turgidly down Main Street. I'd taken a seat near the back, well away from the other passengers, and from that isolated corner peered through the window, passing Variety Store, then the post office, and finally reaching the town park with the Confederate monument, where I'd noticed Lola Faye Gilroy in her grief and isolation, her head in her hands, her shoulders trembling slightly, a vision that seemed to mirror my own fierce sorrow.

"Numb, like you said," Lola Faye added. "You were sitting in the back. I looked up and there you were, sitting in the back of the bus. And you looked numb." She said nothing for a moment, only stared at me as if I were a riddle too complex to solve but at whose myriad intricacies she'd been working for a long time. "Numb," she repeated. "That always seemed strange to me, because you'd sold the house and had money to leave Glenville. You were on your way to a bright future."

"Yes," I said. "But so much had happened. So much death."

"So many innocent people," Lola Faye said.

"Innocent, yes."

She lifted one hand but left the one on the canvas bag in place.

"Your daddy."

One finger popped up, then a second.

"Woody."

A third finger rose.

"Me."

She drew in a breath and moved to lift a fourth finger.

"My mother," I said before she did, and saw at that instant the deadly accuracy of her perfect timing.

"Your mother?" Lola Faye asked pointedly.

"Well," I said quickly, like a man rubbing out his own dusty tracks, "she seemed the most innocent of them all."

"Innocent?" Lola Faye asked. Her hand slowly fell to her lap. "What do you mean, Luke?"

"That she was innocent," I answered and heard my voice break as I spoke. "She didn't deserve what happened to her."

Lola Faye's gaze was strong and steady. "That she died, you mean?"

I felt a great swell of suppressed feeling rise up from my secret depths. "Not exactly," I said as it crested.

Lola Faye watched me for a moment, and then, in what seemed a great giving in to the dark scheme of things, she said, "Oh, Luke, can life really be like that?"

CHAPTER
TWENTY-EIGHT

Oh, luke, can life really be like that?

Something in those words, so simple and sad, opened the floodgates.

"There's no statute of limitations on murder," I said to Lola Faye. "You remember telling me that?"

Lola Faye nodded solemnly.

"It's true," I said. "Even if you're never caught."

With those words, I felt the air heat up around me, saw the trees grow thick with foliage as the fullness of that long-ago summer settled over me again.

"Well, good night, Luke," Debbie had said.

She'd gotten out of the car and was leaning into its open window.

"Be careful driving home," she added.

I'd stared at her angrily, still seething, not only because she had to get back to her mother but also because this was the least of my scalding troubles, the hopelessness that had fallen upon me since my father's murder and my mother's illness.

"You're okay, right, Luke?" she asked.

"Sure," I'd answered coldly and, with no further word, stomped the accelerator and sent the old Ford surging backward out of Debbie's unpaved driveway and onto the open road.

It was nearly ten miles to Peanut Lane and all that way I'd simmered in the cauldron of my misfortune, all that I'd lost or would soon have to forfeit, the fact of the matter starkly put to me in the latest letter from Harvard, warning me that I had only a week left to respond to the acceptance letter: *If we do not hear from you by . . .*

By the time I reached home, I felt nothing but my own inner boiling. The hope I'd once so ardently pursued and worked so hard to achieve was now worth no more than my father's bankrupt store and the empty promise of his insurance policy.

"Hi, Luke," my mother said softly as I came through the door.

She was sitting at the kitchen table, frail already, and getting more so every day, the quickness of her eyes and the keenness of her perception all that remained of the mother I'd once known.

"Hi," I said sullenly.

"Did you have supper?" my mother asked.

"No."

"I'll make you a . . ." She started to get up, a gesture of self-sacrifice I suddenly resented, perhaps even reviled, as if it were a trick, a form of sly manipulation, her way of holding on to me by emphasizing her selflessness.

"No, don't," I said curtly. "I'll do it."

I strode to the refrigerator and yanked open the door. The scraps of yesterday's supper rested in a

320

plastic container, and the very look of it, cold, flavorless, utterly unappetizing, struck me as the perfect symbol for the life that lay before me.

"There's buttermilk," my mother said softly.

"Buttermilk?"

"I had Mr. Klein bring buttermilk."

"Why?"

"Because you like it."

"Like it?" I cried. "I hate buttermilk!" I slammed the door of the refrigerator and spun around. "I'm not my father, Mom! I'm not your loving husband."

My mother looked at me as if I'd slapped my dead father's face.

"No, you're right, Mom," I said mockingly. "You're absolutely right. We should have buttermilk. Have Mr. Klein bring gallons and gallons of it. Enough for my whole life. Because you're right, Mom. You're absolutely right. I am just like my father, and I will have the same life."

Suddenly I felt every cell in my body grow leaden. I was nothing but dead weight, and I would rest like an anvil in Glenville forever.

"I'm going to my room," I said dully.

I stepped toward the door, and as I passed her, my mother took my hand.

"Luke?"

I didn't turn to face her. "There's nothing you can do, Mom," I said.

Her hand fell away, and I heard her release a weary breath.

"There's nothing you can do," I repeated, and with that, I was gone.

My room upstairs was as bleak and uninviting as a prison cell. I dropped onto my unmade bed and stared at the great histories I'd collected over the years: Herodotus, Thucydides, Gibbon, Michelet, Burke, Macaulay, Carlyle. Each volume was a mocking grin, taunting and accusatory. I closed my eyes against them, and after a time, fleeing into a welcome oblivion, I fell asleep.

The sound that awakened me was a low groan.

I opened my eyes, unsure that I'd heard anything at all, waited briefly, and heard it again. It was my mother, the sound she made as she mounted the stairs each night groaning slightly as her hand gripped the banister, and the groan carried the full burden of an exhaustion that was physically real but that I now found emblematic of the grim and insurmountable obstruction that had been laid in my path, a conspiracy waged against me that had turned all my hopes into false hopes, made me see life itself as an invisible and malignant force that nailed me in place and thwarted my every effort to rise, that choked off every avenue of opportunity and buried all my striving beneath layer upon suffocating layer of dreadful circumstance. A fury seized me, and in the grip of it, I leaped from my bed, raced to the door, and yanked it open.

"Do you have to make that racket?" I cried.

My mother had reached the top of the stairs and was holding precariously to the rail. "Sorry," she said weakly. "Sorry, Luke."

322

"Just be quiet," I said sharply. "Just be quiet . . . please!"

With that, I slammed the door and returned to my bed.

But this time, I didn't fall asleep.

Instead, lying fully awake, I listened as my mother padded about in the adjoining room. She was walking very softly, so I knew she was trying with all her might not to disturb me. I heard her move to the bookshelf in her room, linger a moment, then walk away from it and into the bathroom. I heard the soft squeak of the medicine cabinet door as she opened it, the sound of water filling a glass, the soft shuffle of her feet as she made her way back to the bed, the cry of the springs as she lay down.

After that, silence.

Too long a silence, because my mother usually tossed about on the bed, or made low moans when the pain hit her. I listened for these sounds, angry even in the anticipation of them, angrier still when I didn't hear them, and at last I rose and walked to my mother's room.

She lay on her back, her body draped in an old terry-cloth robe. Her feet were together, and her pale hands rested motionless, one atop the other, on her stomach. Her eyes were closed, and there was nothing to indicate anything but a deep sleep.

I walked to the bathroom, turned on the light. The medicine cabinet was slightly ajar. I opened it all the way, and in that garish light, everything came clear.

She had shielded me from harm and herself from further investigation by leaving the bottle in the medicine cabinet, the vial now filled with pills less lethal than those she'd swallowed. She had done this so methodically and well that I knew that no one, not Sheriff Tomlinson, or those later summoned to retrieve her body, or the people she had gone to school with, or her friends and neighbors, or even the devoted Mr. Klein, would ever guess what she had done.

I raced over to her bed, pressed my ear to her chest, and listened to her heart. The beat was slow but still strong, though when I straightened up again, I noticed the stillness that was steadily calming the short twitches and aching movements that so often racked her sleep.

And so I bolted to the phone on the other side of my mother's bed, yanked up the receiver, and started to dial 911.

Then, as if he had returned to me to strike back in this searing moment, I saw my father slouched in the shadowy corner, just as he had been in my mother's hospital room so many months before, saw him exactly as I had seen him then, heard the dreadful thought that had come to me at that instant: *You know you want her dead*.

The phone trembled in my hand. I glanced toward the mirror and saw myself in its reflection, the smartest boy in Glenville.

You know you want her dead.

I stared at the receiver, my finger poised above that last 1.

You know you want her dead.

I put down the phone, then seconds later snatched it up again, my hand shaking like something torn by storm, all my mother had done for me, her years of sacrifice, the love she bore me and that I had returned, all of that arrayed against Harvard, books, escape, the full lethal tide of my own grand dream.

You know you want her dead.

And it was true, I knew, as horribly true as anything I'd ever known.

I felt my breath stop, hold, release, hold again, like a man in the process of strangling himself.

You know you want her dead.

I heard the low whisper of my mother's fading breath, and in that suspended interval, I felt the dying ache of my own soul, an unfeeling void at the center of myself, one I could not act against or ever again deny. I could feel all of my earlier being, every capacity for sensation, now in the process of a radical deflation, a numbness settling over me and sinking into me so that it seemed almost unwilled when the phone finally dropped from my hand and I slumped down on my mother's bed, and then simply sat, still and stony, as her breath grew yet more shallow, and her eyes grew yet more still, and whatever feeling remained in either of us finally fell away.

"I let my mother die," I said to Lola Faye. "I just sat there and let her die. Because I wanted to leave Glenville, and the only way I could do that was by selling the house."

Through this wrenching tale, Lola Faye had kept her gaze fixed on the playground. At the end of it, I'd expected her to react with either sympathy or contempt. But instead, she remained silent for a long time, careful, it seemed to me, to avoid my eyes.

"We should walk now," she said finally. "We should take a long walk, Luke."

The walk turned out to be very long indeed, Lola Faye and I moving slowly down countless deserted streets until, finally, we reached the great, gleaming arch of the Gateway to the West, where, at last, we sat down on one of the benches in its surrounding park.

"Okay, Luke," Lola Faye said. She reached into her bag and removed something I could make out only as an irregular shape covered by a plastic grocery bag. "Here's what I came to bring you."

I unwrapped the package she handed me and found a small trophy. It had a marble pedestal that was perhaps three inches square. A column rose up from it to a height of perhaps six inches. A gilded young man stood atop the column, his arm raised, a torch in his hand. A small plaque rested on the base of the pedestal: THE SMARTEST BOY IN GLENVILLE.

"Your daddy had it made," Lola Faye told me. "It came to Variety Store a few days after he died. I meant to give it to you, but after Woody, that note he wrote, I was afraid to talk to you." She drew in a long, troubled breath. "I've had it all these years. But I couldn't go without giving it to you."

"Go?" I asked.

She nodded, and as she did, I recalled her earlier indifference to anything that might hurt her "in the long run."

"I see," I said.

She looked at me quite frankly, and with no sign of seeking pity.

"It was nice, though, wasn't it, Luke?" she asked. "Having this last talk."

I could see the fear that gripped her and recalled the one hope she'd had, and at that moment, I heard Julia's question once again: *So, Luke, what is the last best hope of life?*

I knew its answer then.

The last best hope of life is that at some point during living it, all that you did wrong will suddenly teach you to do right.

Three Months Later

"How's it going?" Julia asked as I opened the trunk of the car and deposited her bag.

"It's hard work," I answered.

"That's the best kind."

She'd flown into Birmingham, then taken the bus to Glenville, where she'd arrived at the same station from which I'd departed so many years before.

"So this is Glenville," she said.

As we drove through town, she glanced up toward the mountain whose treacherous roads I'd driven with Debbie, then to the park where the Confederate monument still stood with its squat statue of warrior and musket, and finally to the various shops that lined Main Street, many festooned with signs in Spanish, a Chinese restaurant where Variety Store had once been.

"Not exactly Faulkner," she said.

"It never was," I told her.

The house was small, but I'd found it surprisingly comfortable, with its old wood stove and creaking floors. It had the gritty feel of all who'd lived within its walls, the mill workers and pulpwood haulers, the common people of my region who had proceeded on through war and depression and social upheaval, and about whom I'd decided to write a small remembrance, little more than a memoir to start, but enough for the moment. Still, there'd been times when I'd felt the texture of their vanished lives, the crinkly surface of the faded wallpaper, the splintery edges of a doorjamb, the rounded handle of a mop or broom, the heft of an iron skillet, and recalled, not without pleasure, the grander vision of my youth.

"Cozy," Julia said. She smiled as she stripped off her coat and unwound the scarf from her neck. "Small and warm."

"Yes, it is," I said.

It had been so long since I'd kissed her that I trembled when I did it.

"Thanks for coming," I said.

"It's good to see you, Luke," she said.

"Want some coffee?"

"Sure."

The kitchen was tiny, with a few cabinets and a wooden cupboard with chipped paint and one door, solid enough, but with loose hinges, a thing both slack and sturdy, and that, in its strength and imperfection, reminded me of my father. There was a table by the window. It had a badly scratched Formica top and dented aluminum legs, another piece scavenged from the town thrift shop, and thus marked, it seemed to me, by the tender hieroglyphics of its use.

I made a pot of coffee and poured each of us a cup.

"You've become quite the little homemaker," Julia said with a soft laugh.

"Yeah," I said.

We sat down at the table by the window. Julia craned her long white neck, getting the kinks out from her flight and bus ride, then leaned forward and looked out into the backyard. The large oak was bare, save for the wooden swing that hung from one of its limbs. A light snow was now falling, unusual for Glenville in March.

"It was snowing that night too," I told Julia. "Did I mention that?"

Julia shook her head. "No."

I'd called her from the hotel and told her everything about my last talk with Lola Faye. My voice had broken as I spoke, reduced as I'd been at that moment to the raw essentials of myself. Her response had been quick and sure: *It's the right thing to do, Luke.*

And so I'd done it, explained to the college that I would not be returning, then headed to Glenville and set up shop, assembling the fundamental tools for the task I'd set for myself: an ancient manual typewriter, for the feel of the keys; a few reference books; even a tattered old *Bartlett's* to remind me of my many lapses, of all the little forgeries of my life, of what can rightfully be claimed as one's own and what must be acknowledged as another's.

A rustling came from a distant room.

"She's awake," I said.

Julia set down her cup and followed me out of the kitchen, past the stove and the little desk where I'd placed my typewriter, and finally down the short corridor that led to the back bedroom.

"Hi, Luke," Lola Faye said as we came into the room. A smile struggled onto her lips, weak but radiant. "You must be Julia."

Julia immediately offered her hand. "Nice to meet you, Lola Faye."

Lola Faye's eyes sparkled briefly. "You want to watch a movie? Luke bought me a DVD player. We watch old movies a lot. The black-and-white ones."

"I like those too," Julia said.

"It's not a black-and-white one today," I said.

Lola Faye struggled to lift herself, and with her movement, Julia and I took up our positions, one on either side, and lifted her from the bed. Lola Faye laughed as we did this and seemed to think something in the awkwardness of it all quite funny.

"I feel like a big old sofa," she said. "Like you're having to move a big old sofa." She laughed again, this time her gaze on Julia. "You've got plenty of experience with this, I guess. Being a nurse and all."

"Yes, I do," Julia said.

We placed our arms snugly around Lola Faye's waist, and, now secured, she took a slow, ponderous step. "How long are you staying, Julia?" she asked.

"As long as you need me," Julia answered.

Lola Faye chuckled. "It's really Luke that needs you."

We moved her at this same slow pace, one step at a time, to the old couch in the living room, and then, positioning ourselves again, Julia and I lowered Lola Faye down onto it.

"All right then," Lola Faye said, as if she'd achieved a small victory. "Made it." She reached over to the little table to her right, grabbed her glasses, and put them on. Her blue eyes were gigantic behind the thick lenses. "So, what are we seeing today, Luke?"

"*Legend of the Lost*," I said. "I know you like John Wayne."

I walked to the television, took the DVD from its case, inserted the movie, and then walked back to the sofa.

"Why'd you pick that one, Luke?" Lola Faye asked jokingly. "You feeling lost today or something?"

"Well, we are none of us found, Lola Faye," I said, also jokingly. "We're all just lost in different ways."

Lola Faye released a raspy laugh. "I bet you copied that from *Bartlett's*."

I nestled in beside her and hit the Play button on the remote. "I probably did."

"Well, nobody's perfect, Luke," Lola Faye said. She looked at Julia. "Did Luke tell you about me tracking him down in Saint Louis?"

"Yes," Julia answered. "He said you had a great talk."

"Yeah, it was nice."

"And it wasn't the last one, either," I reminded her. "Not the last one by a long shot."

Lola Faye took my hand, and in her touch I felt every whorl of her fingertips, every tiny scar of her hands, the memory of old cuts and scrapes and burns, along with the healing tissues that had mended all these life-inflicted wounds, and by whose reviving power she had proceeded on.

"But a good talk," I added.

"Yep, a good one," Lola Faye said with a laugh. "And I really liked that appletini."